Even when it wasn't you

This is a work of fiction. Names, characters, places, and incidents either are the product of the author's imagination or are used fictitiously, and any resemblance to actual persons, living or dead, business establishments, events, or locales is entirely coincidental.

Cover Design: Lorissa Padilla Designs

Editing: EditElle

For my husband,
who is my forever happily ever after

PLAYLIST:

If you like playlists with your books, here's a short list of songs that inspired me while I was writing *Even When It Wasn't You*. Enjoy!

The 1 by Taylor Swift
Infinity by AJR
Still Into You by Paramore
To My Parents by Anna Clendening
Would You Love Me Now? by Joshua Bassett
A Thousand Years by Christina Perri

CONTENT WARNING (SPOILERS):

I was really excited to write *Even When It Wasn't You* and, in many ways, this was my dream project. I really put Nate and Macy through the wringer for this story. Don't worry! There are plenty of laughs and swoon-worthy moments (and a happily ever after!), but I think it's important to give a heads-up on some potential triggers.

If you don't want spoilers, stop reading now!

In this story, the main character experiences sexual assault (one incident, implied, off-page) and pregnancy loss. I know these are heavy topics, and I did my best to address them with sensitivity. I hope that you will read this story and find hope in the midst of trauma. And that you will love it as much as I loved writing it.

 Kayla

1

THE PRESENT

MONDAY

Good friends and delicious lattes. I dare you to find a more iconic duo.

Thankfully, I can find both of these at Spill the Beans. Our local coffee shop makes the best matcha lattes I've ever tasted. I would gladly walk in every day and give them all my money in exchange for their drinks—and I'm not just saying that because my best friend and her fiancé own the place.

Most days, Evie is hiding in the back office, but today, I've pulled her away from the endless paperwork that comes with running a small business. We're tucked away in a booth toward the back of the store discussing some last-minute wedding plans. She's getting married next week, and I've agreed to do her floral arrangements and bouquets.

Is it a little ambitious to be her florist and her maid of honor? Maybe, but Evie is my best friend—has been my best friend for almost a decade. There isn't anything I wouldn't do for her. Not only will I be the best bridesmaid in the whole world, but she'll also have the best flowers in Belview. This will be the best wedding ever and I can't wait!

"Okay," I say, taking a sip of my drink. "So after talking to the suppliers, I really think you should replace the tulips with ranunculus. They're a little more expensive, but are more vibrant, and give a funkier vibe without being too trendy."

Evie's dark hair is in a messy bun on the top of her head. It bobs back and forth when she shakes her head. "Macy, I literally do not care what you decide to do. I could walk down the aisle with a Publix bouquet and be happy."

Even though I know she won't do it, my eyes widen in horror. Flowers from the grocery store are fine for a weekly pick-me-up. They're fine for small holidays if you don't need something with a personal touch. But they are absolutely not okay for your wedding day.

"You are *not* walking down the aisle with something that costs the same price as a latte. I refuse to let you."

She laughs as she wipes away some water from the table with a napkin. "I appreciate your concern, I do, but I want you to enjoy this next week with me, not stress because you're overthinking every stem and piece of greenery."

"What if I promise not to overthink it?"

"Is that even possible for you?" She rolls her eyes at me before they go to the table where her phone buzzes. The screen lights up with multiple text messages. A crease forms between her brows as she reads them silently.

"Everything okay?"

She shakes her head. "Mom is freaking out. Something about Nate, but there are so many typos I can't figure out what she's trying to say." Her fingers tap across the screen as she responds.

Nate.

For her, it's one syllable in a long string of other words. The same cannot be said for me. Just the sound of his name makes my breath catch.

She's still looking at her phone when it buzzes again. "I guess he's coming home early. She's panicking about sleeping arrangements and asked me to bring my air mattress over."

"When?"

"Right now."

My eyebrows shoot up. Evie moved to Belview after college, but her parents still live an hour away in Oak Ridge. "She wants you to drive to her house right now to bring her an air mattress?"

"Yeah. He's coming home today."

"Today?"

I've been trying to prepare myself for the inevitability of seeing Nate again, but I was working under the assumption that he wouldn't be here until the rehearsal dinner on Saturday night and that he'd be gone again after Sunday's ceremony. Twenty-four hours, give or take.

If he shows up today, that's almost six more days of potentially running into him before the wedding.

Evie looks up and gives me a sympathetic smile. "I know. I'm sorry."

Regardless of what happened between me and Nate, he's still Evie's brother. I should be happy he's here early and they'll get to spend more time together. This week is about my best friend. Not me.

"No. Don't be," I say, forcing a smile. "I'm sure your family is going to be thrilled for the extra days together."

Evie's phone buzzes. Then buzzes again. Her eyes flicker across the screen. "I'm sorry, Macy. I know you wanted to go over the flowers, but I trust you. Get whatever you want and don't overthink it, okay?"

"Okay."

She gathers her wedding planning notebook, some bridal magazines, and her phone and shoves them in an oversized tote bag that she then slings over her shoulder. "I gotta go before Mom starts losing her mind and calling my sister or other brothers."

I wave her off. "Go. I'll figure it out."

She's halfway to the front door when she stops and turns. "Are you still planning on coming to Katja's with me tomorrow?"

"Of course." I've only got a few clients this week. That means I'm free to go to any of Evie's last-minute appointments with her until I start working on her arrangements.

"Thank you, thank you, thank you." She puts her hands together in front of her and gives me one last look before racing out.

I sigh and pinch the bridge of my nose as I lean back in my booth. There's so much to unpack from the last five minutes and most of it was a whirlwind I haven't quite processed yet. Nate is coming to town early. I start dreaming up scenarios when I see him. I imagine what he'll look like and what I'll say, but I don't get too far in my imaginary conversations because I can't conjure up what a conversation with him will actually look like.

With a sigh, I open my laptop and look at what's available from my regular suppliers. Though the bulk of the flowers for Sunday's ceremony will be arriving soon, ranunculus keeps pushing its way to the front of my mind. It just feels right for them to be a part of the bouquets. After making a few phone calls to confirm they will get here in time, I place the final order for Evie's wedding.

It feels good to cross one thing off today's list and the endorphin rush is just what I needed. I lean back against the booth and take a sip of my drink as I relax for a moment.

That's when my world tips upside-down.

I don't get a clear view of his face, just a quick glance at his profile. Even though I haven't seen him in almost four years, it's enough for me to know that it's him.

It's Nate. And he's here. Not in Oak Ridge. Not just a few days early. But here, here—just a couple of feet from where I sit.

One minute, I'm blissfully sipping on a lavender matcha latte in a small booth on the side of the room, the next I'm spilling the green liquid on my off-white jeans in shock. Thankfully, the drink isn't so hot that it burns through the fabric, but there's enough on my leg that it looks like I got into a fight with Kermit the Frog–and it's unclear who won.

I grab the small napkin they put between the mug and saucer and start wiping, but it only makes it worse. Instead of a green blob, I now have a green blob *and* little pieces of partially disintegrated green napkin stuck in the heavy weave of my pants. My favorite pair of pants.

I could get up and ask one of the baristas if they have any towels I could use to get the matcha out of the fabric. I even debate whether or not to go to the bathroom to rinse them in the sink with some cold water. But both options require me getting up and I am completely rooted in my seat right now. I don't think I could move if I wanted to.

My eyes are glued to Nate and I can't make myself look away. I barely register the other people in line. There's a girl in the front, a mom and her toddler, an old guy. But if someone offered me a million dollars to identify them in a line-up, I wouldn't be any richer than I am now. Every bit of my attention is on the guy at the back of the line.

Every bit of my attention is on Nate.

I still can't see his face, but I take in the parts of him I can see. I can't help but notice the way his jeans fit snugly around his butt and thighs. The sleeves of his t-shirt are tight around his biceps. He's still lean, like the last time I saw him, but he somehow looks stronger.

Nate has spent the last few years in law school. Last time I checked, pouring through legal textbooks didn't build a physique like that. Does he work out? Does he moonlight in some physically demanding job to look like that? I know nothing about him anymore. Nate could be excavating mines for priceless treasure earning all sorts of humanitarian awards. He could be the villain mastermind trying to steal the treasure for financial gain for all I know.

This man I'm watching stand in line is a stranger. He isn't the Nate I once knew. Not in the big things, like his career path and whether or not he's the bad guy in a Nicholas Cage movie. And not in the little things, like what he drinks.

The Nate I knew didn't drink coffee.

My mind continues to fill with questions as I watch him. He's completely disinterested in the people in front of him. His posture is stiff as he stares at the hand-drawn chalkboard menu. His dark hair, the same deep brown as everyone else in his family, is cut short—a far cry from the shaggy style he wore the last time I saw him.

After a moment, he starts to look around at the art on the walls. It's a rotating collection, and this month's artist is someone from Tampa with a love for pop art. The bright paint on canvas is in stark contrast to the exposed brick walls on which it hangs. The cheery scenes are at odds with the overall industrial feel of the coffee shop.

His eyes continue to scan the art, and I realize too late that his gaze is slowly moving in my direction. If I don't move, he's going to see me.

Unfortunately, the open layout of the shop means there's nowhere to hide. I squeeze my eyes shut and shift back and forth in my spot as I try to decide whether I'm going to jump from my seat to the one opposite of me so that my face is turned away from him, or if I'm going to fully commit and step outside like I'm taking a phone call.

In my moment of complete panic, however, my brain chooses neither of these and lands on the worst possible option. I slide down the edge of my seat and start to move under the table just as Nate turns all the way around. His eyes lock on mine, and I'm staring at him like a total freak with my body folded beneath me and my chin resting on the counter. My heart skips a beat before painfully pounding against my ribs.

Nate's body goes unnaturally still except for his eyes, which widen for the briefest moment and then narrow. "Macy?"

Never have I wished that the world would open up and swallow me more than I do right now. My knees rest painfully on the ground, but I'm not moving. It's like sleep paralysis, except this is no nightmare. I am completely awake.

I stare at Nate in horror. He's even more beautiful than I remember. Any traces of youth are gone from his face. A strong jaw peaks out from two-day-old stubble covering the lower half of his face. His normally full lips are pressed together in a thin line as his hazel eyes continue to look into mine.

He takes a single step forward, just past a customer walking to the front counter. "Macy Wagner."

My breaths come in shallow pants. I open my mouth to say something—I know I should say something—but nothing comes out. People in the coffee shop are looking at us. The pressure of having them watch me face the person I've avoided for four years is too much. In an act of defeat, I let myself completely slide off the seat and land hard on my butt.

My face is burning. I hold my breath and pray that he'll keep walking. With any luck, Nate Delaney will decide that he was incredibly lucky to get away from

Florida and the weirdo under the table when he had the chance.

I watch as his jean-covered legs walk over to the table. I can't see anything above his thighs, but his feet are easily visible. He's wearing Chucks—I guess some things don't change—and those worn-out shoes stop right in front of me, the toes pointing in my direction like a hunting dog.

She's here! She's hiding here!

He's already seen me. Still, I cover my face and close my eyes in a last-ditch effort to avoid being spotted. It's the most pathetic game of peek-a-boo in the history of the game, and I'm losing.

A rustling of fabric is followed by his long sigh. "What are you doing down here?"

His voice is so close. It's deep, warm, familiar. Hearing it again after so many years is enough to bring back memories I've fought hard to forget. Memories like the time he told me I was the most beautiful girl he'd ever seen. Or when he told me he loved me.

I spread my fingers so that my eyes are no longer covered. Then, reluctantly, I open them. Nate's balancing on the balls of his feet in a crouch, his arm is stretched out above him, resting on the counter for balance. There's a slight tilt to his head as he watches me.

"Oh, hey." My voice is overly friendly. "Nate? Is that you?"

What a dumb thing to say.

Apparently, he thinks so too. He closes his eyes and presses his lips together.

"Of course it's you." I clear my throat. "You're here for Evie and Matt's wedding, right?"

His mouth is a straight line when he opens his eyes again.

"And this is her coffee shop. Well, hers and Matt's. She didn't open it all by herself. Not that she couldn't." I laugh nervously. "She's amazing. But you already knew that. She is your sister and all."

My brain is screaming at my mouth to stop talking, but she's got a mind of her own and it's filled with nonsense.

"What are you doing on the floor, Macy?" he asks again.

I look around and take in my surroundings for the first time. As many times as I've been in Spill the Beans, I can't say I've ever experienced all its glory from this angle. There are crumpled-up napkins pushed up against the wall, some large crumbs from a muffin scattered about the floor, and a piece of gum stuck to the underside of the table.

"I was . . . looking for my . . . " I see a spoon next to me. Who knows how long it's been here or whose mouth it's been in. I try not to wince as I grab it and put it out in front of me. "This. I was looking for this."

Nate lifts his brows. "You dropped your spoon?"

He doesn't believe me. Of course he doesn't. I nod my head vigorously. "Uh-huh."

"And here I thought you were hiding from me."

"Hiding from you?" I scoff. "Why would I be hiding from you?"

"You tell me."

Those three words poke an old wound. "I wasn't."

"Okay." He draws out the second syllable, then jerks

his chin up. "Well, now that you have your spoon, do you want to get off the floor?"

No, I'd much rather stay here forever. I could gather enough discarded napkins to make a little pallet bed and live off people's dropped food. I've already proved that I have no problem grabbing strangers' discarded items. There's no HOA or utilities. I'd see my best friend whenever she came in. I could make a happy little life down here and live out my days like a troll under a bridge.

I force a smile. "Of course."

Nate straightens from his crouch and steps to the side. I'm left with only a view of his feet and a growing sense of dread.

We'll be seeing a lot of each other as we go through the different celebrations that come with Evie and Matt's wedding. As much as I wish I could, I can't run or hide from Nate.

I need to face this situation head-on. I wish I could do it gracefully, but I'm already on the ground, and there's no easy way to get back up. There's a giant bar under the table, and I have to crawl on my hands and knees as I maneuver from my spot. When I'm out from under the countertop, a tanned hand appears in my line of vision. I follow it up to Nate. He's standing there patiently while he waits for me to grab it.

It's an olive branch, I'm sure of it, but there's no way I can touch him right now. Ignoring his hand, I pull myself up using the corner of the booth cushion. Then, of course, my shoe gets stuck under the table, because this isn't humiliating enough, and I have to bend back down to get it.

He watches me the entire time, but his face doesn't give anything away.

Once I'm satisfied I have all my articles of clothing on and accounted for, I slide back into my seat and set the spoon on the table. Nate takes the seat across from me. We sit in silence, just looking at each other for a long time. I'm still in awe at how he's grown into his body in the time we've been apart. He's always been good-looking, but my memory's smoothed out how striking his features are. There was a time when I could stare at his face for hours. Now, it's almost too painful to look at him.

The gold flecks in his pupils sparkle with curiosity as he looks at me. His gaze is intense, as if he's trying to read my mind or see into my soul. Both possibilities are equally terrifying.

Sitting on my hands, I resist the urge to tuck my hair behind my ear or bite my lip or tug on my ear as he continues to watch me. Now that we're across from one another, it's vital that he doesn't realize how affected I am by him. I need him to think I'm okay. That I'm just fine without him.

But I'm not fine. I wonder if he can tell—what he sees when he looks at me.

Other than some small signs of aging, like faint lines at the corners of my eyes, I think I look similar to how I looked in high school. My strawberry-blond hair falls in loose curls around my shoulders, a style I've worn for as long as I can remember. I still go light on the makeup, and I'm most comfortable in a pair of jeans and a t-shirt. But as much as I might look the same, I'm not that same girl anymore.

There's so much I want to say, but I have no idea

where to start. This isn't like meeting an old friend for a coffee date, and it's not like getting to know a stranger. Nate and I are in a category with no easy solution.

My hands shake as I release them from the prison under my thighs and lift the mug to my lips. I take a sip. "You came home early."

He shrugs. "I had some things to do."

I'm dying to know what those other things are, but I settle on awkward small talk instead.

"You look . . . good." I inwardly cringe.

"Thanks." He looks down at his fingers as they run over the corner of the table. "You too."

"And you're doing well?"

"Yeah." He looks back up and meets my eyes. "You?"

I plaster on a smile. "Yep. Uh-huh. Really good."

Other than seeing my ex-boyfriend for the first time in four years and getting caught hiding under a table . . .

My smile falls as we sit in uncomfortable silence. My toe taps violently beneath the table. The urge to say something is an itch beneath the surface of my skin, but there's only so much one can say in a situation like this. My eyes go to the chalkboard menu, and I'm reminded of the fact that he was in line when I first caught a glimpse of him. "You didn't order a drink."

He leans back. "I didn't really want anything."

I wave my hand at the register. "You were about to get something two minutes ago."

"I was." He taps his finger against the table. "And then I saw you. I thought I should come over."

I knew I should have run away when I had the chance. Sitting across from him is hard. My mind is working overtime to form coherent sentences while trying to build a wall around itself so I don't show too much emotion. I've never had a good poker face, but I'm trying to act like seeing him—like being this close to him—isn't affecting me. I'm nervous that he can see right through it, and it might kill me if he could see how much I still wish we were together.

I clear my throat. "What were you going to get? Before you came over."

He grimaces. "I don't know. Black coffee?"

A black coffee? In my mind, black coffee is reserved for bitter old ladies and angry middle-aged men—not Nate. If his tastes are anything like they used to be, he will absolutely hate drinking something without any sweetness to it. I decide to extend an olive branch of my own. "You might like the Kit Kat matcha latte. It's not coffee, and it has chocolate in it."

He looks down at my mug. "Is that what you're drinking?"

I shake my head. "This is a lavender matcha latte."

"Lavender? That's a scent, not a flavor."

"It's both."

"Is it any good?"

I furrow my brows. "Do you think I'd order something I didn't like?"

"I don't know what you'd do," he mutters and looks down at his hands. Just like that, our little truce seems to have come to an end.

I don't know what to say. People grow so much in their twenties that our teenage relationship shouldn't still have such a chokehold on me. Some people wouldn't think twice about the guys they dated when they were in high school and early college. But Nate isn't just some guy. He was the love of my life.

"Get the Kit Kat matcha latte. I don't know anyone who doesn't like it." I shut my laptop and tuck it under my arm. I take one last sip of my drink and scoot to the edge of the bench to get up.

"Where are you going?" he asks.

"I have things I gotta do."

It's as vague as his earlier answer, and while I do actually have quite a few things to do, I don't have to race out the way I am. I certainly don't have to explain to him what I'm doing either. Those days are far behind us.

I stand and give him one more look. And I realize too late that I'm drinking him in faster than my matcha latte.

For the last four years, I've only had an old picture that I pull out from time to time when I'm sad. It's the only way I've seen him since I refuse to seek him out on social media, and I make myself scarce whenever he's in town. My eyes are greedy for Nate in the present. They look at his eyes, his nose, his mouth. They look at him until my vision blurs and I remember that I don't get to stare at him like this. Not anymore. I am the one who gave up that right.

I blink away my tears and give him a tight-lipped smile.

His face is pinched. He opens his mouth like he wants to say something. I desperately want to know what that something is, but I'm too scared to actually hear it.

"I'll see you around," I say before he can speak.

He nods once, like he understands my urgency to get away. "Thanks for the drink suggestion."

"Of course."

I walk away and set my cup on the small counter for dirty dishes. I leave without giving Nate another glance.

Seeing him now is like meeting for the first time all over again, but so much worse. The first time we met, it was as awkward as this. The difference was, back then, there was so much possibility. Now, I'm just faced with the memories of him. Memories without a future.

2

THE PAST

SOPHOMORE YEAR OF HIGH SCHOOL

I STILL CAN'T BELIEVE my dad thought pioneer reenactment camp was something worth missing a week of school for. He's been drilling the importance of school and good grades for the last three years, and missing an entire week of my sophomore year—the first year I'm actually taking an AP course—goes against everything my dad has taught me.

At least the mid-January weather isn't terrible. Right now, we have sunny skies and highs in the sixties. I guess that's why the River Rendezvous is in January instead of the summer. The idea of living that pioneer life in Central Florida in June and July sounds miserable. No AC in the middle of swampland? No, thank you.

Of course, having to make up a week's worth of schoolwork because I'm missing so much time right after Christmas break isn't exactly ideal either, but some of my teachers gave me assignments to work on while I'm gone. I'll have plenty of time to finish all my work since there's nothing else to do but stand around and marvel at the fact that we are living without the luxury of any modern conveniences.

The fact that people travel from all over the country to visit Florida and live out their pre-1840s LARP-ing fantasies is bizarre. Even more bizarre is that they've been doing this for longer than my dad has even been alive.

The only saving grace has been the fact that my dad decided to let us camp out on the "modern" camping side in an RV instead of making us pitch historically accurate tents without any electricity. It's considered cheating among the hard-core campers, but I would have one hundred percent revolted if I didn't get to use a regular toilet.

I'm sitting at the small dining room table that doubles as a living room, working on an Algebra II assignment, when my dad walks out of the master bedroom. I don't look up right away. When I do finally see my dad, my mouth falls open.

Even though I'm fully aware of the strict dress code whenever we spend time in the campgrounds, it's still shocking to see him all dressed up in his pioneer gear. He's a big guy, 6'3" and two-hundred pounds, and I rarely see him wearing anything other than a suit and tie.

Now, he's standing in front of me wearing linen pants, leather boots, and a long-sleeve white shirt that has laces up the front. He looks like he's trying to be on the cover of an old-time romance novel, which sends a shudder through me because who does he think he is?

He smiles wide and does a turn like a model on the catwalk. "How do I look?"

I try to keep the scowl I've had on my face for the last day in place, but I can feel a smile fighting against my lips. Even though I'm still peeved about being here, I can't deny how funny it is to see my dad fully committed to pioneer times. "Do you want the honest answer?"

His smile falls. "What? I followed the rules completely. No modern fabrics, no zippers, no collars. For so many restrictions, I think I look good."

I grab my phone and keep it hidden under the table as I tap the screen and pull up the camera. "You're right, Dad. You look amazing." I lift it and snap a quick picture. "I think your clients would like to see you like this. You can put it on your business cards."

His eyes go wide before he laughs a deep belly laugh. "Good luck getting their numbers. There's such a thing as patient-client confidentiality, you know."

"But I do have your coworkers' numbers." I tap my chin.

"You wouldn't."

No, I wouldn't. No matter how upset I am, I'm not going to risk his reputation at the law firm he helped build. I set my phone down. I'm keeping the picture, but I won't send it to anyone. "Don't worry. Your secret double life is safe with me, Superman."

He snorts and takes a seat next to me. "What about you, Mace? You ready to get dressed and go check out the campgrounds?"

I'm currently wearing leggings and an oversized school shirt. I'm cozy here in the RV, wearing my "modern textiles," and I'm hesitant to go explore the campgrounds. But we're here for the entire week, and I know I will need to leave the comforts of the twenty-first century eventually. There's only so much schoolwork I can do before I go crazy and basket weaving begins to look appealing.

I close my math book with my assignment on the page I'm working on and set it aside. "Fine, let me get into my *Little House on the Prairie* outfit, and we'll go out on the town."

He shakes his head at me, but he's smiling. This trip means a lot to him and we're here for an entire week. Even if there are a million other things I'd rather be doing, I need to make the most of this situation. I shut the bedroom door behind me, since it's the only place we can escape each other in this small space, and pull out my clothing.

It took hours of scouring thrift stores to find stuff that I was allowed to wear. I have a couple of long cotton skirts with elastic waists that aren't exactly authentic, but with flowy cotton blouses landing past my waist, no one will ever know. I put on a shirt and skirt, then slip on my leather booties and walk out.

My dad stares at me when I reemerge. He chokes on a laugh.

"Don't." I lift my finger at him, but I'm still fighting the smile from earlier. It's hard to stay angry when we both look absolutely ridiculous.

He puts a leather satchel across his chest and opens the door. The sky is overcast, and there's a breeze bringing the cooler air into the RV. Goosebumps pop up all over my arms, so I grab a crocheted cardigan—feeling very much like an old lady now—and step outside with my dad. The modern camping side of the Rendezvous is lined with campers and RVs of various sizes and conditions parked in the grass lot. There are old vans with pop-up tents on the roofs, Winnebagos, and newer RVs like the one we're staying in. Music and the hum of generators fills the air.

My dad waves at a few people lingering outside their vehicles before we make our way over to the main campgrounds. It's a five-minute walk through overgrown grass to get to the actual Rendezvous. The sounds from the modern side fade out, and we're met with early morning silence. Birds chirp loudly to one another, and the wind blows through the branches of oak trees that are scattered throughout the massive property. As we get closer, a plethora of uniform, white tents come into view—many with fire pits and wooden chairs set up outside. It's like stepping through a portal into a completely different universe.

Several people are starting fires to heat water for coffee or cook eggs in cast-iron pans over the open flames. The smells carry on the wind and my stomach growls. Even though we brought Lucky Charms, we haven't eaten breakfast yet. My dad wants us to have something from the campgrounds so that we feel completely immersed in the atmosphere of the 1800s. I just hope that whoever is cooking puts more emphasis on food safety than they did two-hundred years ago, because dying of dysentery on the Oregon Trail doesn't sound all that appealing to me.

"Can you imagine camping out here for the entire week?" Dad asks as we continue to make our way through the tents. His voice is filled with wonder.

Mine, not so much. "You're right." I wave my hands at

the scenery. “Who wouldn’t want to give up the comforts of home for this?”

He gives me a side-long look as we continue to walk across the grass, still wet with morning dew. The moisture is turning the leather of our boots dark. “Do you see all the tents?”

“Um. Yeah.” I’d be blind not to. There are hundreds of them, and we are right in the thick of it.

“Those are the people who want to do this. And there are plenty of them.”

I groan. “And yet I haven’t seen a single person my age. Everyone I’ve seen is middle-aged.”

“Give it time. We just got here. I’m sure that there are a lot of kids that come to this every year.”

“I didn’t realize there were so many parents willing to drag their kids from school to dress like Laura Ingalls.”

“Well, most of the kids here are from homeschool families.”

That makes sense. No schedule means they can do whatever weird crap they want, whenever they want. And now I get to be part of it too. *Yay*. I look at my dad. “I bet they don’t even have to buy new clothes since they’re already used to wearing long dresses. Making their own butter? That’s child’s play.”

He jabs me with his elbow as we continue our walk further into the encampment. The map we were given shows the general layout of the grounds. There’s an area where people sleep, a small market area that includes different places to get food, a gathering spot where they have nightly bonfires, and a shooting range at the far end of the camp. If I’m remembering it right, he’s leading us toward the food.

"Be nice," he says. "Just because you go to a private school doesn't mean you're better than them. These families are making decisions that they think are best for their kids."

"Keeping your kids isolated from other kids their age isn't a great idea, if you ask me."

He snorts. "Literally no one asked you, Macy."

I roll my eyes. "Have you met homeschool kids? They are so freaking awkward."

"That's not nice."

I lift my hands. "But am I wrong?"

"I'm sure there are homeschoolers who are"—he drops his voice to a whisper—"socially awkward. But that doesn't mean everyone is." His voice returns to a normal level when he adds, "Aren't there kids who act a little different from others at your school?"

I think of some of my classmates. There's the artsy kid who only ate things that were orange for a month to make a statement. He ate so many carrots, his skin actually started to turn orange. I'm pretty sure his parents made him put an end to his "art installation" after that. Then there's the girl who shaved her head in an act of rebellion against the patriarchy. When the administration kindly pointed out that it was against the dress code, she ended up wearing a wig until her hair grew out enough to call it a pixie cut.

I clear my throat. "Yeah, okay. There are some . . . interesting kids at my school. But that doesn't mean I'm wrong about homeschoolers. They're total freaks."

"Macy," he chides as we slow down to a stop. He's looking around at the different tents. "Like I said, most of the people here are homeschooling families. Not everyone is willing to take their kid out of school for a week to experience pioneer life."

"Only the lucky few."

He chuckles. "What I'm saying is, let's not burn any bridges before we've had a chance to meet them. You might find out you have more in common with them than you realize."

"This sounds like a cheesy PSA about being kind to everyone."

He sighs. "Would it kill you to try?"

"Fine," I say. "No more making fun of homeschool kids. Scout's honor." I hold up three fingers.

"Glad to see those five months of Girl Scouts stuck with you." He gives me a sly smile.

They didn't. I don't know if that's the actual salute, and if it is, I'm pretty sure I learned it from TV, not my Brownie troop. "Oh yes. I'm a regular survivalist. What can I say?"

He chuckles. "I know this is a different type of vacation. You're used to the beach or the mountains. I like those places too, but my hope is this will be the kind of experience that brings long-lasting memories."

My eyes follow a couple wearing clothing similar to ours. They're walking in the opposite direction, and it hits me how everyone is going to be dressed like that all week. There's something about seeing actual grown-ups dressing up on purpose that makes me question everything I know about life. "Oh, I'm sure we're going to make memories."

"I'm not saying this has to be your favorite trip we ever taken, Mace. But I am asking you to have an open mind."

I know he's trying to make memories with me, and I should be happy that he actually cares. Despite the high demands of his job, my dad always finds time to do stuff with me. He never lets a day go by without telling me how happy he is that we are in this family together. That's a lot more than I can say for the woman who birthed me —and then left a few short years later.

This less-than-conventional trip to the reenactment camp is his way of trying to have some father-daughter bonding time. I know that. And that's the only reason I'm able to lift my pinkie finger to him. "I'll do my best."

He entwines his pinkie with mine and squeezes. "Thank you." He smiles at me. "If you hate it, I promise not to make you ever do this again."

I snort. "I might emancipate myself if you try to make me do this again."

"How about this? If I ever bring you back, I'll help you fill out the paperwork myself."

I grin. "And if I promise to make the best of this week, can I pick the next trip?"

"Sure."

"Overseas?" I ask, my voice hopeful. I've wanted to take a trip to Greece ever since I saw pictures of all the blue and white buildings of Santorini.

He levels me with a look. "U.S."

"Alaska?"

"Continental."

"You're no fun," I say with an exaggerated pout, so he knows that I'm not actually upset. There are plenty of places that are worth visiting. Hiking the Narrows at Zion is still on my bucket list, and I mentally put it at the top for next year.

"What if I go buy hand pies for breakfast?" He points to a tent where a woman is putting out a wooden sign advertising the different flavor pies they have. There's cherry, blueberry, and rhubarb. The aroma of fried dough fills the air, and it's probably the closest thing I'll get to donuts the whole time I'm here.

"That sounds good."

"Go find a spot for us to sit while I go buy some." He jerks his head over to an area with wooden tables and benches. A few families are congregating over there, and I know this is his way of telling me to go and make friends.

I widen my eyes in mock horror. "With the homeschoolers?"

"They don't bite."

"What if their awkwardness spreads through saliva droplets? I might catch it."

"I'm sure going back to school next week will be the perfect remedy. Now go."

I stick my tongue out at him before walking toward the tables. I've only made it a few steps before I hear a voice say, "You're wrong, you know."

I stop at the words. I turn to find the source of it and see a boy standing a few feet away from me. He's about my age. Shaggy dark hair falls into his hazel eyes. He's tall and skinny, all long limbs and sharp angles, and he's wearing a plaid button-up shirt. The collar and buttons have been removed, and it looks like it's been stitched up the center to keep it closed. His khaki pants are rolled up at the ankles and his bare feet are brown from dirt.

"Excuse me?"

The boy shrugs. "It's not saliva droplets. It's skin-to-skin contact."

It takes me a second to register what he means. When I realize he's talking about catching social ineptitude from homeschoolers, I'm furious. In what universe did he think it was okay to eavesdrop on my conversation with my dad and then interject with his own thoughts? It wasn't like I was having a deeply personal heart-to-heart, but that conversation was between me and my dad, not this boy standing here.

I cross my arms over my chest. "Rude much?"

"Not unlike calling a whole group of people awkward?"

I should be embarrassed to be caught talking the way I did, but I'm too irritated to care. "Case in point? You telling me that you spread like a contagion."

He raises his brows at me. "You're the one who started it when you speculated that it was saliva."

"Isn't that the way most viruses spread?"

"So now homeschoolers are a virus?"

This isn't going well. This boy is super annoying, but I promised my dad I wouldn't burn any bridges. I promised on all my honor as a scout. I close my eyes and take a deep breath while I count to ten slowly.

When I open them, he's looking at me with a strange expression. "You okay?"

"Just trying not to say something I'm going to regret."

"Like calling homeschoolers viruses."

I ball one of my hands into a fist at my side and hope he doesn't see it. "I shouldn't have said that."

He watches me for a long time before his mouth

spreads into a wide smile. "No, you're totally right. We are weird. Spending a week pretending that running water and electricity don't exist? That's not exactly normal behavior."

My eyes widen.

"But that doesn't mean it isn't fun." He sticks out his hand. "My name is Nathaniel, by the way, but everyone calls me Nate."

The only people I shake hands with are my dad's coworkers or clients. Not kids my age. I stare at his hand for a moment before finally putting my palm in his. "Macy."

"First time here?" He releases my hand, and both our arms fall back at our sides.

A corner of my mouth lifts. "That obvious?"

His eyes travel from my head to my feet. They stay there. "You guys did a good job with the clothes, but most of us don't wear shoes."

I look down at my shoe-covered feet. I just got a pedicure before we came. My toes are pretty and polished. I don't want to ruin all that hard work by walking through the dirt. "I'm keeping my shoes on."

He wiggles his toes. "Suit yourself."

"So"—I clear my throat—"it was the shoes that gave us away?"

He nods.

"And here I thought it was the way we stumbled through camp like lost sheep."

Nate chuckles. "You did look a little lost and the shoes were a dead giveaway, but it's also the fact that most of us do this every year and know each other. I've never seen you before." He glances over my shoulder. "At least your dad picked the best place to get food."

I turn to see my dad in line at the hand pie place. He almost looks like he belongs there. As if he knows he's being watched, he turns. When he spots me, he waves. I wave back.

"The blueberry ones are the best," Nate says. "They always sell out before noon, so if you think you'll want one, get it early. And the owner loves show tunes, so if you want extra filling, just talk to her about your favorite musical."

I wave my arms out at our surroundings. "Doesn't seem historically accurate to be singing *Annie*."

He shakes his head at me. "It's 1840. *Les Mis* is much more appropriate."

My dad took me to see that one on Broadway last year. I didn't think I was going to end up liking a musical about the French Revolution, but I found myself crying twice. I immediately bought the soundtrack and listened to it on repeat until I learned every song. The fact that *this* is the musical he chose makes me stop and really look at him.

"Have you seen it?" he asks.

I nod.

"What's your favorite song?"

This is too weird. One minute, he criticizes me for calling homeschool kids weird. The next he's asking my favorite song from *Les Mis*. His sudden change throws me off, but the answer is easy. "'On My Own.'"

"Huh."

"Huh? What's that supposed to mean?"

He rocks back on his heels. "It just means that it's alright."

He says 'alright' like I answered wrong. I cross my arms over my chest. "Oh yeah? And what's yours?"

"'Master of the House.'"

I can't help it. I laugh. For some reason, the comedy number seems to suit him, even though I don't actually know him.

My reaction seems to make him happy because he smiles again before looking over my shoulder. "Well, looks like your dad got your pies. He's coming this way."

I lift my hand and cross my fingers. "I hope he got the right flavor."

"If not, there's always tomorrow."

"'One Day More.'"

He scrunches up his face. "Did no one tell you this is a weeklong event?"

"I meant . . . like the song."

"I know what you meant." His smile grows. "It was nice to meet you, Macy." He sticks out his hand again.

I shake it. "You too, Nate."

"I'll see you around." And then he's gone, walking toward a group of kids of all different ages.

I'm watching him pick a little girl up and put her on his shoulders when my dad stops beside me. He's got two pies and he hands me one. The smell of the cooked dough is heavenly, and there's a blue-purple glaze spilling from the inside.

He hands me one. "Looks like you're already making friends."

"And I didn't even catch anything yet."

"Give it time," my dad jokes before extending his arm toward a table.

We sit and enjoy our breakfast—the blueberry is as good as Nate says it is—while we look over the itinerary for the rest of the week. The idea of axe throwing and basket weaving still isn't something I'd choose to do, but maybe I can make it through the week and things won't be so bad.

3

THE PRESENT

MONDAY

THIS IS SO BAD.

I'm still shaking when I get to Oops a Daisy. It takes me three tries before I finally get my key into the lock.

I wish I could say it's because I drank too much caffeine, but I know it's because of my run-in with Nate. Seeing him after all this time is unnerving. It's strange how you can simultaneously want to run *from* and run *to* a person at the same time. It was that internal tug-o-war that had me racing out of Spill the Beans as quickly as I did.

If I had spent one more minute sitting across from Nate, who knows what would have happened. I might have tried to hug him. I might have begged him to take me back. I might have explained all the things I couldn't tell him four years ago.

No, the best thing was for me to leave and hope I can spend the next week avoiding him. My hope is that if I spend a few hours in my shop, I'll be able to calm myself down before figuring out what the rest of this week looks like. I still have small jobs to finish before all my attention is focused on Evie's wedding flowers.

As I walk inside, I flip on all the lights. The space I rent for Oops a Daisy is nothing special, but it's centrally located in Belview, and the rent is cheap. I think it's so low because I don't really need anything from my landlord. He gave me a loft—a blank slate—and I transformed it into the business of my dreams.

I put shelves on the walls, with some help from Matt—Evie's fiancé—and my dad. Vases of various colors and sizes fill the shelves and give the wall a nice pop of color.

There's a large counter where I make my arrangements in the open so that anyone coming in can watch me assemble bouquets right before their eyes.

And then there are my side-by-side floral fridges. They are my favorite part of the shop. The glass fronts allow my finished creations to show off to the world. *Look at me*, they say. *You can take me home and bring some joy into your life.*

After all, that's the reason I started Oops a Daisy in the first place: joy.

I open the first box of blooms and pull them out, one by one, to strip the leaves before cutting a small amount of the stem from the bottom. Then they go in a five-gallon bucket with plant food to keep them nice and happy while I decide where every single flower and piece of greenery will go.

I have a couple of part-time employees, and sometimes Evie will come and keep me company, but for the most part, my shop is a one-woman show. I put on some music to keep myself company while I work. Today's playlist is a Broadway hits shuffle, and after a few songs, I can feel some of the tension leaving my body.

I'm singing songs from *Beetlejuice* and *Dear Evan Hansen* as I clean flower after flower. I don't even think about Nate (that much) until a song from *Les Mis* starts playing over the speakers. My heart skips a beat as the familiar melody begins. I grab my phone and skip to the next song as quickly as possible, but not so fast that an image of Nate, current Nate that I just saw at the coffee shop, pops into my head.

It's silly, I used to love *Les Mis*, but now I can't hear a song from the musical without thinking about Nate and getting sad. It doesn't even make sense. He wasn't the one who took me to see it on Broadway, but talking about hand pies and our favorite songs from *Les Mis* the first time we met was enough to ruin the soundtrack for me.

I lean against the counter as a song from *Wicked* starts playing. It takes a few moments for my heart rate to return to normal, and a few extra for me to stop picturing Nate in my mind. It turns out, getting those stupid hazel eyes out of my head is much easier said than done.

When the next song in the shuffle starts, I decide I've spent enough time thinking about him, and that I need to focus on the bouquets that are going out today.

After I finish my prep, I start arranging flowers for an anniversary bouquet. I place the greenery first and have just moved on to adding flowers when a song from *Hamilton* begins. I'm totally in the zone and start humming along as I place stems at varying angles. Before I realize it, I'm belting out "Satisfied" alongside the woman who plays Angelica Schuyler.

Okay, it's more screaming than singing as I get to the

end, but I'm alone in the store and I don't care. In my mind, I'm on the stage singing away the pain that has resurfaced with Nate's appearance. I will never be satisfied without him. I know that, but I can never tell him. The only consolation is I won't be doing the toast at his wedding when he marries someone else, unlike poor Angelica from the musical.

At one point, I grab a rose and hold it up to my mouth like a microphone. I'm so into my little performance that I don't even look for thorns. They should have been stripped off by now, but I must have missed one because a thorn pokes through my thumb with a small pop.

"Son of a . . . " I drop the flower and press my thumb against the fabric of the apron I'm wearing. This isn't the first time I've bled over my business. It won't be the last. But I still don't like it when I do something stupid like this.

Music continues to play in the background as I grab a Band-Aid from my first aid kit and wrap it around my finger. It stings a little, but the pain always goes away relatively quickly. I wish the same could be said for Nate.

I sigh as I allow him to enter my thoughts . . . again. I rest my elbows on the counter and put my head in my hands. This is getting ridiculous. I've been trying so hard not to think about Nate, but no matter what I do, my mind keeps wandering to him.

The best thing for me to do right now is to get out of this place and talk it out with someone I trust. Since Evie is on her way to Oak Ridge with an air mattress, that only leaves my dad. It's almost noon, and it's not unheard of for the two of us to go out for a lunch date during the week to catch up on life. I text him and ask if he wants to get something to eat. I suggest Antonio's, which is a nice Italian restaurant, and hope he doesn't think I've completely lost my mind. It's more expensive than our usual places, but tiramisu sounds really good right about now, and they happen to have the best in town.

His response comes back almost immediately. We make plans to meet there in fifteen minutes, and he tells me he's happy to pick up the tab. He really is the most amazing dad ever. Without even knowing how wild today has been, he just intrinsically knows I need him to go with me and not ask questions—not yet.

I clean up my workspace, flip my sign so it says closed, and start walking toward Antonio's. It's only a few blocks from my storefront, and the weather doesn't feel like walking on the surface of the sun yet, so it's an enjoyable stroll down Oak Street.

I only look around once—okay, twice—to make sure I don't bump into Nate. I can't imagine he'd be walking around downtown at the same time as I am, but I also didn't expect to see him at Spill the Beans or sit across the table from me either. Anything is possible at this point.

When I finally make it to the restaurant and step inside, my dad's already sitting down at a table. There are two glasses of water in front of him. He must have left as soon as I texted to get seated before I arrived. He smiles when he sees me and deep creases form at the corners of his eyes. I grin back as I walk through the restaurant toward him.

He stands and gives me a hug when I get to his table. "Hey, Mace."

Dad's wearing his usual suit and tie, and I realize too late that I still have a green stain on my pants. It matches the green stains on my fingertips from working with plants for the last couple of hours. He is the sophistication to my hot mess. Total opposites. A stranger wouldn't guess we were related unless they really looked at our faces. We have the same coloring, the same nose, the same eyes.

I give him a sheepish smile as we sit. "Hey, Dad."

His eyes fill with concern when he takes in my appearance. "Everything okay?"

I take a sip of water from the glass in front of me. "Not really."

"Want to talk about it?"

"Maybe after we order?" I don't want to start baring my soul and then have to pause to tell my server I want a salad with dressing on the side.

We spend a few minutes looking over our menus in silence. When the server returns, my dad and I order the soup and salad combo because that's what we always order, no matter where we go. But I do add tiramisu to come out with my lunch.

When our server walks away, my dad lifts his brows at me. "Antonio's? Dessert with lunch?"

I sigh as I slump down in my seat. The entire reason for asking my dad to eat with me was so I could talk to someone about Nate. My hope was that talking about it might make me feel better, but the idea of unpacking how I feel after seeing Nate is exhausting too.

My dad leans forward. "What's going on?"

I rub my temple. "Something really weird happened to me at Spill the Beans today."

He adjusts the fork on the table in front of him. "Oh, yeah?"

"I saw Nate."

His fingers still. "Nate Delaney?"

"Is there another Nate that would have me ordering tiramisu for lunch?"

He clears his throat. "I guess not."

"And I shouldn't be surprised to see him. Evie's getting married this week, so it was inevitable." I rub a knot that's formed in the back of my neck. "It's just weird that he's here so early."

"Did he say why he came back early?"

"You're assuming that we talked."

He raises his brows. "Did you?"

I sag in my seat. "Yeah."

He leans forward. "How did that go?"

I worry my lip. How did it go? Let's see. I made a fool of myself. I realized how much I missed him. I ran out before I could let him see how much he still affects me. "Okay."

"And he didn't say why he was in Belview?"

I shake my head. "No. Just that he had some things to do. Whatever that means."

"And does Evie know why?"

I trace the condensation on the outside of my glass. "If she does, she didn't tell me. But in all fairness, she seemed as caught off guard as I was. So who knows." I sigh.

"Hmm." He nods. "Okay."

I scoot my chair closer to the table. "Why are you so invested in why he's here?"

"I'm not. I'm just thinking."

"About what?"

He folds his hands on the table. One of his fingers

taps against the back of his other hand. "Maybe his early return is an opportunity for you to talk to him. To explain what happened."

My heart races, just like it does every time I think about the events that led to our eventual breakup. The pain surrounding those months is a physical thing I can feel deep in my gut. It's something so deeply personal. Only my dad, Evie, and my therapist know the full extent of it. Everyone else just knows that I broke up with Nate without an explanation.

Nate's only here for a week. I can't imagine ripping myself open after all these years because my ex is here for a few more days than I'd planned. "Why would I do that?"

My dad reaches across the table and grabs my hand. He squeezes it. "Because you never know what the future holds. Time is a precious thing. I don't like the idea of you holding on to your past. I want you to be happy."

The way he says the last part gives me pause. I pull my hands back and stare at him while I attempt to decipher what he's really saying. A sudden fear grips me. "What's going on?"

He turns his hands so that his palms are facing up. "Nothing."

"Are you sick?"

"Macy."

My eyes widen. "Wait." My voice cracks. "Are you dying?"

I feel like I'm going to throw up. Is that why he didn't bat an eye when I asked him to come to Antonio's? Is that why he arrived early? Why he's talking about time being valuable? He knows his time is running out and—

"I'm not dying," he says.

"Then what's going on?"

"Nothing." He closes his eyes for a moment, as if searching for the right words. "There was a time when you and Nate were inseparable. Maybe there's a way to rebuild that relationship."

That's what this is all about? Me building back a relationship with my ex? I snort. "I think that time has passed."

"But you can't pretend you don't care. Don't forget, Macy. I was there."

For everything.

My dad is in his fifties, and has plenty on his plate with work, but he's been with me through the hardest things I've ever experienced in my life. First, when Mom left. Then, when I ended things with Nate. He took time off. Took me to the beach for a week. Let me cry for hours on end. Got takeout from my favorite restaurants. Helped me start Oops a Daisy.

"I'm not pretending not to care." I run my hands over my thighs. "I just don't know how to talk to him, and I don't know if I should even do that, considering he's leaving in a week."

"Maybe that's not for you to decide. Maybe you've made enough decisions for him and it's time to be honest."

I blink at him in disbelief. I don't understand where this is all coming from. Why he's choosing to tell me all this now. He says he's not dying, so why does he care so much about what happens with me and Nate?

"I'll think about it."

"I know a lie when I see it, Macy." He shakes his head.

"But I really do hope you'll consider talking to Nate. I know it's scary, but maybe you'll discover you can heal better if you stop holding onto the past like it's yours alone to bear."

I make a non-committal noise because I'm sure there's some truth in what he's suggesting.

"There was a time when you could talk to Nate about anything. I don't expect you to be like that again, but maybe you can be friends."

I laugh bitterly. It's one thing for my dad to suggest talking to him and trying to gain closure. It's quite another for him to think we could actually be friends. I could never be friends with Nate. It would never be enough. It's much easier to keep him at a distance.

Thankfully, the server brings our food at that moment. She places a house salad, baked potato soup, and a giant piece of tiramisu in front of me, then a Caesar and minestrone soup in front of my dad.

My dad inhales deeply. "Antonio's was a good choice."

I look down at his food. "It's just soup and salad."

"Yeah, but this is a lot different from soup and salad from a quick-serve place. They have a chef. They make stuff from scratch."

"I guess."

He lifts his fork and waves it at my dessert. "Plus, there's that tiramisu."

"You think I'm going to share?"

"After what you just told me? Probably not." He jabs his fork into some lettuce and takes a bite. "But that doesn't mean I don't know how delicious it would be."

I roll my eyes and take a bite of my food. Even though the tiramisu is calling to me, I am reasonable and start with my salad. We eat in relative silence for a moment. Could I really be friends with the boy I once loved? It seems impossible. And really, what would be the point? We've both been just fine living our separate lives for the last few years. There's no sense in forcing something unnatural. I can just go through the motions and hope the week flies by.

Because I don't want to think about Nate anymore, I ask my dad about work. He launches into a spiel about some issues they're having with the electrical and how they've had three companies come out to look at the wiring this week. After that, he asks me how everything is going at my job. I tell him about some new vases I found from a local potter that I'm excited to use for premade bouquets. It's almost enough to keep my mind off Nate. But even as we move from one topic to another, his face keeps popping into my mind.

Is it because I'm still in shock from seeing him, or some kind of sign that my dad is right, and I should talk to him? I don't know. There was a time when I could talk to Nate about anything. Even when we were first getting to know each other, conversation flowed easily. I think we're beyond that now. Now that's just memories.

4

THE PAST

SOPHOMORE YEAR OF HIGH SCHOOL

I KEEP bumping into Nate all over the River Rendezvous.

It's not that I think he's stalking me or anything. It's just that the campgrounds are small enough that we keep seeing each other in random places. He always initiates a conversation, and I never know what to expect when he talks to me. Sometimes our exchanges are filled with random facts about the River Rendezvous. (I know more about the history of early Florida settlements than I ever expected.) Other times, Nate asks me about my favorite movie or book or show. With every conversation, I'm learning little bits about this homeschool boy, and with every conversation, I'm thinking he's less weird than I'd originally imagined.

Our little chats break up the monotony of the days, and I find myself looking forward to them. He lives in Oak Ridge, which is about an hour from where Dad and I live. His family is huge, though I haven't met any of them yet. He likes poetry, and his favorite food is French toast. I know he's collecting little facts about me too. Like how I live in Belview with my dad. I don't like poetry, and my favorite food is tacos.

I enjoy our short conversations, but I'm always left confused by them as well. He stops to talk to me for a few minutes at a time before he runs off with a group of friends.

This morning, I'm in line for hand pies and Nate is behind me. I place my order, step off to the side, and after Nate places his, he walks over to me. I wonder what weird thing he's going to say this time, and how I'm going to respond.

"What are you up to today?" Nate asks.

It's a normal question, with a normal answer, all things considered.

I shrug. "Oh, you know. I thought I'd maybe weave another basket, eat a thousand hand pies." Anything to avoid walking around anymore. These stupid leather booties are hurting my feet terribly. I have so many blisters and no amount of bandages or toilet paper folded up and shoved between the shoe and my heel is helping.

Nate adjusts the pack of arrows that's slung over his shoulder. "Feel like coming to an archery competition?"

I bark out a laugh. "I've never shot an arrow in my life."

He looks down at his feet. "I meant, do you want to come watch me compete in an archery competition?"

"Oh." The invitation catches me off guard. I've spent some time talking to different people here and there, but this is the first time someone has directly invited me to something. My dad and I usually just find events in the master schedule and show up. Nate inviting me almost feels like I belong here after wandering the campgrounds for days without making a strong connection with anyone. My only hesitation is the distance. I don't want to walk across the campgrounds if I can help it. "When?"

"Now . . . " He tilts his head. "Well, after I get my pie, that is. If you don't mind eating one pie instead of a thousand, it would be cool if you came."

"Uh."

"If it helps, my sister will be there too. You won't have to sit by yourself."

The magical word "sit" is all I needed to hear. The idea of sitting and relieving the pain is enough to convince me to go. It's a hike to get to the range, but maybe the competition will take a really long time and I'll have the perfect excuse not to walk around for a while. "Okay."

Nate grins wide. "Cool."

The guy behind the counter calls mine and Nate's names, we grab our pies, and I follow Nate toward the range. I'm trying to walk as normally as possible, ignoring the stinging pain of the leather rubbing against my raw skin.

We haven't made it very far when a girl comes up and starts walking on the other side of Nate. She has dark hair that is pulled back in a long braid down her back. There's a straw hat on her head, her long, cotton dress is covered in light-blue flowers, and she has a basket in the crook of her arm.

"Hey," she says. "So, just a heads-up, I have a bet with Wes about whether you choke at the last minute and lose."

"And, hello, to you, too, Evie."

"Hello." She bumps her shoulder against his. "But

also, I need you to win today."

"Don't I usually?"

"Yes, but just in case you thought about not trying or something."

Nate snorts. "Yes, because everyone knows how tempting it is to lose for fun."

"You know what I mean."

"Fine. I'll try not to lose. What's the wager?"

"Well . . . " She clasps her hands in front of her and tilts her head toward Nate. "Wes is offering up all of his Cokes if you win."

"Really? How'd you convince him to bet those?"

She shrugs. "I think the prize if you lost was too high for him to refuse."

"I'm almost afraid to ask." Nate chuckles. "But what does he get if I don't win?"

She clears her throat and lowers her voice. "All of *our* Cokes."

"What?" His eyes are wide. "Yours *and* mine?"

"You just told me you were going to win."

"What if I lose? We'll be stuck drinking water for the rest of the week. It really will be like pioneer times then. How will I make it?"

The utter defeat in his voice makes me laugh. "Wait. I thought you guys liked being here."

Two sets of eyes snap toward me. I've been walking with them the entire time, but I think they somehow forgot I was here. Evie raises her brows as she gives me an appraising glance.

"Oh, right." Nate waves his hand between the two of us. "Macy, Evie. Evie, Macy."

We both say hi to each other.

"Evie is my sister."

"Big sister," she corrects.

"Only by a year," he says. "And Macy . . . she's the girl I met the first day."

"The one who was freaked out by homeschoolers?"

"Yeah," Nate says.

My face burns. For one, because I'm a little embarrassed about saying that. If I've learned anything in the last few days, it's this: homeschoolers are the ones who fit in here. Not private school girls like me. But more so, I'm embarrassed because I realize that he's been talking about me to his sister. How many other people around the Rendezvous know I was making fun of homeschoolers? Is that why it's been so hard to make friends here?

"And for the record, yes, we like it here," Nate continues. "But Coke is the one modern thing our parents let us bring to camp, so we get a little stingy with them."

Evie puts her finger up. "Which is why you're going to be thanking me when we have four more to add to our stash."

"And how do you expect me to act when we lose everything and have to spend the rest of the week without that sweet, sweet bubbly treat?"

Evie rolls her eyes. "Don't lose."

"Easy for you to say. You're not the one who has to hit the target."

She scoffs. "You could hit the bullseye with your eyes closed. So don't be an idiot."

The two continue to bicker playfully until we arrive at the range. And not a minute too soon. The backs of my heels feel wet, and I'm almost afraid to look at the carnage caused by my boots. I hope I'm not leaving a trail of blood that leads to the archery range. At least if I disappear because of disgruntled homeschoolers, the search party will be able to find me.

As Nate signs in, I look around the range. There are a dozen targets set up in a mostly dirt field. Even more guys and girls are gathered around with their bows and arrows. The crowd is mostly dressed in long dresses and linen pants. Some of the guys are shirtless with leather vests, and I count two with large hats that have long feathers coming out of the side. According to the schedule posted on a rudimentary bulletin, they had the preliminary rounds yesterday and this is the final tournament.

"Wish me luck," Nate says.

Evie says, "You better not lose, loser."

It's so weird, and I laugh at the absurdity of the entire situation. As an only child, I don't know what it's like to have a sibling, but watching them makes me wish I did. They seem so comfortable with each other.

Nate walks toward the crowd and I'm left with Evie. She smiles at me. "Do you want to go sit down?" She points to a bench that is in the shade of a giant oak tree. It's not super close to the range, but we'd be able to see everything just fine from it.

I practically moan at the idea of taking the pressure off my feet. "Yes, please."

She hooks her arm in mine and pulls me over. "I can't believe this is the first time I've met you," she says. "You'd think we would have seen each other with how much you and Nate have talked."

"It hasn't been that much."

"Oh, really?" She scrunches up her face. "The way he

keeps mentioning you made me think you were hanging out a lot."

"Nope." I shake my head. "Just a few random conversations around camp."

"Hmm."

"What does that mean?" I ask, sitting down.

"I just think he might like you." Her eyes widen. "Actually, pretend I didn't say that."

I laugh. "It's okay. It's not like that. I think he's just taking pity on me because I don't know anyone here." I bend over and loosen the laces of my boots. I wince as I slip my feet out. The cool air feels so good on my blisters. "And I'm thankful for a friend."

"Well, I can be your friend too," she says before she plops her basket in her lap and pulls out two cans covered by small brown bags. I can see the telltale red color poking through the top of the bag. It's two of their precious Cokes. She hands one to me. "Want one?"

I grab it from her. "I'm surprised you are even allowed to have these here. They aren't exactly authentic."

She shrugs. "As long as we keep them covered, we're good."

I turn it over in my hand. "I feel like I'm sneaking beer in a gas station parking lot."

She laughs and opens her can with a satisfying pop. "I've never thought about it like that, but that's a pretty fair assessment."

"Glad I can be a bad influence on you guys."

She shakes her head. "I promise us homeschoolers aren't as perfect as you think. Just the other night, I went to bed without saying my prayers. I still can't think about it without getting nervous."

My mouth falls open. That's her idea of rebellion? Forgetting to pray one night?

She laughs loudly. "Wow. You really do think we're crazy, don't you?"

I look down at my yet-to-be-opened soda. "I guess I only have stereotypes to go off of."

"Well," Evie says. "Yes, we do go to church, and I do say nightly prayers, but I promise we're not total freaks."

Apparently, they aren't jerks either. The fact that she's still sitting here, offering to be my friend, is a little confusing. I don't think I'd want to talk to someone who made fun of me for being a spoiled rich kid. Not that I'm complaining. I'm thankful for the company. There's only so much time I can spend with my dad before needing to hang out with someone closer to my age.

"So do you think Nate will win?" I ask, popping the top of my soda as well.

She leans back and takes a sip. "Not a question."

"I'm guessing he's pretty good?"

"He is." She nods, her attention on the range. "Nate has a natural talent when it comes to archery. He gets first place every year. There are quite a few adults who are not looking forward to when he officially joins the adult division." She laughs. "He'll smoke 'em all."

"Seriously?"

"Yeah."

I look at the range. Nate is standing off to the side as another guy fires an arrow at the target. It hits the ring around the bullseye. "I've gotta be honest. I have no idea what's going on."

"That's okay. Just know that at any given time, Nate is probably winning."

"That's pretty amazing." I take a sip of my soda. I've had plenty of Cokes in my life, but I doubt any one of them has tasted as good as this one. It's refreshing after days of only drinking water. "So what do you do when you're not pretending to be a pioneer?"

She tucks one of her legs under and turns to face me. "Well, my parents have a small family farm. We spend a lot of time tending to that when we're not doing school."

"Really? What's that like?"

"About as fun as you can imagine. We take turns waking up early to milk Betsy, that's our dairy cow. And then there's feeding the chickens and collecting eggs."

My eyes are the size of saucers. This is so unbelievable to me. I can't imagine living like that. We have a lawn guy who comes out to cut the grass and a cleaning lady who comes once a week to mop and vacuum the house. It's so vastly different from my life.

"But then I like to read."

"Oh, yeah? What kind of books?"

She looks down at her drink. "Romance mostly."

I perk up. "I like romance too."

She gives me a relieved smile and we spend the next several minutes talking about our favorite books and authors. I don't know what I expected, but I'm pleasantly surprised to discover we have some of the same favorites—and we both hate love triangles.

When I tell her I play tennis, she tells me she likes the table variety. When I tell her my favorite band, I find out we have the same favorite song. I'm having so much fun talking to her, I don't even care that I don't fully understand what's happening on the range. Time goes by so quickly that I'm caught off guard when Nate makes his way to us.

"Oh look. Here comes the show-off now," she yells to her brother.

I lean over and whisper, "Does that mean he won?"

She gives a small nod.

"Don't be jealous because you can't hit the bullseyes even if you were allowed to walk up to the target with the arrow in your hand," he says as he gets closer. He has a bow in one hand, a trophy in the other, and his pack with arrows strapped to his back. He plops down on the ground across from us.

"When am I ever going to need to be proficient with a bow and arrow?"

"When the world collapses and we need to hunt to eat?" He pulls the arrow bag over his head and sets it next to him.

"If that happens, just let the wolves take me."

"Maybe they'll accept you as one of their own," I say. "Then you wouldn't have to worry about hunting or shooting an arrow."

Nate laughs. "Looks like you guys are two peas in a pod."

"Really, Nate." Evie winks at me. "We don't even need you anymore."

"But who's going to make sure you don't lose all our soda to Wes?"

"Hmm." She turns to face me. "What are you good at besides tennis? I don't see them putting up a court anytime soon."

"Uh . . . " I grimace. "I know all the lyrics to 'Ice Ice Baby'?"

Evie gives an exaggerated huff. "Yep. You're useless."

"Hey."

"But I think I'll try to convince the wolves to let you join our pack because I still want to be your friend."

"I'm not sure if I should be flattered or offended," I say.

"Definitely flattered," she says at the same time Nate says, "Offended."

I laugh.

"That said. We'll need to help you look the part if you plan to join us." She lifts a strand of my hair and lets it drop loosely. "Tell me, how do you feel about wearing fur?"

"Uh."

"There are some lovely raccoon fur hats at a few of the tents. We should get you one." Evie points in the direction we came from—all the way across the camp. The idea of walking again makes me want to cry.

"Don't look so sad," Nate says. "They're really nice hats."

"It's not that. It's just . . . " I lift up the hem of my skirt and show them my feet.

Evie gasps. "Oh, Macy."

"You're still wearing those stupid shoes?" Nate's voice is hard. It makes me jerk back and even Evie gives him a look. He runs a hand through his hair. "Sorry, I'm not mad at you, but your feet look terrible. I just hate that you're hurting because you thought you had to wear those."

Oh.

Evie bends down and grabs my shoes. "He's right. Your feet look terrible, and as your new friend, I refuse to let you wear these anymore." She shoves them in her wicker basket, next to our empty soda cans.

I open my mouth to argue, but there's nothing to say. I'm embarrassed that it's taken me this long to realize that it doesn't matter if my feet get dirty. Mud can wash off, but the blisters are there long after I leave the Rendezvous.

When I stand to walk barefoot, I'm surprised by how much my feet still hurt. I unsuccessfully try to hide my wince.

"They still hurt?" Nate asks, this time, his voice is much gentler.

I force a smile. "I'm fine."

Nate sighs and hands his arrow pack to his sister before he faces his back toward me. "Hop on."

"What?" I giggle nervously as I look back and forth between him and Evie.

"It's not a big deal," he says. "Hop on my back and I'll carry you."

My eyes widen. It was one thing for me to take my shoes off and walk through the campgrounds, but quite another to get a piggyback ride. "I'm too heavy."

He turns back around and smirks. "I promise you're not."

I look at Evie and she shakes her head. "You're not. He can carry me, and we're about the same size." When I hesitate, she adds, "I really think you should let him do it. He'll be insufferable if you don't."

Nate's smirk turns into a giant grin. "She's right."

"Okay." I still can't believe I'm letting a boy I barely know carry me, but when he turns his back to me again and crouches down, I hop on.

I'm pretty sure the last person who carried me like this was my dad, and I was about ten years younger. I don't know where to put my hands, and I realize too late that I'm choking Nate.

"Mind easing up on my windpipe," he manages to choke out. Evie laughs, but my face burns. I try to wiggle off, but Nate holds my legs securely against his waist. "I've got you. I just need to breathe."

I stop fighting and let him carry me through camp. I was sure I would be a spectacle, but hardly anyone looks at us as we pass them, other than to give us friendly smiles. And really, it makes sense. This place is another world. People wear raccoon hats and feathers and leather and every other weird thing you don't see in normal life. Is a teen boy carrying a girl on his back that unimaginable? No.

When we get back to the part of the camp with the shops, Nate finally set me down. It still hurts to walk, but it's a much more relaxed pace, and he and Evie give me plenty of breaks. Evie and Nate try to convince me that I need a raccoon hat, but I draw a hard line there. We eat dinner together and end up sitting around the giant communal bonfire after the sun sets.

After days of feeling like I'm a stranger looking in, I finally feel like I belong. The more we talk, the more we tease each other. I can't remember the last time I've laughed so hard.

I won't see them again after this week, but I can say without a shadow of a doubt that I won't forget them. I'm happy that I got to meet them and spend this small bit of time with them this year. These are memories I'll cherish for the rest of my life.

5

THE PRESENT

TUESDAY

THE SMALL VELOUR sofa I'm sitting on is surprisingly comfortable. I sink back against the plush cushions and let out a long breath. I've been hanging out in the waiting area of Katja's, a bridal boutique in downtown Belview, for the last twenty minutes while Evie gets the final adjustments on her wedding gown.

She's standing on a small platform in front of three floor-to-ceiling mirrors angled toward her so she can see her reflection in all its glory. The dress is a simple shape without any embellishments and shows off her natural beauty. It fits nicely, but the seamstress says it can be better.

The seamstress in question is a petite woman in her fifties with thick, red frame glasses that take up half of her face and is currently kneeling on the ground in front of Evie with pins between her teeth.

Katja Khamitova is not known for her bedside manner, but every single bride that comes here walks away with their dress fitting like a magical glove. Rumor has it that she used to make dresses for the wealthy in Russia before moving to the United States. I wouldn't doubt it. The woman is talented with a needle and thread.

Because of the nature of my job, I've had many run-ins with Katja over the years, and her relationship with fellow wedding vendors is no less harsh than the way she approaches her clients. The first time she told me my bouquet looked sloppy, I cried, even though she was right. Since then, I've improved my skills and learned to take her sass and give it right back to her. She still might not like me—and she might still hate my arrangements—but she doesn't insult me anymore.

Unfortunately, Evie has not learned to talk back to Katja, and she's been yelled at three times for squirming in the ten minutes we've been here.

"But my feet are starting to hurt," she says through clenched teeth after Katja threatens to poke her with a pin.

"You know you're going to be standing in front of everyone for a lot longer than this when you actually get married," I say.

She pouts. "Way to be sympathetic."

"I'm being realistic. How long is the ceremony?"

"Thirty minutes? An hour? I don't know."

"Maybe that's something you should have found out *before* picking your shoes."

She grimaces. "I didn't think it would be a big deal."

I'm sorry she's hurting, I really am, but the poor thing has been caught up in the wedding glow. She sees everything through *Canon in D* glasses. Everything is "just fine" in her eyes—until it isn't.

"I did tell you that three-inch stilettos were a bad choice for your wedding day."

She avoids my eyes when she says, "I don't remember that."

"Seriously?" I sit up. "As I recall, I told you that they were really pretty, but you were going to get blisters. And then *you* said that they weren't uncomfortable. I think your exact words were 'they feel like I'm walking on a cloud.'" I do air quotes and say the last part in my best imitation of her voice.

A slight blush hits her cheeks. She can pretend that she doesn't remember that conversation all she wants, but we both know it happened. "They didn't hurt then."

"You wore them for two minutes. You can wear anything for two minutes and they won't hurt."

"Anything?" she asks.

"Yeah."

"What about hot coals?"

"Don't be silly. Coals are a wildly impractical choice for wedding shoes. You'd burn the church floor and cause all kinds of drama." I wave my hand in front of me.

Evie sighs. "I just gotta get through the wedding ceremony, and then I'll be fine."

"And pictures."

She narrows her eyes at me. "Again, thank you for your support."

"You know it's because I love you. I want you to be happy on your big day, not miserable and bleeding all over the dance floor."

"I know." There's a hint of defeat in her voice.

"Maybe it's not too late to change shoes?" I suggest.

Evie looks down toward her feet. I can see she's

considering it. I'd be happy to run down to the store and grab the first pair of white flats I can find in her size and charge them to my card if that meant she'd be more comfortable. All I need is for her to give me the green light.

"No," Katja says, her Russian accent thick. "You will not change your shoes."

I snort. "She's paying you to alter her dress, not pick out her shoes. Shouldn't she be comfortable when she gets married?"

My comment earns a scathing look from Katja. "She can look perfect or she can look comfortable. She cannot be both. Right now, she's a masterpiece." She looks up at Evie, and I swear there is the smallest glimmer in her eyes—like she is a proud mother—but it disappears in an instant. "You will wear these shoes."

Evie agrees, but I can still see the pain in her eyes.

I give her a what-the-heck look in the mirror as soon as Katja goes back to the dress. The Evie I know prefers comfort to aesthetic, but it looks like she's not immune to wanting to feel like a princess on her wedding day—even if that means her feet will hurt for a week.

She bites her lip and gives me a look that says she doesn't have a choice.

"You can always take them off at the reception," I say, hoping to give her some light at the end of the tunnel. "That way you can still dance to the DJ you hired."

"Sounds like a good compromise."

Katja mumbles under her breath. It's not English, and I'm afraid to know what she's saying about us. Probably something about Americans being unrefined and unwilling to bleed for fashion.

Evie ignores her. "Okay, so tell me more about what happened with Nate."

My smile falls. I already told her a little bit last night on the phone, but she's refusing to move past the part where I hid under the table.

"Why? You already know your favorite part."

She laughs, earning not only *another* glare from the seamstress, but one from me as well. "I'm sorry. I know it's not funny. But seriously, you're twenty-three years old. You didn't think he was going to just pretend he didn't see you there?"

"I was hoping he would think to himself, 'Wow, she must not want to talk to me if she's sitting on the floor. I won't make things harder on her than they already are.'"

She arches a brow at me. The motion is eerily similar to her brother's. "Since when has Nate ever done anything to make someone feel comfortable?"

I know she's referring to the way he makes conversation with random strangers and forces them into conversations whether they like it or not. She's not talking about him going out of his way to be a jerk. That's just not him. Or, at least, it wasn't.

"Maybe just this once, he could have let it slide."

Katja has moved on to the dress's sleeves. Evie lifts her arm to give the seamstress better access to the fabric. She tips her head slightly around Ms. Khamitova so she can look at me. "Did you ever stop to think that maybe things are awkward for him too?"

Of course I have. When Evie first told me that Nate and I were going to be in the wedding party together, I was shocked. As far as I knew, Matt didn't really know

Nate, but he wanted to honor Evie's family by including any of her brothers who wanted to be a part of it.

Thankfully, Nate and I don't line up, so I won't be walking out with him for the recessional. But the idea of spending so much time with him is still stressful.

"Is it awkward for him?" I ask. "Or does he even care?"

She looks at me. "Do you really want to know?"

Yes.

No.

"I don't know," I say, exasperated, because I really don't know how much I want to know. I don't want him to be secretly pining away after me all these years later. I know what that feels like, and believe me, it sucks. The idea of him being happy with another person hurts just as much. I guess I just want to know what to expect. Do I need to prepare for a potentially heart-wrenching experience on my best friend's special day? I run my fingers over the soft fabric of the couch. "How about this? Did he bring a plus one?"

I know he's not married, but that doesn't mean he's not in a serious relationship with someone who fulfills him like no other.

She shakes her head. "He didn't bring a plus one."

And because I can't help myself, I ask, "Is he dating anyone?"

Surprise is written all over Evie's face. I've never, ever asked her this question, no matter how many times I've secretly wondered. Her face softens. "Honestly, I'm not sure."

"Really? I'm surprised it wasn't the Spanish Inquisition at your parents' house last night."

"There was too much chaos for a real interrogation.

But don't worry, first chance I get, I'll put him in a dark room with a spotlight pointed in his face and ask him about his darkest secrets."

"Or you could ask him nicely." I smirk at her reflection in the mirror. "You could say it's a wedding present."

"Great gift idea. It's a well-known fact that newly married couples love knowing about the bride's brother's secrets on their honeymoon."

"Well, they say you marry your spouse's family when you tie the knot."

She scrunches up her face and looks off into the distance. "I knew I should have been more worried about the way Matt looked at my brother."

"Sit still," Katja snaps.

Evie and I share a smile at how hard Katja is working to keep us serious. "Okay," I say, "so it was chaotic. That's nothing new for y'all."

"No." She purses her lips. "But my parents made a big deal about the fact that we were all under one roof and it wasn't even Christmas. So we cooked a big meal, and between that and wedding chatter, everyone was fighting for attention. We all wanted to talk to Nate, but Catherine held him captive talking about her favorite books."

"Of course she did."

Catherine is Evie's niece, daughter of her oldest sister Joanna, and the cutest four-year-old on the planet. Her hair is the same dark color that everyone in the Delaney family has, but she also inherited her dad's curly hair, so it's ringlet city. Her cheeks are chubby and dimples appear every time she smiles. Plus, she just so happens to have the vocabulary and disposition of a much older kid, so it's a trip talking to her.

It's no surprise that she would steal Nate's attention from everyone else.

"He hasn't been forced to read *Green Eggs and Ham* a million times like everyone else, so she was delighted that he read it to her three times without so much as a sigh." Evie laughs, earning a glare from the seamstress.

He might not have sighed, but I do.

Nate is great with children. Always has been. It's no surprise to me that he would cheerfully read the same story over and over again to Catherine. I'm sure he's a great uncle.

"Did they get the sleeping arrangements figured out? Is he sleeping on your air mattress?"

"No, they did some shuffling. Catherine is going to sleep with Joanna and Lucas. That way, Nate can sleep in his old room. Just between us, I think it's Mom and Dad's way of trying to hit him with a big dose of nostalgia. If he spends enough time reliving happy childhood memories, maybe he'll decide to come back home."

"That's a lot of pressure to put on *Star Wars* sheets."

"You and I both know how much he loved that bedding."

Despite myself, I laugh. He really did.

"All done," Katja says. She stands back and looks at Evie and nods. "You will be a beautiful bride."

There are pins in the dress, and I can't see the final product like the seamstress can, but I agree. Evie is going to look amazing. Matt is one lucky guy.

Evie's cheeks turn pink and she smiles. "Thank you."

"Now go get dressed," Katja says sharply, breaking the sweet moment.

I smirk at Evie in the mirror, and she giggles as she walks back to the changing room.

A phone rings in the other room. Katja trains her eyes on me. "Tell Evie to hang her dress there when she gets out." She points to a metal rack. "Can you do that?"

"Got it." I nod. "Plop the dress right on the ground before we leave."

She narrows her eyes at me.

I sigh. "Yes. Dress on the rack. I can handle it."

She huffs before disappearing into another room, muttering under her breath once again. I pull out my phone and start scrolling when the bell on the door chimes. Katja is on the phone and Evie is getting changed, so I turn around to tell the new customer that someone will be right with them.

The breath leaves my lungs when I realize the new customer is, in fact, Nate.

What is even happening with my life right now? Every time Evie disappears, Nate shows up. I know it's not intentional, Evie wouldn't do that to me, but the timing is uncanny and doesn't bode well for the rest of the week. How am I supposed to avoid him all week if we keep bumping into each other?

He stumbles when he sees me. "Macy?"

At least I'm not hiding under a table when he sees me this time. I force a smile. "Hey."

"Uh." He looks around the room. "Is Evie here?"

I hitch my thumb at the dressing rooms. "She's getting dressed."

"Oh, okay." He sticks his hands in his pockets and leans back on his heels.

"She should be out in just a minute."

"Great."

Silence stretches between us. It was never like this before, even when we first met. I run my fingers through the ends of my hair and look at the artwork on the walls. Nate stays standing several feet from the couch I'm sitting on.

I look back at the dressing room. Still no sign of Evie. She was just wearing jeans and a t-shirt. It's not that hard to take off a dress and put your regular clothes on, even with the dozens of pins Katja put along the seams. Evie could alter the dress herself in the time it's taken her to come out.

"Were you able to get the rest of your work done yesterday?" Nate asks.

"Yeah." I face him and nod. "I just needed to order the rest of the flowers for Saturday."

"That's right," he says. "I heard you were doing the flowers. I looked at the website. You're really good." His voice is quiet. It feels intimate. Even though we're alone in the front of the store right now, I know it would feel no different if the room were packed.

I can't stop my body from warming at the compliment. "Thanks."

"You're welcome." His eyes look deeply into mine.

It's too much. I turn back around. Ok, seriously. Where is Evie? Or, for that matter, Katja? There's no way she would let a customer stand unattended for this long —especially left alone with me.

"I'm not sure what's taking Evie so long." I stand up because I'm tired of twisting back and forth in my seat. Even though we're now facing each other, there's still several feet between us.

"That's okay." He rubs the back of his neck. "I know you were busy yesterday, and I'm sure you don't want to, but I think we should talk at some point."

My heart picks up its pace. Even though I know talking about things is what a mature adult would do in this situation, I really don't want to. I just want to make it through this week with minimal embarrassment and pain.

"I don't think that's a great idea." I look down at my feet. "Evie and I rode together. She's got a bunch of things to do, and I don't want to hold her up or end up stranded downtown."

After the final alterations, Evie is going to her house so she can get some work done before having dinner at her parents' with the rest of the family. I mean it when I say I don't want to get stranded downtown, but I also don't want to feel trapped with Nate having the dreaded talk.

"I don't think you need to worry about that," he says.

"Oh yeah?" I raise my brows. "Why is that?"

He tips his head toward the dressing rooms. I turn just in time to see the rustling of the heavy drapes that cover the doors leading into the dressing room area like someone was just there. I should have known better. It doesn't take that long to get dressed. I *knew* that. Evie has been spying on us this whole time.

I turn back to face Nate. "How long has she been watching us?"

He shrugs. "Not that long. She started walking out, but when she saw us talking, she just kinda stood there watching us."

I groan. Nothing like an audience to make an uncomfortable situation even more awkward. From the looks of it, I'm guessing Evie will be fine waiting for me to get this conversation out of the way, but I still hesitate.

"I'm not asking for your day, Macy." I hate the way my name sounds from his lips. Even after all this time, it sounds perfect. He rubs his face. "There's just a few things I want to talk to you about before this week gets away from us."

My conversation with my dad pops into my head. He really wanted me to understand that time is precious. He thought I should try to make amends with Nate. Maybe this really is why he returned to Florida early, so I would have this time to talk to him. The way he keeps insisting we talk makes me think he needs this too. As much as I don't want to admit it, I think I might actually owe Nate an explanation for why I pushed him away.

It won't change anything in the present, but maybe Nate will know that there's nothing wrong with him. Then maybe I'll finally be able to let go.

I turn back around and this time I catch Evie watching us. She doesn't hide this time. She jerks her head in the direction of Spill the Beans and mimics taking a sip from an imaginary cup. Spill the Beans is just a block from Katja's, and I imagine this is Evie's way of telling me to go get a drink with Nate.

I summon all my courage when I look back at him. "Are you hungry?"

"I could eat."

"Wanna grab a quick muffin from your sister's shop?"

I hope that he catches the emphasis on *quick*. Muffins are in the display case and need no prep. We can buy our food, get this awkward conversation over with, and be on our merry way.

His shoulders relax. "Sure."

I glare at Evie and raise my voice loud enough so she can hear me. "I will be telling them it's on the house."

"If that makes you feel better," she says back.

Oh, it absolutely makes me feel better. When I turn around, there's a ghost of a smile on Nate's face. When he catches me looking, it falls.

"Let's go," I say, and walk out the front door. Nate follows behind me.

We walk in silence toward the coffee shop. I'm hyper aware of his every movement as our steps falling in line with each other so we are walking in sync. My hand itches to reach out and grab his. There was a time when they would find each other without thinking. I look over at him in my peripheral vision. His hands are in his pockets. I wrap mine around my waist.

When we get to Spill the Beans, he steps in front of me to grab the door. He holds it open while I step inside.

"Thanks," I mumble.

"You're welcome."

Silence again as we stand in line.

"Can I get a chocolate chip muffin, please," I say when we get to the register. "Evie said it's on the house."

I always pay for my things when I come in, which is more often than I should, and the employees all know I'm best friends with their boss, so the barista doesn't even bat an eye when I say it.

"Make that two," Nate says, and pulls his wallet from his back pocket. "And I'll pay for them both."

I look at him in question.

"Doesn't feel right to steal from my sister."

I sigh. "Suit yourself."

Nate pays for our order and the guy working the register hands us two small white plates, each with a muffin on top. We grab them and take a seat across from each other at a small table.

"I'm glad you agreed to talk to me," he says.

It's not like I had a choice. I pick at the top of my muffin, causing some crumbs to fall onto the plate. "Yeah, of course."

"I know this week is going to be really . . . " He pauses and I know he's searching for the right word. I know this because I've been doing the same thing since I saw him yesterday. "Different."

"You could say that."

"And I know you weren't expecting me to come back until Friday, so I'm hoping my sudden appearance won't make things too difficult for you."

I wonder if this is when we pull out our calendars and start planning out who gets Evie on what days leading up to the wedding. The rehearsal dinner and wedding will be busy enough and will have enough people that it shouldn't be so bad. But days like today? I guess it's better to have a plan.

"But I really do need to talk to you sooner rather than later, so I'm glad today worked out."

My stomach churns. I knew this was coming, and yet I don't feel ready to talk about it. I don't know if I'll ever feel ready to tell him why we couldn't be together. I hold my breath and wait for him to say something.

"I came back early because I have a job interview."

When I don't immediately respond, he adds, "Here . . . in Belview."

"What?"

I feel like I've been sucker punched. And then kicked —hard.

I've been sitting here thinking that this is a "different" situation for both of us. I thought maybe I'd have to endure listening to him talk about his girlfriend and maybe see her at the wedding. That would be unbelievably hard, but this? This is next level, because what he's saying is that there's a real possibility that he's going to move home. That he's going to live here. When he marries that perfect woman, I'm going to be forced to see her all the time because he will *live* here. I will never be able to forget him. I will be forced to see what I have to live without for the rest of my life. No matter how hard I try, I will never be able to move on.

This is so much worse than the scenario in my head.

My breaths come in shallow pants. I'm lightheaded. My mouth is dry and I can't swallow. If I can't get my body under control, I'm going to pass out. I know there are things I'm supposed to be doing right now, exercises my therapist has taught me for whenever a panic attack begins, but I forget them all.

I can't breathe.

"Macy, look at me."

I struggle to suck in air, but my chest feels so damn tight.

"Macy." Nate's voice is strong, commanding.

My eyes find his. He's watching me carefully. His voice is soft when speaks again. "I want you to try to match my breathing. Ready?" He takes a deep breath, his eyes never leaving mine. "And out." He releases it through his mouth.

He does this over and over again. I watch the way his chest rises with each inhale, and the way his lips form a small O when he exhales. His breathing is slow and steady. It doesn't change. I can't match his pace, but as I continue to watch him, I can feel my heartbeat begin to slow. I'm able to inhale for a longer time after several attempts, and my breathing begins to return to a normal rhythm. I don't know how long it takes, but he doesn't stop his exaggerated breaths until I'm breathing normally again.

It's not fair. How can the person who just sent me spiraling also be the one to help me relax?

He gives me what I imagine is supposed to be a comforting smile. "You okay?"

No, I want to scream. *I'm not okay. I can't face the idea of you moving back home.*

Instead, I nod.

"It's just an interview, nothing is set in stone," he says. "But I thought it was only fair to let you know that it's a possibility."

I take a shaky breath. "Does your family know?"

He looks down at his hands and shakes his head.

"Why are you telling me this? Why not tell them first?"

He looks up. "Because they'll all be thrilled if I get a job here." He clears his throat. "I'm not sure you'll feel the same."

Again, I hate how pathetic I must seem compared to him. Nate seems totally unaffected by being here. Of course, it doesn't seem like a big deal for him to just move back to Florida. Meanwhile, I'm having panic attacks in the middle of coffee shops.

I want him to be happy. I really and truly do. I just want him to be happy far away from here.

"There's something else you should know," he says.

I don't know if I can handle any more shocks to my system.

"Okay," I say in a quiet voice, bracing myself, but nothing could prepare me for what he says next.

"My job interview. It's at Wagner and Stein."

Is this a joke?

Wagner and Stein is like a second home to me. I spent many of my summers helping file non-confidential paperwork and other menial tasks as my first job. The employees there send me birthday cards every year. I've watched carpet be replaced, walls get repainted, the landscaping change. I've seen the building morph over the years and can remember every reiteration.

Wagner and Stein is woven through my life, because it's been my dad's law firm for as long as I can remember.

Everything suddenly snaps into place.

The way my dad took me to Antonio's for lunch without a single argument. The way he went on about the importance of making amends. I can't believe I actually thought he was sick. Turns out, he was saying and doing all that because he knew. He knew the reason Nate was back in Florida before the rest of his family. He knew that I wouldn't take the news very well.

I cannot believe the one person who has been there for me my entire life could do something like this to me. I cannot believe he's actually considering hiring Nate.

I can count the times my dad has let me down on one

hand. He's always been great—until now. This is one of the deepest betrayals I've ever felt. The fact that it comes from the one man I thought I could trust hurts more than I can stand.

I let that hurt grow into something I can handle. Anger.

For the second time in so many days, I storm out of Spill the Beans, leaving Nate alone at a table thinking I'm incapable of actually finishing a conversation like a civilized adult. But I don't care because this time I really have things I need to do.

I need to talk to my dad.

6

THE PAST

JUNIOR YEAR OF HIGH SCHOOL

"I DON'T WANT to be here."

My dad laughs, but it lacks any joy or humor. It sounds exactly like I feel: exhausted. He runs his hands through his hair. "Trust me, I know."

I lift my finger in front of me. "You said that if I didn't like it, we'd never have to come back."

"Macy . . . "

"You promised."

My dad stands in front of me inside the RV. His hands are down at his sides. "Yeah, well, I think we both know I'm not the only one with a problem of breaking trust in the family."

I cross my arms over my chest. "You act like I haven't already learned my lesson." I feel like I'll never stop paying for that one stupid mistake.

"I know you have. That's part of why we're here. You need a chance to unplug and separate yourself from it all. I'm hoping spending some time away from school will help."

"Being here isn't making it any easier." Nothing is going to make the last month any better. I'm shaking and I can feel the start of angry tears forming in my eyes.

"I love you. I only want what's best for you."

"And missing school to come to the Rendezvous is somehow supposed to help?"

"I'm hoping getting away from your"—he lifts his fingers to do air quotes—"*friends* will help."

"You don't know anything about my friends." I stamp my foot and immediately feel childish. I *am* childish. I can't be in this small space with my dad right now. I just can't.

I'm not wearing shoes when I storm out the front door of the camper and make my way from modern camping to the main campgrounds. The door slams behind me as I speed away.

It's a chilly January morning, so I have leggings under my long, flowy skirt and a heavy sweater over my shirt. I wrap my arms tightly across my chest as I walk across the empty clearing leading into the campgrounds. My feet are freezing, and little pieces of the overgrown grass stick to them as I walk. I don't stop to pick the pieces off. I don't go back for my shoes either. I'm too angry to look at my dad right now and would rather lose a toe to frostbite than face him.

After several minutes, the sea of white tents comes into view. I don't slow as I enter the campgrounds. The layout hasn't changed since last year, and I make my way to the large tree. If the Rendezvous is an old town, the tree is the town square. It's central to almost everything, and can easily be found from almost anywhere on the campgrounds. Normally, there are a lot of people in the area, but it's still early enough that people only walk with specific destinations in mind instead of lingering to visit with friends.

The tree's canopy reaches over a dozen picnic tables and several of its branches are low-lying enough to touch the ground. I plop down at a picnic table, sitting with my feet facing out and my back against the table. I cross my arms over my chest. I'm still acting like a toddler, but at least I'm far, far from my dad, and no one here seems to care about me pouting.

"Look what the private school dragged in," a familiar voice says from behind me. There's no unkindness in the tone, just gentle teasing. His voice is exactly how I remember it.

I turn in my spot just in time to watch Nate sit on the bench opposite of me with the table between us. The table shakes a little as he sits down. My eyes take him in. He looks the same, but not. He's filled out more from the previous year. Less bony. Less angle-y. And even though we're sitting, I swear he looks taller. He's wearing a thick flannel shirt with suspenders over his shoulders. His dark hair covers his hazel eyes ever so slightly as he watches me. There's a pie in his hands. Steam pours off it, and the smell of dough and blueberry fills the space between us.

I know Nate and his family come every year. I shouldn't be surprised to see him, but considering the year I've had, this *would* be the one time that his entire family got the stomach bug and skipped out on the Rendezvous. I continue to stare at him, the ghost of a smile on my lips.

"Gotta say, I'm surprised to see you." He turns the pie

in his hands, drawing my attention to it. He hasn't taken a bite yet.

I raise my brows. "Oh yeah?"

"Not that I'm complaining." He grins at me. "But there was something about the way you said, 'This was fun, but I'm never coming back,' last year that made me think you were a one and done kind of girl."

"Trust me when I say no one is more surprised than me." I run my fingernails over the woodgrain, leaving faint marks on the table.

"So what changed? Did you regret not getting the raccoon skin hat?"

I snort. "I did feel like there was something missing from my fall wardrobe."

"Well, I bet the store's open. We could go now and grab one." He waggles his eyebrows.

I snap my fingers in front of me. "Too bad I left my wallet in the RV." I'd been in such a hurry to get out of there, I hadn't thought to bring anything with me.

"So you're penniless, now. My, how the tables have turned, rich girl."

"You caught me. I'm hoping to find a wealthy prospector to fill my coffers."

"Prospector? Coffers?"

"They're real things," I say, slightly defensive.

"I know. It's just funny to hear you talk like that."

"What can I say?" I wave my hand at the campground. "The atmosphere has a way of changing you."

"Ain't that the truth." He laughs. "Okay, but back to the lack of money. Is that why you haven't started stuffing your face with hand pies yet?"

I place my hand to my chest. "I'll have you know, I would never stuff my face."

He leans down so he can look under the picnic table. "Just like you would never go barefoot?"

I lift my bare feet up so they are hidden beneath my long skirt. "A lot can happen in a year."

"Again, not complaining." He continues to turn the pie in his hands.

The smell is driving me crazy. And I'm not sure what to say in response to his last comment, so I do something impulsive. I don't know why I do it. Maybe the last month has finally caught up to me. Maybe it's just the otherworldliness of this place. Without asking permission, I lean forward and snatch the pie from his hands. I take a big bite before putting it back.

I'd forgotten how delicious these things were. I barely hold back my moan as the blueberry filling dances over my tongue. It's so good, I almost forget the reasons I'm back here in the first place.

He looks at me and down at his pie, and then back at me again. His eyes are wide. "You weren't kidding about this place transforming you. You're positively primitive."

My mouth is still full when I say, "And it's only been an hour and a half."

He laughs before taking a bite. He doesn't even hesitate. Nate just puts his mouth where my mouth just was like it's no big deal. When he holds the pie out to me, my stomach does a little flip. If I eat after him, my lips will be where his were. I've never kissed a boy, which means this is the closest I've ever gotten to it. I know it's silly, but the idea of sharing a pie with Nate is enough to make me have a mini-freak out.

But I'm hungry and I'm still feeling reckless. I pretend not to care as I take the pie from his hand. I hope he doesn't see the way my hand shakes when I grab it this time. Even though I try to take a reasonably sized bite, there's so much filling, some of it spills out the side and down my fingers.

"Do you have any napkins?" I ask.

He shakes his head. "I'm capable of eating without making a giant mess."

I roll my eyes and hand him the pie. Then I do the only thing I can think of. I lick the side of my finger.

When I look up, Nate is staring at me. He clears his throat. "Actually, I think I'm done with this. Do you want the rest?"

I want to say no because I feel like that pie is more trouble than it's worth, but the thought of it being tossed in a trash can makes me want to cry. I reluctantly grab it from Nate, but am much more careful to take more strategic bites that won't make a mess this time.

After taking another bite, I ask him what he's up to this morning.

"I have an archery tournament later." He shrugs.

"Are you in the adult division this year?"

"Yep."

"That's so cool. Are you nervous?"

"Not really, but I don't think I'll get the first place trophy this year."

"I bet you do." I don't actually know what I'm talking about. I'm only going based off what his sister told me last year.

He chuckles. "I guess we'll see. But other than that, I'm pretty free today. What about you?"

I wave my hand at the clearing. It's still relatively empty. "This is it."

"Don't let it be said that the River Rendezvous isn't exciting."

"It's quite stimulating," I say without any emotion in my voice. I take another bite of the pie, and there's just enough left that Nate could get the last bite. I feel bad that I've eaten most of it when I know they're his favorite. "You sure you don't want any more?"

His answering smile is warm. "I'll be fine. And if I get hungry, I can buy another one. My coffers are filled to the brim."

"Must be hard to carry all that money around since they don't have banks yet." Or, at least, I don't *think* they had banks in 1840.

"How do you think I got all these muscles?" He lifts his arms and flexes. He's teasing me, but I'm surprised that he actually does have muscles. His biceps are huge.

My eyes dart away. "Guess I know where to go if I end up homeless."

"Yep. And all you gotta do is share a tent with my giant family."

"Every girl's dream."

He laughs. "You mean, other than owning a raccoon hat."

"Obviously."

Nate stands. "Well, I'm happy to help you fulfill one of those dreams. Since we don't have anything else to do, this is the perfect time to get that hat."

"Are you serious?"

He's bouncing on his toes. "You know I am. Come on. There's a place just a few tents down."

I sigh as I push up from the table and adjust my skirt.

Now that we're standing side by side, it's obvious how much he's grown. Last year, we were almost the same height. Now, he's got several inches on me.

We start walking and quickly fall into step.

"I don't know. I think a raccoon hat would be a giant waste of money. I wouldn't actually wear it."

"Don't be such a party pooper." He bumps his shoulder against mine. "I'll buy you a hat, and if you wear it every single day, I'll give you a prize when the week is over."

I lift my brows. "Oh, yeah. What kind of prize?"

"To be determined."

"And I'm just supposed to believe this prize is worth a week of utter humiliation?"

We pass by a group of middle-aged men, all decked out in the traditional clothing that is required at the Rendezvous. They are laughing loudly as we walk by them. They are all wearing raccoon skin hats.

"You think anyone is going to notice if you're wearing one? Honestly, it might be worse if you don't."

"I highly doubt it."

"I guess there's only one way to find out."

"If you say so."

"Don't be scared," he says as we approach one of the many tents that sells hats. He grabs one from the display and sets it on my head. It's off center and falling into my eyes. "What's the worst thing that can happen if you wear this hat for the week?"

I adjust the hat so that it's off my face. "Um, I wear this hat for the week."

"Don't you ever want to live a little? Stop caring what other people think?"

"It's easy for you to say. This is normal for you." I play with the hem of my sweater at my wrist.

"You keep assuming that just because I'm home-schooled, I don't know what it's like to feel embarrassed."

"Have you . . . ever felt embarrassed?"

He barks out a laugh. "You're kidding, right?"

"It's not that funny," I mumble. "It just seems like you're always so confident. I can't imagine you caring what other people think."

"Oh, I care what people think." He picks up a raccoon hat and places it on his head. "I just don't care what every person thinks about me. Only the ones that matter."

Nate's hat is crooked. I reach out and adjust it. "And how do you know which ones matter?"

He shrugs. "You just know."

The problem is, I don't just know. This past year has been tough. My friends and I seem to be slipping apart. They keep doing things I'm not comfortable with, and every time I show the least amount of hesitation, they make me feel bad until I finally give in.

It's my most recent cave to peer pressure that landed me back at the Rendezvous even after my dad promised that he would never make me come back. But I don't want to think about that right now. I want to enjoy this moment with someone who genuinely seems to want to spend time with me, and the worst thing he's trying to force me to do is wear a raccoon hat for a week.

I bit my lip. "If I let you buy these hats, you have to let me pay you back."

"No, I don't."

"Fine. If I let you buy these hats, you have to let me buy you a hand pie every single day for the rest of the week."

He shakes his head. "Nope."

I make an irritated noise. "I don't want you to feel like you have to pay for this just because I don't have my wallet. I'm fully capable of buying my own stuff."

"I know you are."

"And I don't want to take advantage."

"You're not." He pulls his wallet out of his pocket. "How about this? If I buy these hats, you have to promise to wear yours all week."

"Isn't that the bet already? I thought I was getting a prize if I did that."

"You can still get the prize. Me paying for it is just a bonus."

"Fine." I point my finger at him. "But you have to wear yours every day too."

"Oh, I was already planning on it." His accompanying smile is so wide, I can see almost all of his teeth. He looks happy, but he's also gloating.

I don't care. I'm happy too.

After Nate pays, and we make sure our hats are placed just so on our heads, we continue walking through the campgrounds. I won't admit it to Nate, but I actually like the hat. Or rather, I like the way it's keeping me warm. It's still early enough, and there's enough wind that the air is biting cold. Having the hat, no matter how ridiculous it looks, is helping me feel more comfortable in this weather.

"So, are you going to tell me why you were so unhappy to be here when I first saw you?"

I sigh. "Was it that obvious?"

"You looked like my younger brothers when Mom won't let them play video games for three hours straight."

"You think I was pouting?" I say, aghast.

He grimaces. "Maybe pouting is the wrong word. But you looked sad. Is everything okay?"

"Not really."

"I know you might not want to talk about it, but you can . . . if you want to."

I let out a long breath. Talking about it sounds nice. "Are you sure you want to listen?"

"How else am I going to get my *Pretty Little Liars* fix since we can't watch TV?" I narrow my eyes at him and he raises his hands in surrender. His teasing smile drops. "Seriously though. I don't mind. I'm a pretty good listener."

We pass several more tents before I speak. I start with the easy stuff. I tell him how I'm struggling to keep up in my AP classes. This year's workload has been horrible. School doesn't come naturally, and I've had to work my butt off to maintain straight As. If I get a B, my dad will ground me. It doesn't matter that I'm not the one who wanted to take the stupid classes in the first place.

Then I tell him about tennis tryouts. They start the week after I get back from the Rendezvous. I've been working really hard to get to the number two spot. I want to play on the top doubles team, and the girl who is currently in that spot is really good. Nate reassures me that the number three spot is good, too, and I should be proud to be in the top five, no matter where I fit.

Not exactly helpful, but I know he's trying to make me feel better, so I don't press it.

The next part is where I struggle to come up with the right words. I'm worried that I'm going to confirm every private school stereotype.

"I don't think I have any real friends," I say, and tip my face toward the ground. My bare feet peek out from the bottom of my skirt with every step.

"Why do you think that?"

"Promise you won't laugh."

He steps in front of me and stops. He's so close, I have to crane my neck so I can see his face. His expression is serious. "Macy. I know sarcasm is your second language. I'm pretty fluent myself. But if you're sharing something that is genuinely hard for you, I'm not going to laugh."

It's strange. I barely know Nate, but I believe him. I take a deep breath and step around him so I can keep walking. I don't want to be still for this. I don't want him to be able to watch my every facial expression when I tell him how much I feel like a stranger in my own life. He doesn't hesitate and walks beside me, easily falling in step again.

"I've been friends with the same group of girls since third grade. We do everything together. Birthdays, dances, whatever. Things used to be really easy, but this last year has been weird. They keep pushing the limits and I can't keep up."

"What do you mean?"

"Oh, you know, just regular stuff." I wave my hand in front of me like it's no big deal, because it seems so normal for everyone else, but deep down I know that it is. It's a big deal to me.

"Like, they all started having parties and things just started escalating really fast. It started with drinking, which whatever, that's fine. But then someone had pot at one, then another person brought some of their dad's painkillers to another. And—"

"That's not normal, Macy."

"Well, that's the thing. I didn't think it was either, but then everyone started doing it. And I felt like a weirdo being the only person who didn't drink. My friends stopped inviting me because they thought I was judging them, which okay, maybe I was. But then I just felt so lonely, so when my dad went out of town for a work trip, I thought I'd have a party. Prove to them that I wasn't this nerd who didn't know how to have fun. Of course, that's the one time my dad decided to come home early. When he saw what was happening, he lost it. Told me I wasn't allowed to hang out with them anymore."

Nate whistles low. "Wow. That's . . . Honestly, I'm surprised he brought you here. I think my parents would have had me digging my own grave in the backyard before taking me on vacation."

"Well, I think he's trying to get me to hang out with people less likely to get into trouble."

"And he thinks homeschoolers are all mild mannered and good?"

I nod. "Yeah. I think the plan is for me to hang out with you and Evie, get some candle making under my belt, and hopefully flush the desire to hang out with my friends ever again. But he doesn't need to worry about me hanging out with them anymore."

"Why's that? Did you learn your lesson?"

"Not exactly." I snort. "After my dad caught us, he called every single parent to tell them what their kid was up to. I've never gotten so many horrible texts before in my life. I had to stop reading them all, but the message was clear. They never want to hang out with me again."

"I'm so sorry. I can't imagine how rough school has been, having to face them after that."

"It just sucks, you know. I didn't even want to throw that stupid party. I just did it because I wanted to keep being their friend, but it just made things worse. Now, they refuse to even acknowledge me in school, unless they're making mean comments under their breath. It almost makes me wish that I could join the homeschool crowd beyond the Rendezvous."

"Don't say that. You know we're all a bunch of freaks."

I know he's trying to lighten the mood, so I give him a small smile.

"But seriously, I'm really sorry."

"Thanks." I let out a long sigh.

"Did you explain everything to your dad?"

I nod. "Yep. And I don't think he's actually mad at me. Just trying to help. Unfortunately, his help is not really all that great right now. And now we're here, and I wish I could just rewind and redo the last few weeks. Maybe I'd still have friends and I wouldn't feel so lonely."

Nate is quiet, and we walk in silence for a while. I'm not crying, but I'm afraid I will start if I keep talking. Plus, I'm dying to know what Nate thinks.

We reach the far end of camp. Before we turn around and start walking back, Nate stops and looks at me. "Macy. I can't imagine what that must feel like, but I don't think those girls were ever really your friends. They wouldn't have made you feel bad for not wanting to drink and do drugs. They wouldn't have bailed just because your dad called their parents. That's what parents do, and it stinks that it was at your house, at your party, but if it wasn't there, it would be another party, at another house."

"I just don't know what to do," I whisper. "I feel so alone. I just wish I still had friends, you know?"

"You're not alone. I'm your friend. Evie is your friend. That's two. Come back to my tent with me. We'll have so much fun, you'll forget how bad those other girls made you feel."

"That sounds as bad as promises of candy if I get into your white van."

He laughs, loudly. "I promise I'm not kidnapping you. You don't even have any money. What are you good for?"

"My stellar fashion sense?" I point to the raccoon hat on my head.

"I already got that." He points to his. "But seriously. Come hang out with me. Meet the rest of my family. I'm sure they'll like you too."

"How can you be so sure?"

"Remember what I said earlier, about knowing when people matter?"

I'm holding my breath when I nod.

"You matter, Macy. I'm sorry that your friends don't realize that. But you do."

I bite my lip. I'm not sure why this strange boy telling me I matter means so much, but it does. I'm happy he thinks I'm worth knowing and I'm happy he wants to include me in his life, no matter how brief.

"Come to my tent," he says. "And if you're lucky, we'll have candy."

7

THE PRESENT

TUESDAY

I STORM past Dad's secretary and into his office without stopping—without thinking. I'm so focused on talking to him right now that I don't even consider the fact that he might be in an important meeting with a client.

He's not, but I don't think I'd care even if he was. I'm so angry that I'm not worried about making a scene. The only thing I care about is figuring out why the hell my dad thought it was a good idea to interview Nate for a position at Wagner and Stein. What a major violation of trust.

My dad is sitting behind his giant mahogany desk and staring intently at a piece of paper in his hands, his reading glasses perched on the tip of his nose. When he registers my presence, he sets the paper on his desk.

"You *knew* that Nate was in town."

He doesn't respond.

"You *knew* the reason he was in town."

He still doesn't say anything, but his face softens.

This is how I know that this isn't some misunderstanding or cruel joke. His expression is how I know that Nate really is applying for a job at Wagner and Stein, and my dad knew about it long before I did. Not only did he know, he kept it a secret.

"How could you?" I'm surprised by how quickly the tears come. My vision goes blurry and my dad becomes a blob of colors and vague silhouettes.

"Macy." His voice is soft. "Please come sit down."

I shake my head. There's no way I can sit right now. There's too much energy coursing through my body. I want to run. I want to punch something. I want to . . . I don't know what I want to do. I settle on pacing back and forth in his office. "I can't believe you didn't tell me."

"You know it's not appropriate for me to discuss potential candidates with you."

I stop my pacing. "We're not talking about some random graduate from Yale who found you on LinkedIn. This is Nate."

"What do you want me to say?"

"I want you to say you're not going to hire him."

He rests his elbows on the desk and rubs his temples.

I take a step toward him. "Dad?"

"I know Nate would not be your preference, but—"

"No. My *preference* is not to listen to country music. I *prefer* pepperoni on my pizza. I *like* it when my floral shipments come in on time. But this?" I laugh bitterly. "This is more than a preference. You're talking about hiring Nate at your law firm."

My dad motions for me to take a seat. "Please."

I begrudgingly sit down in one of two leather chairs that sit opposite of him. My knee bounces wildly as he reaches under his desk and pulls out a bottle of water. He slides it across the wood toward me. I grab it and start picking at the plastic wrapper. "What am I supposed to do if you hire him? How could I ever come to see you at work? How could I leave my house?"

My dad's face softens. "I'm sorry, Macy. I really am."

I stare at him, waiting for him to continue. How can he say he's sorry when he's the one doing this? "Why are you doing this to me?"

"Believe it or not, this has nothing to do with you."

Easy for him to say. It feels like it has everything to do with me. It has the potential to upset the delicate balance I've found in my life.

My dad sighs. He looks tired. "His résumé is very impressive."

My face scrunches up. "Didn't he just finish law school? How impressive could his résumé be?"

In what universe does a recent graduate get an interview at one of the most prestigious law firms in Belview?

"He graduated at the top of his class at NYU. Passed the BAR exam on the first try. Was in Phi Alpha Delta. He worked part-time at a local law office while taking an impressive course load. He had glowing recommendations from the senior partners at that firm."

My head is spinning with all this new information. I knew he was going to law school, but I didn't realize he'd done so much. He's been racking up awards and accolades while I've spent the last four years in Belview. College dropout with a silly, little floral business.

There have been many times when I've felt the sting of defeat. There have been moments I've felt like I couldn't go on. But this is a special kind of failure. Nate has managed to accomplish the academic success my dad always dreamed for me. And now he's here to join the ranks at Wagner and Stein.

Never have I felt worse about where I am in life.

I don't cry or pout. I don't scream or even speak.

I'm completely numb.

I set the water bottle I've been holding onto my dad's desk. I pick my purse up off the ground and put it over my shoulder. I don't say goodbye before standing up. I hear him calling my name as I walk out of his office, but I don't stop.

It looks like Nate is returning to Florida for good, possibly Belview, and there's nothing I can do about it.

I'M SITTING on my couch with a giant tub of mint chocolate chip in my lap when I hear the knock at my door. I've been at home for a few hours now. My hair is in a messy bun on the top of my head. I still have faint mascara lines at the corners of my eyes from crying, and my bra has long since been discarded to the depths of hell.

In other words, I'm in no condition for company.

I ignore whoever is on the other side of the door and take another bite of ice cream.

"Macy Wagner. If you don't answer this door right now," Evie yells from the other side of the door.

I can choose to ignore her. But if I do that, I'm sure she'll just use her spare key to let herself in. I sigh and set the carton on my coffee table before I answer the door.

The last time I saw my best friend was at Katja's. She was practically pushing me to go talk to Nate with a sly look on her face. Now, Evie looks as upset as I feel. She pulls me in for a hug. "Nate told me what happened at the coffee shop."

I wonder which part. Was it when he told me he was applying for a job at my dad's firm or when he had to calm me down from a panic attack before I almost passed out? Maybe he told his sister about how I stormed out on him for the second time in two days. There's just so much material, it's practically writing itself at this point. I feel like the main character of some tragic story.

Evie releases me and pushes past me to the living room. When she sees the almost empty carton on the coffee table, she raises her brows. "How full was that when you started?"

I look down at my feet. "I bought it on the way home from my dad's office."

"Oh, Mace." She finds the lid and puts it on top, then disappears into the kitchen. I hear the sound of the freezer door opening and closing. When she returns, I'm sitting in the same spot I've been in for the last couple of hours, my legs tucked under me.

She sits next to me. "I thought y'all were going to have some kind of closure talk. I was looking forward to the possibility of you becoming friends. I promise I didn't know why he came home early."

I nod because I know she didn't know about the interview. If Evie had any clue what was about to happen, she wouldn't have let me go off with Nate by myself.

"When he came back to Katja's by himself, I knew something was wrong. He didn't tell me. Just drove me back to my house in silence. It wasn't until we were all at my parents' for dinner that he shared the news that he was interviewing for a job at Wagner and Stein."

The ice cream churns in my stomach. "I feel so silly. It never even crossed my mind that he would apply for a job at my dad's law firm. Of all the places in all the cities in all the world, *this* is where he chose to send his résumé?"

Evie bites her lip. "It wasn't the only place he applied."

I sit up. "What do you mean?"

"Well, I asked him the same question when he told me. I asked him why he wanted to work at Wagner and Stein when there were so many other law firms. He told me he sent out his résumé to a lot of places, mostly in Belview, but some in New York. This was one of the few places that actually called him back for an interview."

My head spins with this new information. "Does that mean he has other job offers?"

"Please don't ask me that."

"What do you mean?"

Evie grabs one of my throw pillows and hugs it to her chest. "I've spent the last several years putting you in your separate little boxes. I can't talk to you about him. I can't talk to him about you. It's tough. Two people I love and care about in their own little worlds. And now you want to know if he is dating anyone, if he has other job offers. He wants to know how you're doing and how long you've had Oops a Daisy. I'm getting major whiplash here, Macy. From both of you."

My mind stumbles on the part where she mentions Nate was asking about me. What does that mean? I shake the thought away and focus on Evie. She has a point. I'm sure this is super weird and confusing for her too. Probably for everyone involved.

I need to do my best to get through this, and that means putting on my big girl panties. There will be plenty to sort out everything when the interview is over and the "I do's" have been said. I can't pretend that Nate moving home won't affect me in a big way. What I can do is push any of those thoughts to a place where I don't let them get to me until after the wedding.

Evie said she's been putting me and Nate in two separate boxes for the last several years. Even now, I can tell she's not sure what she should say and what she shouldn't. It's not fair to her.

"So, all awkwardness aside, are you excited about the idea of Nate moving back home?"

She looks at me, uneasiness filling her features.

"It's not a trap," I say. "He's your brother and I know you miss him."

She tucks some hair behind her ear. "Of course, I'm excited. And yeah, I've missed him. I was closer to him than any of my other siblings before . . . " She stops and clears her throat. "Before he left for school. I'd like to think we could rebuild that relationship if he was closer."

"Well, I hope that it works out for both of you."

"Thank you," she says. "I know how hard it must be for you, so it means a lot to hear you say that."

"I mean it."

"I know you do. And that, combined with the fact that we're already talking about him, is why I'm going to say one more thing about my brother. I know things are really awkward with Nate, but it would mean a lot to me if you tried talking to him."

"Evie—"

"I know." She holds up a hand. "It's hard. And listen, I'm not mad at you for what happened. I understand, really. But if there's a chance that he is moving to Belview, I need there to be some kind of peace between you."

"I don't think I can be friends with him."

"I'm not asking for friendship, Macy. It's just, he and I used to be really close. And the last few years have been hard for me too. I don't want to have to plan my life around your schedules."

"You won't have to."

She levels me with a look. "Really? Because right now, my best friend literally rents a cabin in North Carolina every Christmas, which just so happens to correlate with the one time of the year Nate comes to visit his family."

I sigh. She's right. I can't just take vacations every time I might bump into him. For a split second, I consider buying my little cabin in the woods, but reality comes seeping back in. I was serious when I said Nate and I can't be friends. Looking back, I don't think friendship was ever an option.

But that doesn't mean I can't work through what an amicable relationship with him looks like. I promise Evie I'll try, then make a mental note to schedule something with my therapist soon, because navigating my relationship with Nate, without letting the past get in the way, isn't going to be easy.

8

THE PAST

JUNIOR YEAR OF HIGH SCHOOL

It's the second to the last night of the Rendezvous, and my dad and I are walking to the bonfire together. We've made up from that first day, and have had plenty of heart-to-hearts in the time we've been here. As hesitant as I am to say it, it's actually been an enjoyable week. The two of us have spent a lot of time together participating in activities the campgrounds have to offer. But he's also been giving me a lot of space to spend time with people my age.

This is part of his not-so-subtle plan to help me see beyond the people I used to consider my friends—and I don't hate it. Spending a lot of time hanging out with the Delaney family was overwhelming at first. The chaos that comes with such a large family had a bit of a learning curve. But once I got everyone's name down, other than the twins who I still get confused about, it made things a lot easier.

When I'm not spending time with my dad, I'm usually hanging out with Evie and Nate. They're the closest in age to me, and they seem to have a closer relationship with each other than with the rest of their siblings. I dare to say, they've become my friends in the short time we've known each other. They might be my only friends considering the drama back home. I'm not sure if I should be happy to finally have people who like me just the way I am, or if it's pathetic that my only friends have only known me for a combined two weeks.

It's cold, and the campgrounds are dark, as my dad and I walk toward the bonfire. Without streetlights or flashlights, we have to rely on the light from the fire to get us there. Thankfully that thing is massive. The flames tower over the crowd gathered around it. While I can't say I'm an expert on bonfires, I still know that this is one for the record books.

There are several log benches surrounding the fire, and the sound of string instruments carries over the breeze. The bluegrass music they're playing isn't something I would listen to on my own, but I like it. It's fitting for evenings at the Rendezvous.

My dad and I are careful to avoid large rocks and sticks as we continue to walk toward the fire. As we get closer, I spot the Delaney clan. Nate's parents are sitting on a log bench together while their children talk to their friends. Wes is laughing with a girl his age, the twins are throwing small sticks at each other like they're much younger than fourteen, and Evie and Nate are standing close to the fire.

"I think I'm going to talk to Esther and Michael," my dad says, pointing to Mr. and Mrs. Delaney. "If you want to go hang out with your friends."

I rub my hands over my arms. "Oh, I'm totally getting

closer to the heat." I try not to think about how cold it will be when the fire dies down. Or how miserable it will be walking back to the modern side of the campgrounds. Right now, I just want to get to where it's warmer so I'll be more comfortable.

Evie notices me right away and waves me over. When Nate notices his sister's movements, he turns toward me. I can't see him clearly because of the darkness, but where the fire illuminates his skin, I can see a giant grin spread across his face. He's smiled a hundred times around me in the last week, but something about the way he looks at me right now makes my heart stop.

Images from the past week flash through my mind. The way he cheered me up when I first arrived. The way he brought me back to his tent and introduced me to the rest of his family and included me in different events. I think about the way he won the archery tournament again and how we celebrated with smuggled Cokes in brown paper bags. I remember all of our conversations as we walked around the campgrounds, and the way he kept reminding me that I was worth it.

Oh crap. I think I might have a crush on Nate Delaney.

I stumble with the sudden thought, and of course, he notices. His smile falls as he walks over.

"Are you okay?" he asks, his voice full of concern, when he reaches me.

My cheeks warm. I've never been so thankful for the darkness as I am now. I nod. "Yeah. I just tripped over a small rock."

He looks around me at the ground for the treacherous rock, but he won't find it. There was no rock, just a girl who had sudden awareness that her friend is hot. But it's not like I can tell him that I tripped over my own feet because some kind of switch was flipped inside my body and I just realized I'm attracted to him.

When I shiver, it's not from the weather.

He notices the movement and his eyes widen. "Sorry, Macy. You were coming over to the fire, and here I am holding you up." He grabs my hand and drags me behind him. "Come on, let's get you out of the cold."

My mind focuses on the place where our skin meets with laser-like precision. His hand is warm as it wraps around mine. He squeezes it with the smallest amount of pressure as we get closer to the fire. His fingers bend in a gentle curve. Meanwhile, my hand suddenly feels like it's made of concrete and I can't move my fingers even the slightest bit.

It's a miracle I'm able to move any part of my body with the shock I'm experiencing, but somehow my legs carry me to where Evie is standing next to the fire. Her eyes go to where our hands are still joined. Nate notices her staring and instantly drops mine. The cold air rushes over the places where his skin warmed mine.

I'm trying not to wiggle my fingers or stand too still or look at Nate. I want to act natural, but my mind has irritatingly gone blank.

This isn't the first time he's touched me, but this is the first time he's touched me since I realized that I might actually like him, and I don't remember how I would have reacted before. Scratch that. I know exactly how I would have reacted. I wouldn't have thought about it at all. I would have acted like nothing happened and moved on with whatever activity we were doing.

Too late for that now.

My breath catches in my chest, my heart is racing. Too many seconds have ticked by, and I'm still inside my mind trying to figure out how I'm supposed to be acting right now, but I am convinced that I'm doing the complete opposite of playing it cool right now.

"Macy, you ok?" Evie asks.

"Yep," I answer too quickly. "Totally fine."

When I look over at her, she's watching me with a strange expression on her face.

"She's cold and tripped over a rock," Nate says. He wraps his arm around me and starts rubbing the side of my arm. "Give her a minute to warm up and then we'll get our regular Macy back."

I go completely still.

Nate has so much confidence in me, but I'm convinced I just ruined one of the best things that ever happened to me: easy friendship with people who like me for who I really am.

Nate eventually takes his arm back and I hold my hands out to the flame like I'm still trying to warm myself.

"What took you so long?" Evie asks. "You missed old lady Tabitha dancing around the fire without her bra. All the guys were trying so hard not to look."

Nate laughs through a cough. "She was really into it. Jumping all over the place."

The mental image is too much. I cover my mouth to hide my laugh. Tabitha is about fifty years old and well-endowed in the chest region. I'm sure there were several young boys who were traumatized tonight. Several adults too. I feel guilty for being late since what I was doing was more enjoyable than watching Tabitha's performance. "I guess I won't tell you where I was then."

"No, now you have to tell us," Evie says.

"I can't."

"Was it because you were doing something similar to Tabitha?"

"No," I say quickly.

"Then, just tell us," Nate says.

"But I feel guilty."

Evie smirks. "I'm going to assume it was dancing until I hear otherwise."

"Ugh." I cover my face with my hands.

"Seriously?" Nate says. "Is it that bad?"

I bite my lip, then say in a rush, "My dad thought it might be fun to go get dinner before coming to the bonfire tonight."

"Off site?"

I nod.

Evie gasps. "Tell me you didn't get fast food."

I grimace. "It was Culver's."

"You suck," Evie says playfully and pushes me. It's not really that hard, but I lose my balance and fall into Nate. He catches me in his arms and rights me easily. Again, his hands linger on me. I'm sure that hasn't happened before. I feel like I would remember that, even if everything felt completely platonic, right?

What is happening?

Evie watches the entire interaction. Her eyes narrow in concentration for a moment before she shakes her head. "I, uh, just realized I need to go check on the twins."

"They're fourteen," I say. "Do they really need you to check up on them?"

"I promised Mom I would," she says, and rushes off before Nate or I can argue.

"That was weird," Nate says once Evie is out of our sight.

I clasp my hands together in front of me. I look everywhere but at Nate. "Yeah."

"But I can't say I'm mad to spend more time with you."

I let out a nervous laugh. "We've spent the whole week together. You sure you're not getting sick of me?"

"I don't think I could get sick of you."

My eyes snap to him. Wait. Is he flirting with me?

I shake away the thought as quickly as it enters my mind. Nate always says strange things to me. Our entire relationship has been a series of odd conversations. I'm just seeing it differently because I'm seeing him differently. I laugh again. This time it sounds breathless.

"Macy."

I tuck a piece of hair behind my ear. "Yeah?"

"You don't have to be afraid of me."

"I'm not afraid of you."

He smiles at me. "You're afraid right now."

I look around. Even though it's just me and Nate talking right now, we're not alone by any stretch of the imagination. There are people everywhere. We're standing by the fire where everyone can see us, and if I were to cry out for help, twenty brawny dudes would come to my rescue. "I'm not scared."

"That's not what I mean," Nate answers, as if he can read my thoughts. He reaches out and grabs one of my hands. It's the same hand he held on our way to the fire, and I feel like I might die. "I like you, Macy. And I think you might like me too."

Blood is thumping through my ears in such a loud repeating whoosh, I'm not sure that I heard him correctly.

"You like me?" I say, my voice shaking.

He smiles, a small crooked one I've never seen before that sets my heart hammering. "Ever since I first saw you last year."

"There's no way you liked me when you first met me."

"Fine. Maybe I didn't like you right away."

I make an offended noise.

"But it was only because I didn't know you yet." He looks down at our feet. "I thought you were the most beautiful girl I'd ever seen and wanted to spend more time with you." I can't speak. Nate takes advantage of my silence and continues. "I kept finding excuses to talk to you but got so nervous I kept walking away like an idiot."

I think about all of our micro-conversations from last year. He would talk to me for five to ten minutes and then run off. "I thought that was just the way you acted."

"Because I'm a homeschool kid." He doesn't say it like a question because he knows the answer. But he also doesn't seem angry or upset by the fact that I might have had a teensy tiny prejudice.

A corner of my mouth lifts. "Maybe."

"That's okay." He's still smiling. "I was acting super weird and definitely living up to the stereotype. Then the week was going by so fast and I finally got up the courage to ask you to come watch the archery competition."

The competition where he got first place. My eyes widen. "You were showing off."

"Maybe." He gives me a sly smile.

"But you never said you liked me."

He laughs to himself. "I was barely brave enough to ask you to come watch me shoot targets. Do you really think I was going to tell you I had a crush on you?"

"I guess not."

Honestly, it's for the best that Nate didn't confess his feelings. Last year, I was busy taking in the entire River Rendezvous experience. I don't think I would have reacted well to Nate telling me he liked me.

"But then I saw you this year and I couldn't believe my eyes. It was like I got a second chance."

He approached me on the first day and spent a lot of time listening to me talk about my life back home. He scheduled activities we could do together and introduced me to his family. We've been spending a lot of time together, but he hasn't hinted that he sees me as anything but a friend until now. "Took you long enough."

He rubs the back of his neck. "Well, it turns out Evie likes you a lot, too, and is always around. It's hard to put yourself out there when your big sister is always hovering."

Evie. I've almost forgotten she went to check on her brothers. I look around to see if I can find her, and to make sure she's not on her way back to us now that Nate and I are laying things out there. I see her sitting by herself—not with the twins. She's near the fire so she has enough light to read the paperback in her hands. "Does she know?"

He lets out a self-deprecating laugh. "I think she does now."

I look down at the space between us. Nate's still

holding my hand. He's holding my hand and he likes me. I have no idea what to do with this information. I like him, but the Rendezvous is almost over, and we will be returning to the real world in one more day. It seems silly to start something when we have less than a day left. I sigh. It feels so unfair that it took me this long to see Nate this way or for him to confess his mutual feelings.

His face falls. "Am I totally misreading this?"

I bit my bottom lip, my eyes going to where he's still holding my hand. "No, I like you too."

"But . . . "

I look at his face. He's watching me, waiting patiently for me to continue. "I don't think it's a good idea."

"Macy," he says. "If you don't want to do anything, we go back to being friends, and it's not a big deal."

It's not that I don't want to be something more than friends. I just wonder where it can go. We live an hour away from each other and my dad won't like the idea of me looking at any boy in a romantic manner. I'm too young. The risk of heartache or becoming a teen mom isn't worth it. Dating is something I can consider after I graduate from college, but not right now. He's made that clear time and time again. My dad will definitely lose his mind if I tell him I want to start dating.

"How would it work?" I ask.

"Maybe we only see each other once a month. I don't care. I'll take you however I can get you." His face is so earnest as he says, "We have phones. We can text. We can FaceTime."

I can't believe I'm actually considering it. Not because I don't think he's worth it. I do. And I don't think he'll grow bored of me after a month and change his mind. There's no way he'd ghost me in an attempt to get rid of me. I barely know Nate, but I've seen enough of his character that I know he means what he says.

The fire continues to crackle next to us. A particularly loud pop makes me jump and Nate's hand tightens around mine. He hasn't let go of it the entire time we've been talking. I'm glad he hasn't. I squeeze back. It feels like I'm standing on the edge of a cliff overlooking the water. The view is amazing. I could stay here and take it in for hours and it would be fine. But I want to jump. I want to feel the rush of falling. I want to know what the water feels like on my skin. I don't know what's going to happen when I resurface, but I take the plunge. "Okay."

If I thought the smile he gave me before was brilliant, it was only because I haven't seen this one before. The joy that radiates from his expression right now warms me from the top of my head to the tips of my toes. "Yeah?"

I nod. "Yeah."

He pulls me into a tight hug and swings me around a few times. My long skirts flow beside me as we spin. I laugh into his neck and breathe him in.

If I knew the happiness that would come from just hugging Nate, I would have been begging my dad to take me to the River Rendezvous all year. I'd mark down the days on the calendar. I would run over to the historic campgrounds the second we arrived and never return to the modern camping side.

I don't know how long he twirls me, but Nate eventually stops. When he sets me down, I wobble on my feet. His hands land on my arms and steady me. He looks down at me, his smile still as breathtaking as it was when he first picked me up. "You're not going to regret this, Macy Wagner."

I don't know what a long-distance relationship is going to look like. I don't know what's going to happen when I tell my dad. But what I do know is I won't regret taking this leap with Nate.

9

THE PRESENT

WEDNESDAY

The drive to Evie's parents' house gives me plenty of time to regret my decision to join her family for dinner tonight.

This is one of the last nights before the wedding celebrations officially begin—Evie's bachelorette party is Friday, the rehearsal dinner the next night, then it's wedding day—so Mr. and Mrs. Delaney thought it would be a great time to have a big family dinner. Aunts and uncles and cousins from across the country are all going to Evie's parents for a giant cookout, and I'm invited. As much as I would love to come up with an excuse not to go, I'm the maid of honor and it would be terrible to miss. So, here I am.

My car jostles up and down as I make my way down the long gravel driveway that leads to their house. The Delaneys live on three acres. They have a large garden, fruit trees, and a small amount of livestock, including chickens, quail, and goats. Their house is everything you'd expect from a homeschool family that took their seven children to a pioneer reenactment camp every year when they were young.

I park next to some familiar cars that belong to Evie's parents and siblings.

There was a time when this place was like a second home to me. I spent many days helping Evie and Nate feed the animals, collect eggs, and harvest veggies. Their parents insisted that I just walk in and make myself comfortable. They always invited me to stay for dinner and never made me feel like I overstayed my welcome.

That was before we went off to college, and Nate and I eventually broke up. I was too afraid to visit during Evie's college days, and then she moved to Belview after graduation. That means I haven't been here in four years. There's a strange feeling of déjà vu as I walk up the porch steps and toward the front door.

Everything looks exactly how I remember it, with only small differences. There's a doorbell camera now. The rubber welcome mat has been replaced with a rough jute one. Potted plants hang from the ceiling of the porch.

It's suddenly too much. I take a deep breath to calm myself.

You can do this, Macy.

It's just dinner.

You can always leave early.

My hand shakes as I knock. I doubt anyone can hear it over the loud sound of everyone's voices, but a moment later the front door opens.

On the other side is Joanna, the oldest of the Delaney siblings, and Evie's only sister. She looks like all the other Delaney siblings—tan skin and dark hair. When she realizes I'm the one knocking, her carefree smile transforms into a frown. "Oh."

I force a smile. "Hey, Joanna."

She lets me in but doesn't wait for me to follow her. She disappears, leaving me in the foyer by myself. We never were close, but things took a nosedive when I broke up with Nate. I've only seen her a few times since, and only because I happened to be around when she came to visit Evie.

Standing in the foyer is even stranger than standing on the porch. Everything is exactly as I remember it. The hardwood floors, the floral wallpaper, the family pictures on the wall. The carpet-covered stairs that lead to the bedrooms on the second story. It even smells the same.

The strong sense of nostalgia that hits me as I stand there is almost enough to make me cry. I linger in the entryway of the house to fortify myself before facing everyone. Laughter floats to me from the other room, and I don't want to be the reason it stops. Tonight is an extension of Evie's wedding, and I need to be really careful about not making this evening about me. I need to pretend that I'm unaffected by Nate's presence. I have to act like I don't notice the dirty looks from Joanna. I have to find a way to be happy.

The sound of steady footsteps pulls my attention to the stairs. The first thing to come into view is worn-out Chucks. A pit forms in my stomach as they continue to make their way down the steps. I watch as more and more of the boy I once loved appears before me.

When Nate notices me standing at the bottom of the stairs, he stops. He's still several feet above me, and I have to tilt my head back to see his face. Our eyes meet and I swear time stands still. Every memory of me waiting downstairs for him to come down from his bedroom floods my mind at once.

"Macy." His hand grips the banister. "I didn't realize you were here."

"Evie invited me." The words sound defensive, like I need to prove that I have every right to be at his childhood home. I don't know if I'm trying to convince him or me.

He shakes his head. "No, I know. I wasn't sure if you were coming tonight."

Is it because I keep running away every time I see him? Probably. I shrug. "Figured I shouldn't miss it."

Nate takes the rest of the steps down so he's standing a few feet in front of me. "She'll be happy you're here."

That may be true, but I'm already second-guessing myself. I'm ready to walk back out the front door and take the return trip to my home, especially when his eyes travel over my body, leaving a trail of heat in their wake.

He swallows. "You look beautiful."

I look down at myself. I changed half a dozen times before settling on the outfit I'm wearing. It's a simple A-line with a floral design. It does amazing things for my figure while still being comfortable. My hair is in its usual style but I did spend a little extra time on my eyeliner. There's no use in fooling myself. I made a conscious effort to look nice tonight knowing Nate was going to be here, but actually hearing him say I look beautiful makes the pit in my stomach change into a flutter.

"Sorry." He runs a hand down his face. "I shouldn't have said that."

"It's okay," I say, even though it's really not.

I still don't know if he's dating anyone. If he is, that comment is wildly inappropriate. If he's not, my behavior is. I ended things between us. I shouldn't have dressed up for him, and I shouldn't enjoy the fact that he noticed.

We stand there careful to avoid making direct eye contact. I feel his eyes on my face when I look at my feet, but when I tilt my face up, he looks at the wall. It's a delicate dance as we try to look at each other, while not actually looking at each other. I look at his arms—strong, corded muscle peeks out from his t-shirt. I glance at his jaw where a subtle bit of stubble shadows his skin. I peek at his face, still marveling at the way he's grown up in the years we've been away from each other.

He clears his throat. "How are you doing today?"

Other than standing in the hall with my ex? "What do you mean?"

"Yesterday, you had a panic attack at Spill the Beans. Are you better?"

My face burns. Oh right. That wonderful incident when I found out that Nate sent his résumé to my dad's firm. "Yeah. I think I was just surprised, that's all." *Liar.* "I thought you liked New York."

Nate shrugs. "It was okay, but I missed my family."

Family has always been important to Nate. It was why everyone was so shocked when he changed his mind last minute and went to NYU. It coincided with our split, but no one expected him to react like that. No one expected he'd be gone for four years.

"So why not get a job in Oak Ridge?" I ask.

"I thought about it, but Evie's in Belview." He shrugs. "It would be nice to be near her."

Understandable. We stand in silence for a moment

longer before I finally ask the question I really want to know. "Why Wagner and Stein? Why try to get a job with my dad?"

There's a long pause before he opens his mouth. "I—"

"There you are." Evie burst into the room. She stops short when she sees Nate and me standing close to each other. A deep line forms between her brows as she looks between the two of us. "I just wanted to let you know that Dad is almost done with the burgers if y'all want to come get plates."

She gives us one more look before turning back toward the kitchen.

"We should probably go." I jerk my head in the direction Evie walked off.

"Yeah."

Nate lets me go first and stays a couple of feet behind me as we walk through the house. The kitchen is a large space that opens up to an outdoor patio. There's a slight breeze and the mosquitos aren't bad yet, so the French doors are open and people are spilling outside.

"There you are," Mrs. Delaney says, walking up to me, her arms outstretched. She pulls me into a hug. "I'm glad Evie convinced you to come tonight."

I squeeze her back, enjoying the fact that her embrace is still warm and familiar. "I wasn't sure if it was a good idea."

I've tried my best to avoid the rest of the family whenever I can. Coming to an event meant for those related to the Delaneys feels wrong.

She leans back, but keeps her hands on my shoulders so I can't run away. "Macy. You've always been welcome here. I've never stopped loving you." Her eyes flit to something behind me and her expression turns sad. I turn to see Nate talking to one of his brothers.

I'm hit by a pang of regret. I loved Nate and I loved his mother. I've missed the natural way they pulled me into their family. Mrs. Delaney was the mom I never had when I was younger. She taught me so much in my junior and senior years of high school. She took me prom dress shopping, taught me how to bake, and taught me how to mend a button. All the things my dad didn't know and didn't realize I wanted to learn.

"Make sure you grab a few cookies when you go through the line." She tilts her head toward the food table.

Someone pulls her away because they've run out of baked potatoes, and I'm left standing by myself. I can feel people's eyes on me—family members I haven't seen since high school. I don't know them well, but I imagine they're wondering what I'm doing here. Why would Nate's crazy ex be at this family celebration?

I look around the party for a familiar face. Thankfully, it doesn't take me long to spot Matt across the patio. He's standing with his brother, Joey. They're laughing hard, but when his eyes catch mine, his smile falls. He says something to his brother and starts walking toward me.

Tonight, Matt has half of his long, black dreads pulled back in a hair tie off his face. He's got several inches on Nate, and I crane my head back to say hi to him before he pulls me in for a hug.

"Evie told me she saw you and Nate in the foyer," he says quietly, so no one else can hear. "Are you doing okay?"

I don't think Evie has told Matt my entire history with her brother, but he knows enough to know that this week will be difficult. And just knowing that there's someone here who isn't loyal to Nate through blood makes me relax—a little.

I step back and smile weakly. "I think so."

"You sure?"

"I don't know, but I don't want to think about Nate too much if I can help it."

He scrunches his face up in mock confusion. "Nate? I don't even know who that is."

My smile grows. "Thanks. Did you already eat?"

"I did, but I'm happy to go through the line with you. I might grab some more fruit salad."

"Thanks. I'd really appreciate it."

I didn't realize how badly I wanted him to walk with me until we start going through the line together. I feel better having him next to me as I pile food onto my plate. Just before I scoop coleslaw onto my plate, my eyes go to the one person I'm trying not to look at. I can't help it even though I wish I could. Matt follows my line of sight and frowns. He leans down and quietly says, "If he does anything to upset you, I'll beat him up."

I laugh loudly enough to gain a few curious looks.

I don't think I've ever heard Matt raise his voice, let alone threaten physical violence. It's one of the reasons I love him so much. That, and the fact that he makes my best friend deliriously happy. I raise my brows at him. "You're seriously going to hit your future brother-in-law?"

We finally get to the fruit, and he loads his plate with pineapple, melon, and grapes. "Obviously not, but do you feel better knowing I offered?"

"Sure." I roll my eyes and now it's his turn to laugh.

"Seriously though, if you need a way out of a situation, give me a signal and I'll do what I can."

"What kind of signal?"

"Maybe a toast to the happy couple?"

"Talking in front of the entire Delaney family doesn't feel like a great exit strategy."

He laughs again. "Give me a look, and Joey and I will figure something out. Sound good?"

"Yeah. Sounds great."

I doubt I'll use it, but it does feel good to know there's someone here looking out for me if I need it. I thank him again before walking toward the picnic table that Evie and the rest of the bridesmaids are sitting at. Joanna is there, along with some of Evie's other friends, Lillian, and Rachel.

After I get settled in my seat, I look around and notice that Matt and Joey are sitting with Nate and the twins. When Matt sees me, he gives me a friendly wink. It's a wink that says, you've got this. You'll be fine.

With that assurance, I am able to relax enough to take a bite of one of Mr. Delaney's famous burgers. I groan in delight as I chew. It's even better than I remember. I listen to Evie as she and the other girls at the table talk about her upcoming honeymoon in Fiji and whether or not she and Matt feel confident to leave their business behind for a week.

Lillian, one of Evie's bridesmaids and a girl she's been friends with since college, does most of the talking. She looks at me a few times like she can't figure out why the maid of honor is being so quiet. I think she knows Nate and I dated, but she doesn't know the extent of it. Evie is too good of a friend to air it out for everyone. So I choose to ignore it.

I steal another glance at what I've dubbed the boys' table in my mind. Nate is looking at me this time. I quickly look down at my plate. My hands are shaking, so I rest them in my lap under the table while waiting for the jolt of adrenaline to pass.

Eventually, I take another bite. When I swallow, I look over again. Nate is talking to Joey, but as if he knows I'm looking in his direction, he turns to face me. I don't look away this time, and a corner of his mouth lifts into a small smile.

This continues to happen throughout the meal. Someone makes a joke at Nate's table and everyone laughs. When I look over, he's already looking at me. Someone at my table mentions the fact that he's in town early and I glance over. When I do, he turns to face me.

There's a tether running between us, and we can't seem to go more than a minute or two without looking over at the other person. I can't concentrate on what anyone is saying. I can't stop staring at Nate.

When Evie's older brother, Wes, becomes the stand-in bartender and everyone starts shouting out their drink orders, I decide it's my cue to step away for a minute.

"I'll be right back." I stand up and step over the bench of the picnic table one leg at a time.

Evie raises her brows in silent question. *Are you okay?*

I nod.

Matt also gives me a questioning look, but I mouth that I'm fine.

Because I am. I'm fine. I just don't think I can sit out there anymore.

I make my way through the house and end up on the front porch. The sun has almost completely set behind the horizon, and the outdoor light isn't on, so when I sit down, I'm hidden in the darkness. The cicadas are loud tonight, and they drown out the noise from the crowd out back. I hug my legs to my chest and enjoy a moment of peace. It almost feels like I'm alone.

I look up at the sky, making out the familiar constellations as they start appearing in the sky. My eyes linger on a familiar smattering of stars that make the arms and legs of a mythical being. I sigh and lean my head against my knees.

The front door squeaks when it opens, and light from inside the house spills onto the porch. When I turn, I'm not the least bit surprised to see Nate standing there. With the way we kept staring at each other at dinner, I half expected him to come out here sooner.

"Mind if I sit?" he says, gesturing to the empty space next to me.

I stretch my legs out in front of me. "Go for it."

My eyes drop from the sky and focus on the fruit trees in the yard while Nate lowers his body next to mine.

"It's getting pretty intense back there," he says. "I forgot how loud my family can get when they're all together."

He's forgotten because he's been gone for so long. Because he only comes home for Christmas. Because he went to school in New York.

Because of me.

"Do you miss it?" I ask, afraid to hear the answer. Afraid it will make the pain that's settled in my chest all night grow.

"Of course I do," he says.

I deflate.

"But I think it's been good to be on my own for a while too."

I turn to him and raise my brows. "Oh, yeah? Why's that?"

He shakes his head slightly. "I've only ever known the chaos of a giant family. It was good for me to go somewhere where I could figure out what life was beyond the safety nets."

"And what did you discover?" It's another question I'm afraid to hear the answer to, but I'm still living with safety net upon safety net. I dropped out after one year of college and haven't left Belview since, content to be five minutes from my dad.

There's a gleam in his eyes when Nate smiles. "That I'm capable of doing hard things. I never thought I'd leave Oak Ridge. I never imagined actually finishing law school. I always thought that I'd do something like farming or agriculture, which would have been fine, but I'm proud of what I was able to accomplish."

"That's really great." My words come out forced. I'm happy for him or, at least, I want to be. It was a big thing moving up north by himself and graduating from law school, especially with all those accolades. But it also makes me look at my life—one I thought I was proud of—and try to see it from his perspective.

Not for the first time, I imagine he's thinking he really dodged a bullet when I broke up with him. I would have only pulled him down.

"What about you?" He's still looking up at the night sky. "You started a business. That's pretty incredible."

There's no condescension in his tone, but I still feel like an impostor. My dad co-signed on my business loans. His employees were the first customers. I'm good at what I do, I know that, but I also feel like putting together arrangements is so silly compared to becoming a lawyer.

I run my hands over the wood of the patio. "Yeah."

"I know I already said this, but you're very talented. The pictures on your website were incredible."

"Thanks."

This moment feels intimate and suddenly I need to know if he's dating someone. I don't want to know the answer, not really, and I know this can't go anywhere. But I need to know if I'm crossing some kind of line spending time with Nate alone in the dark.

I tuck a strand of hair behind my ear. "What else did you find in New York?"

He turns to face me. "What do you mean?"

I bite the inside of my cheek and avoid looking at him when I ask, "Are you dating anyone?"

He lets out a long breath and looks at the yard. "No, I'm not dating anyone."

"Oh."

"Law school kept me pretty busy."

"Right."

He stretches his legs out in front of him. "What about you? Are you dating anyone?"

A quick laugh escapes me. "I am not."

"Oh."

Oh, indeed.

Now that we've established that neither of us is dating, the tension in the air becomes suffocating. I thought the tether between us at dinner felt strong, but it's nothing compared to what I feel right now. I'm hyper-aware of everything Nate is doing. Out of the corner of my eye, I see his Adam's apple bob when he swallows. He shifts in his seat as he crosses one ankle over the other.

A small flutter starts in my chest. This is a bad idea, us sitting out here together. We've just established we're both single, and that, mixed with feelings of nostalgia, is a bad combination. As much as I might still have feelings for Nate, it can't happen. I don't want him to get so caught up in the moment, he does something he'll regret.

"I think we should try to be friends," I say quickly.

Friendship is the most I can ever give him, but it still feels terrible. Nate once told me that he would take me however he could get me, but I'm not sure if this is what either of us had in mind at the time.

He's silent, so I keep going. "I know the idea of being friends with your . . . ex . . . " I take a shaky breath. "I know it's uncomfortable, but if you get a job at Wagner and Stein, that will mean a move back home. It will mean living near each other. Spending time with Evie. I don't want us to live in a constant state of avoiding each other."

It's only been a few days of playing the avoiding game and it's awful. I don't want to live in perpetual fear of running into him, and I don't want each interaction to feel short and stilted. It would chip away at me until I became a hermit again. I don't want to be that woman again.

"I don't want that either." He picks at a splinter poking up from the wooden boards of the porch.

"Good," I say. "We don't have to be best friends, but I think we should try."

It's the least I can do for Evie. I know she's tired of

compartmentalizing the two of us. It might be best for us too. It's been so long, we're not the same people we used to be.

"Almost like a fresh start." His voice is quiet.

"We can call it that, if you want."

"Okay." A corner of his mouth lifts. "Is this the part where I put out my hand and introduce myself to you?"

"Seems appropriate."

He sticks his hand out. "My name is Nate, and I hope we'll be good friends."

"Okay, Nate." I stick my hand hoping he won't feel how clammy it is. If we're going to be friends, I don't want him to know how affected I am by him. "I'm Macy."

He wraps his fingers around my hand and gives me a firm, yet achingly gentle handshake. "It's nice to meet you, Macy."

I'm not sure that we'll be good friends. I'm still stepping outside my comfort zone to be regular friends, but I smile at him. "You too."

Nate doesn't release his grip right away. He moves his thumb slightly over the top of my hand. A couple of goosebumps pop up across my skin. When I'm good and flustered, he finally lets go. He sits up straight and pats his thighs. "Do you want to go back to the party? Or are you wanting to hide out here a little longer?"

What I *want* to do is hide here for a little bit and then hop in my car and drive home, but I remind myself that this is about Evie, and I've just agreed to be friends with Nate. Running and hiding are the last things I should do right now.

I stand up and smooth the skirt of my dress out. "I

think I've been out here for long enough. I'm ready to go back."

He stands with me. "You sure? I don't mind going back by myself. Or hanging out with you for a little while. I can go get some soda, and we can sit on the porch and look at the stars for a little while."

Okay. Now I *know* he remembers our time out here together. We spent lots of nights watching the night sky together. He would point out constellations while I tried, and failed, to find them. There are only two I can identify consistently.

I look up at the stars and scan the twinkling lights for the one familiar sight other than the moon. I can feel Nate's presence beside me. "We don't have to go in. We can just stay out here, Macy." His voice is low.

I close my eyes and savor the sound of it. No, we can't stay out here. For the same reason I couldn't take his hand on that first day at Spill the Beans. If I had taken his hand that day, I would have wanted to fall into his arms. If I stay on this porch with him, I will lean against him.

For his sake and mine, I can't do either.

We've agreed to be friends.

I open my eyes and turn my head toward Nate.

He's watching me. "Macy."

I threaten to break when he says my name a second time. I push those thoughts down and put on a cheery smile. "I just needed some fresh air, but I'm good now. Let's go celebrate Matt and Evie."

He looks disappointed, but to his credit, Nate doesn't argue or point out my fallacies, including the part where we were already outside in the fresh air when we were sitting on the back porch. He puts on a matching bright smile and opens the front door of the house. "After you."

The party is in full swing when we reappear on the back porch, and only a handful of faces turn in our direction. Matt, Evie, a couple of her bridesmaids, and Catherine, Nate's niece.

She comes running over to us and jumps into Nate's arms. "Uncle Nate! I was wondering where you went."

He pulls her up into a bear hug and swings her back and forth in his arms. She's absolutely delighted by his attention and squeals loudly when he starts kissing the top of her head. "Hey, Caty-bug."

He looks so natural with his niece in his arms. Even though they haven't seen each other a lot in her short life, it's obvious how much she loves him—and how much he loves her. Joanna and her husband live nearby. If Nate moves to Belview, he'll see Catherine more often.

"I thought you left without saying goodbye." The quiver in her voice makes me feel like an intruder standing here while he shares this moment with his niece.

I start to inch away, but he catches my eyes and shakes his head. He doesn't want me to go, so I stay.

He shifts his attention back to Catherine and adjusts her so she rests on his hip. He looks down at her adoringly. "Why did you think that?"

Her eyes are watery. "Mom said she saw you stalking off, and we shouldn't expect you to come back tonight."

Nate chuckles. "Stalking off?"

Catherine nods her head wildly. "Uh-huh. She said you were probably in a bad mood because of Macy, but I don't know why. Macy is so nice. She gives me flowers whenever I see Aunt Evie."

He raises his brows. "Is that so?"

"Yep. Maybe if you're feeling bad, she can give you some flowers too. They always make me feel happy."

Nate looks past Catherine and meets my eyes. "What do you think, Macy? Would you give me flowers if I was feeling bad?"

I roll my eyes. "I'd let you buy flowers."

"What if I was feeling really, really bad?" He sticks out his bottom lip in a fake pout that I know is for Catherine's sake, but I have to fight from grinning.

"Will you please give Uncle Nate flowers so he doesn't feel bad?" she asks in her sweet four-year-old voice.

I sigh, resigned. "Fine. Come by my shop tomorrow, and I'll give you some flowers so you don't feel bad anymore."

"Thanks, Macy," he says as he winks at Catherine. She giggles at the attention.

"What are friends for?"

10

THE PAST

SUMMER BEFORE SENIOR YEAR OF HIGH SCHOOL

"REALLY?" Nate lifts his arm so that it's standing straight up and he's pointing to the sky. "You don't see that row of three stars right there?"

We've been lying on a quilt in his front yard, looking at the night sky for at least half an hour at this point, and I've yet to find a single constellation Nate has pointed out. Sure, I see a lot of "three stars" *right there* but that doesn't mean I'm looking at the same ones he's looking at. I think we're both getting frustrated by my lack of ability when it comes to stargazing. Our evening is going to go to crap if something doesn't change soon.

"Oh, yeah," I say, grimacing at how fake my voice sounds. "I see them now."

Nate props himself up on his elbow so he's no longer looking up at the sky, but down at me. He's smiling. "You liar."

I cover my face with my hands and groan. "What do you want me to do? I'm no good at this."

And I can think of a million other things I'd rather be

doing with Nate before I leave for my student leadership conference in New York tomorrow morning. I won't see him for two weeks, and will be so busy with seminars, I doubt I'll have much time to call him either.

What I'd really like to do is spend the last of my time at his house kissing that stupid smile off his mouth, but ever since his mom caught us making out in his room, they've enacted a strict no-bedroom policy for me and Nate.

They prefer to have us in their sight at all times, which is the reason we're outside in the middle of June, covered in bug spray, looking up at the night sky. The porch light flicked on at dusk, and Nate's mom hasn't stopped walking by the front window at irregular intervals to check in on us. I know Nate's family likes me, but apparently, my dad isn't the only one worried about becoming a grandparent too soon.

Neither of them needs to worry though. We really haven't done anything but kiss, and honestly, I'm having so much fun figuring that out with him, I don't feel rushed to do anything else.

"Ok, let's try one more," Nate says. "This one is super easy. If you find it. I'll give you a prize."

I move my hands, which are still covering my face so I can look at him. "A prize?"

"Yep. But you only get it if you really find it." He raises a single brow. "And I'll know if you're lying."

I push up on my elbows. "You'll know if I'm lying? Feeling confident, aren't you?"

"You could say that."

"There's this thing called humility. Not sure if you've heard about it."

He taps his lips with his fingers. "Oh, it rings a bell, but I don't think it's for me."

I snort. "Okay, Mr. Arrogant."

"Do you want the prize or not?"

I definitely do. It's become a game of ours. We come up with pointless competitions and give out silly prizes if the other person wins. It's never anything big though, our prizes are a piece of gum or a hug or a wildflower. "Obviously."

"Then stop being such a pain in the butt." He playfully pinches my side, making me squirm. But then he lies on his back, and I fall back next to him. His fingers interlace with mine. "Okay, so this constellation is called Pleiades, and it's one of the most recognizable star formations in the sky."

"With a name like that, I'm sure it's going to be so easy to find."

"It's not that hard, I promise. And if it makes you feel better, some people call it the Seven Sisters."

"I bet a homeschool mom came up with that name to make her daughters feel better about having so many siblings."

He laughs. "You're probably right."

"What is it with homeschoolers and big families?"

"Gotta keep up the homestead somehow." He manages to shrug while lying down. The movement makes the quilt bunch up all funny.

I elbow him in the ribs. "You're so weird."

I don't actually think he and his family are weird anymore. That doesn't mean I don't give Nate crap just to see his reaction.

Once I showed up to his house with my hair in a

single French braid and white Keds on my feet and asked him if he liked my new style. He told me he'd never seen me look more beautiful. Another time, I brought home-made bread with me. It was the hardest, driest loaf known to man. Nate ate an entire slice of it with a smile on his face and then offered some to Evie.

"I'm sure it really is weird, but having a big family is something I want one day," he says. "No offense to your parents, but I don't want to stop at one. It seems way too lonely."

He's right. It is lonely. While there are some very real perks to being an only child, I think I'd prefer to go without some of those things if that meant having a brother or a sister. Or even seven brothers or seven sisters.

He squeezes my hand. "Anyway. I didn't mean to get sidetracked. Let's look at the sky so you can win your prize." He points at the night sky again, and I try to follow where his finger is aimed. "It's a clump of stars all huddled together."

I scan the sky until I see a group of stars. I gasp in excitement. I think I actually found it. It's a miracle. I start counting. One, two, three, four, five, six. Seriously?

I sigh loudly.

"What's wrong," Nate asks.

"I thought I found it, but the stupid blob I found only has six stupid stars."

He rolls onto his side. "That's it."

I roll to face him. "Didn't you hear me? The one I found only had six, and as an expert astronomer, I can tell you the name of this constellation is not, in fact, the Six Sisters."

His laughter sends a whiff of his minty breath my way. "So, I have a confession."

"Is it actually the Six Sisters?"

"No," he says, pushing back a stray strand of hair that has fallen in my face. His fingers linger on my face. "But most people can only see six stars without a telescope."

I grin at him. "That's why you were so sure you'd know if I was lying."

He nods.

"So, does this mean I get the prize you were talking about?"

He nods again. "Yep."

We're so close, our noses are almost touching. Even though I can't make out all the colors in the dim lighting, I can see the way his eyes search mine. My lids lower because I'm really hoping my prize will be a smoking hot kiss I can think about the entire time I'm in New York.

I hear the rustling of his clothing as he moves closer. I hold my breath waiting for his lips to touch mine. But then I feel his lips against my forehead. I make a noise of frustration and open my eyes. Nate is smiling, his eyes twinkling with mischief.

I push his shoulder, sending him falling backward. "You're the worst, did you know that?"

"Nah. you like me."

I bite my bottom lip. Yeah, I do. I like Nate Delaney a lot. Even more than I thought possible when he asked me out six months ago. With every date and conversation, I'm learning more about what makes him tick. I know his favorite flavor of ice cream is vanilla, and his dream pet is a Great Dane. He loves alternative rock, but doesn't own an article of black clothing. He works hard to help his family, and isn't afraid to sweat, but he also enjoys writing poetry. He's so perfect and amazing, I can barely stand it.

"It's okay. I'm head over heels for you too," he says. "But I know my mom is going to make you go home soon, so let's go get your prize."

He stands up and puts his hand out for me to grab. My hand finds his, and he lifts me up, pulling me into him. Nate wraps his arms around me and pulls me tight against him. I slip my arms around his waist and I push my face against his chest. I listen to the steady trump of his heart. I breathe him in. He smells like joy and happiness—which is suspiciously similar to pine and earth. I used to think it was a cologne, but he never changes. And I suspect it's just because of the time he spends outside every day.

Two weeks is nothing, but everything is so fresh and new and I don't want to leave. I want to come out to his house every morning and stay until late in the day. I squeeze him tighter against me, fisting the fabric of his shirt in my hands. I would be content standing like this with him forever.

Nate shifts so he can lean his face down to reach mine. He kisses my cheek and lands a quick peck on my lips. "Come on."

I reluctantly peel myself away from him, but reach over and grab his hand. Our fingers are intertwined when we walk inside his house. The smell of baking fills the air. When we walk inside the kitchen, there's a bright green platter on the island, and on the platter are chocolate chip cookies.

Mrs. Delaney is pulling a fresh baking sheet from the oven and sets it on the stovetop before taking off her oven mitts. She's a petite woman in her forties. And while it's obvious all of her kids got her features, the darker coloring comes from their dad. "I was wondering if you two were ever going to come in," Mrs. Delaney says with a warm smile on her face. "I was afraid they were going to get cold before you had a chance to eat one."

I grab a cookie and take a bite. It's as delicious as ever. "Thank you, Mrs. Delaney."

"Oh, honey, you know I love baking for you."

"Hey," Nate says, reaching for a cookie of his own. "What about me?"

"Yeah, yeah. I love baking for you too. I just know Macy doesn't take it for granted."

I really don't.

While I realize that chocolate chip cookies aren't some major delicacy, it's not like my dad has time to bake. Any time we want a treat, we buy something from the store. I used to think desserts from the grocery-store bakery were something special until I came to Nate's house for the first time. Mrs. Delaney made cookies when I got there, and that was the first time I'd ever eaten them straight from the oven. The gooey dough and melty chocolate were life-changing. I ate half a dozen in one sitting like a half-starved freak.

Since then, Mrs. Delaney has baked them every time I come over. And Nate teases her that she loves me more than him because of it.

"Oh, and so I don't forget." Mrs. Delaney grabs a small brown box from the counter. "I know they aren't warm, so it won't be the same, but I made these for you to take with you to New York. That way, you won't get too homesick while you're there."

I take the box and clutch it to my chest. My dad has helped me make sure I have everything for my trip—enough changes of clothes, toiletries, money, etc. He's wonderful. But Mrs. Delaney has made sure I get to take a bit of home with me.

"Thank you so much." I look over at Nate. "Was this my prize?"

"Prize?" Mrs. Delaney asks.

"Nate was trying to help me find constellations outside and—"

"Is that what they're calling it these days?" Wes says as he bursts into the room. He's Nate and Evie's older brother and looks like an older version of Nate. He's already graduated from high school but is home from college for the summer.

Mrs. Delaney gasps. "Wesley Charles."

Wes swipes a cookie from the platter. "Like you weren't peeking out the window between batches."

Mrs. Delaney's cheeks turn pink. "I just wanted to make sure they were okay."

"We were looking at stars, Wes," Nate says while giving his brother a dirty look.

Wes laughs as he chews his cookie, and I let out a small giggle. Wes is always giving Nate a hard time, especially when it comes to me, but he's never cruel. I like him. Sometimes it feels like he's my older brother, too, even though I barely know him.

"What's going on in here?" Evie says as she walks in. "Oh, cookies." She sits down at the island and breaks a cookie in half. She takes a bite.

"We were just debating whether or not Macy and Nate were kissing outside." Wes waggles his brows.

"We weren't kissing," Nate says at the same time as Evie cries out, "Ew, gross."

Their mom looks at me. I lift my hands. "We really weren't. Nate was showing me different constellations and told me I got a prize if I actually found one."

"Was the prize kissing?" Wes asks and I can feel my entire face heating.

I wanted it to be kissing, but I do not want to talk about that with Nate's brother or sister or mother. Good gracious. We might as well ask Mr. Delaney to come and chime in.

"Enough with the kissing talk." Mrs. Delaney grabs a hand towel in one hand and puts her other hand on her hip. "Wesley, go check on your brothers."

His brows lower. "They're fifteen, Mom. They don't need me to check in on them."

"Go." She shoos him away with the towel.

When he finally turns to go up the stairs, he looks at me and waggles his eyebrows one more time. I cover my mouth to hide my smile.

"You," she points to Evie. "Go find your dad and ask him if he wants any cookies."

Her eyes are wide. "I wasn't doing anything."

"Evelyn Marie."

Evie slides off her seat and grumbles something about how she's my friend too and should get to see me before I leave for New York.

I grab her hand as she walks by me. "We spent all morning together."

"I know, but I'm going to miss you too."

"I promise I won't leave without saying goodbye."

“Fine.” She huffs, but quietly says, “And for the record, I think Nate’s present is worth it.”

My heart skips a beat. Evie knows what it is? That means it’s not just some random thing for our game. There was some intention behind whatever Nate wants to give me. Now I really can’t wait to find out what it is.

“And you two.” Mrs. Delaney points her finger back and forth between Nate and me. “It’s getting late and Macy has an early flight. I’m going to go make sure Wesley isn’t doing anything stupid, which gives you a few minutes of privacy. Don’t make me regret it.”

I press my lips together to stop the smile fighting to surface.

When she disappears up the stairs, I turn to face Nate and start laughing. “That was so embarrassing.”

“Perks of a big family,” he says, but he’s laughing too. “Wouldn’t trade them for anything, even if that means talking about kissing you with my mom.”

I cover my eyes. “I’m not going to be able to look her in the face.”

“How do you think I feel? You’re leaving tomorrow. I’m sure I’m going to get the talk again.”

I groan. “I’m so sorry.”

“It’s okay. Totally worth getting to spend a little extra time with you.” He sobers. “I’m really going to miss you, Macy. I know it’s only a couple of weeks, but I’ve really enjoyed spending time with you this summer.”

“You act like summer is already over. We’ll hang out when I get back.”

“I know.” He looks down at his feet.

“Hey.” I push his arm. “Don’t get all mopey and forget that you still owe me a present.”

"It's a prize."

"That's not what Evie said."

Nate rolls his eyes. "I love my sister, but she's gotta stop butting into my love life."

"Your love life?" I waggle my eyebrows. "Sounds serious."

"Really? A couple of cookies and a few minutes with my siblings is all it takes for you to start teasing me too?"

I grab his hand. "You know I love ya."

Everything freezes.

My eyes are wide.

His eyes are wide.

Neither one of us is breathing.

When I said those words, I meant it in the way you tell your friends that you love them after teasing them. I didn't mean to tell him that I loved him, even though I've known that I do love him for the last few weeks. There have been many, many times I've thought those words, and a few times I've almost accidentally said them aloud. I just haven't had the courage to tell him yet.

This was not how I planned for it to happen.

I'm freaking out. I have to leave to go home in a few minutes, I'm flying to New York in the morning, and I just told my boyfriend, *I love ya.* Ugh. Could this have gone any worse?

Is Nate going to say it back?

Nate squeezes my hand. "Come on, it's in the living room."

I'm still feeling super awkward as I follow Nate into the next room. There's a small pink bag on the table with white tissue paper coming out the top. "Is this my prize?"

He clears his throat. "It's a present."

I pick the bag up and start pulling the tissue paper out. Inside is a small box—a small, jewelry box. I look up at Nate.

"I hope you like it."

My hands shake as I pull the lid off the box. Inside, there is a silver necklace with a pendant on it. It takes me a few seconds to realize it's a constellation. My mouth spreads into a wide grin as I run my fingers over the cool metal. "It's beautiful."

"Yeah?" he asks.

"Yes, you dork." I hand him the box and turn so I'm facing away. I lift my hair up and off my neck. "Help me put it on?"

Nate wraps his arms around me so he can drape the necklace around my neck and clasps it.

I turn to face him. "What constellation is it?"

"Andromeda."

I think back to when Nate was trying to point out different clusters of stars. There was the Big Dipper, Little Dipper and Orion's Belt. But I vaguely remember a woman's name thrown into the mix. "I didn't find this one."

He shakes his head. "No, you didn't."

"What does it mean?"

He looks down at his feet. "Andromeda was a mythical woman chained to a rock. Perseus had to come rescue her."

I choke on a laugh. "Are you serious?"

He looks up at me. "You'd be surprised how hard it is to find a romantic constellation. I thought about Cassiopeia because she was supposed to be really beautiful. But she was really arrogant, so I didn't think that was good either."

He's embarrassed. I hate that. He went through the effort to give me something that was important to him, and he didn't just pick some random design. He put thought into it, even if it doesn't make a whole lot of sense. I wrap my fingers around the charm. "It's perfect."

"Are you sure? I debated whether or not I should get a heart or a flower instead, but that felt so generic."

"This is perfect. I promise. Every time I look at the stars, I'll think about how you tried really hard to teach me something and I couldn't get it."

He groans. "Now I feel really bad."

I take a step toward him. "But you're missing the point. I'll be thinking about *you* every day."

"I'll think about you every day too."

"It's only two weeks. I'll be back before you know it."

He nods and the silence grows between us. I'm thinking this might be when we say our goodbyes and I go find Evie to do the same. I clasp my hands in front of me and lift up to my toes before dropping back down. "Well . . . "

He stops me before I can say anything else. "Macy."

"Yeah?" I look up at him through lowered lashes.

"I, uh . . . " He takes a deep breath. "I'm really glad you are my girlfriend. You're smart and funny and pretty. I like spending time with you and my family really likes you too. And I want you to know that I'm not just saying this because of what you said in the kitchen. I've been wanting to tell you for weeks, and I couldn't let you leave for New York without telling you." He stops and swallows. "I love you, Macy Wagner."

My breath catches. "I love you too, Nate Delaney."

Wonder is written on his face. "Really?"

"Yes, really." I laugh. "I've loved you for a little while, but I've been too afraid to say it."

He pulls me in for a hug. "You don't ever have to be afraid to tell me what you're feeling. You can trust me. I promise."

"I know." I lean into him and revel in what just happened.

Nate loves me.

I love Nate.

I want to jump around the room squealing. I want to run and tell Evie. I want to—

The sound of a throat clearing interrupts my thoughts.

"Sorry, Macy," Evie says from across the room. "Mom said it's time for you to go so you don't get home too late."

I let go of Nate, still feeling giddy from our confessions. I look at Evie, who is standing in the doorway waiting for me.

"I'm going to stand in the hallway, but you need to wrap it up," she says.

When she disappears, I turn back to Nate.

"I'm sorry." He smiles sheepishly.

"It's not like your mom booked my early flight." I rest my hand against his chest. "I'll be back in two weeks."

His hand covers mine. "I'll be here waiting."

I lean up and kiss him. Just the quickest press of my lips against his.

"I love you," I whisper against his mouth.

"I love you too," he whispers back.

"Macy, you gotta go," Evie calls from the hallway.

Ugh. I hate this. I tell Nate goodbye before meeting Evie in the hall. She's holding my box of cookies in her hands.

I grab it from her. "Thanks."

She looks down at my necklace. "I see he gave you the present."

I link my arm in hers as we walk toward the front door. "You were right. I like it very much. Did you help him pick it out?"

She shakes her head. "Nope. He did that all by himself."

That makes it even more special. I'm never taking this thing off. I'm wearing it to New York and school and prom. It's going to become my signature piece of jewelry that everyone will recognize as mine.

"You okay there, Macy?"

"Yeah," I say dreamingly.

"I know I'm going to regret this because Nate is my brother, and gross, but you seem a little more lovestruck than usual."

I stop and turn to face her. "He told me that he loves me."

Evie's eyes widen. "He what?"

"Nate loves me."

She looks down at the necklace and back at my face. "He told you when he gave you that?"

I nod.

"And?"

"And I told him I love him too."

Evie's face lights up and she pulls me into a tight hug. When she starts shaking me up and down, I almost drop the cookies her mom made for me.

"This is the best thing ever," she says into my hair.

I step back and wince. "You sure it's not too weird?"

"Are you kidding me?"

"Well, you didn't seem like you were too excited about the idea of us kissing."

"He's still my brother, Macy. I don't want to see him kissing anyone." She laughs. "But my brother and my best friend love each other. What could possibly go wrong?"

11

THE PRESENT

THURSDAY

I've stopped jumping every time the bell above my door chimes and someone new walks into Oops a Daisy.

The store is officially closed for Evie and Matt's wedding. I'm not taking on new projects, and I have a million things to do before the bachelorette party tomorrow, but I haven't been able to focus because people keep coming through my front door. I keep thanking them for stopping in but have to keep telling them I'm not able to help them with any flowers today. The reactions range from confusion to frustration. I completely sympathize with each emotion because I'm all over the place this morning.

That's what I get for agreeing to be friends with Nate. It was easy to agree when he was being all sweet and his niece was practically setting up a playdate for the two of us. Now, I have to deal with the consequences of my actions, which means working with my lights on and my door unlocked, even though I can't help any customers.

It's my fault for not setting up a specific time for him

to come by. Now I have to make sure I'm here whenever he decides to show up—and I have to make it obvious that I'm inside. I don't want him to make the effort to show up, see my lights dimmed, my door locked, and think I chickened out.

I almost chickened out.

But that will stay my dirty little secret. Nate might know I'm single, but I don't want him to think I've been stuck in Belview pining after him for the last several years. It's better to start our new friendship with him thinking that it is actually possible. As for me? I plan to fake it until I make it. If I tell myself that my feelings for him are simply platonic enough times, I might actually believe it. Eventually.

I'm prepping flowers when the bell above my door rings. I rest my hands on the counter and sigh. At this point, it's getting ridiculous. I should have put a sign on the door that said we're closed for everyone but Nate. I promise myself that I'll do that as soon as I send this person away. But when I look up, it's Nate standing in the doorway. He's wearing jeans and a button-down shirt, with a duffel bag over his shoulder.

He lifts his hand in a small wave. "Hey."

I stand up straight and rub my hands over my apron. I push my hair back from my face and smile. "Hey."

"I heard I might be able to get flowers here." He looks around the shop, which is sadly, wildly, underfilled at the moment. My floral fridges are filled with boxes of unprepped flowers and trimmed stems in five-gallon buckets, but there isn't a bouquet in sight.

"I usually have a lot more," I hurry to explain. "I just blocked off most of the week for Evie's wedding."

"I'm sure it's beautiful."

"It is." I stand there with my arms awkwardly hanging down at my sides.

Nate points to the flowers on my counter. "How are things going for the wedding?"

"They're, uh, they're good. Just getting them cleaned up before I make everything."

He adjusts the bag on his shoulder. "Do you want some help?"

"I thought you were just here to get flowers."

He shrugs. "I've got time."

The drive from Oak Ridge is an hour. It seems like a waste for him to drive all this way just to pick up a bouquet and drive back. Now that I actually think about it, I can't believe he'd do it.

"If you want to help, then I'll take it."

He sets his bag off to the side, follows me to the table, and I give him a quick tutorial on preparing flowers.

We stand across the table from each other, discarded leaves and stems littering the table and floor. Nate takes each individual bud from the shipping boxes and examines them carefully. He gently peels the bottom leaves from each one and sets them on the table in a pile. A small crease is permanently lodged between his brows as he works methodically from one flower to the next.

"You don't have to treat them so delicately, you know." I squeeze my clippers hard for emphasis and the bottom of a stem goes flying through the air.

His hands stop their delicate movements. "I don't want to mess anything up."

"Don't worry. Flowers are pretty resilient."

He nods and when he picks up the next flower, he

pulls the leaves off the stem with a little more force. We fall into a rhythm, but it feels anything but comfortable. I'm as aware of him as I was the night before. I can feel his eyes when they are on me. I fight the urge to constantly look back up at him, even though his fingers caress the flowers as he examines them, and the muscles in his arms flex as he puts a flower into the five-gallon bucket.

Physically, I feel like a string ready to snap, but our conversation is filled with what I would consider typical friend topics. It's a strange thing talking to someone you used to know better than anyone else but haven't talked to in years. I ask if he's had a chance to try the Vietnamese restaurant downtown yet. If he's excited for his sister's wedding. If he thinks they'll ever stop making *Fast and the Furious* movies. And even though it's awkward, it's not so bad. It almost feels like we might be able to do this if we're careful not to delve into anything too deep.

Nate clips a particularly wide stem and the tip goes flying at my head. I see it coming, but there's no use trying to dodge it. I feel the light tap against my cheek.

"Sorry."

I rub the side of my face. The sting has already dissipated. "It's nothing. Just a normal hazard of being a florist."

He stares at me. "Do you like it?"

"Being hit by stems?"

He smiles at me. "Being a florist."

I smile back. "Yeah. I like it a lot."

"What made you start Oops a Daisy?"

It's a natural question, and it's normally an easy one

to answer. But this story starts with the ending of mine and Nate's, so I'm struggling with how to answer.

"Joy," I finally say.

"Joy?"

I take a deep breath and focus on the flower in my hands. I want to tell him, that's something friends would do, but I need to be very careful with my words. "After we . . . " I swallow and try again. "After I left college, things weren't great. I was living on my dad's couch. I didn't have a lot of motivation to do anything. I felt stuck."

"Macy." His voice is so gentle it hurts.

"Please." I put my hand up to stop him. If he talks to me, if he tells me that he was hurting, too, or he would have been there for me, I won't be able to finish telling him how I built this place.

He nods. "Okay."

"I was struggling, and my dad made me start seeing a therapist once a week. She always had a bouquet in her office." I smile to myself as I remember the different colored blooms displayed on her desk. "I would stare at them when we talked. I looked forward to seeing what she had every week, until one week she didn't have any."

I lift another flower and twirl it in my fingers. "I walked in that day. I didn't say hi, I didn't ask her how she was, I just blurted out that she didn't have any flowers. We spent that entire session unpacking what my reaction meant, and at the end of the hour, Dr. Shay suggested I try making a bouquet of my own. She insisted I make one for her as well and bring it to my next session."

"And did you?" Nate asks.

I laugh to myself. "Yeah. I bought a bunch of flowers from the grocery store, and after watching some tutorials online, I discovered it gave me peace. I brought Dr. Shay a bouquet the next time I saw her and have been bringing one by her office every week for the last four years."

"I'm glad you found something that you enjoy."

"Thanks." I bite my bottom lip. "What about you? Do you have something you enjoy?"

"Law school doesn't leave a lot of time for hobbies." He sets the flower he's working on down on the table.

"I imagine not." I pause. "Speaking of law school, did you have your interview yet?"

I'm still wrestling with the idea of Nate moving to Belview and working with my dad. I know it's not a sure thing. There are three potential candidates to fill the opening that has been created with the firm's recent growth. But what will it feel like if he does get it?

He taps his fingers against the table. "Yeah."

"How did it go?" I set my clippers down and give him my full attention.

"It was good." He's looking down at his hands. "I think they really liked me. They asked me to come back in today for another interview."

My mouth falls open. "What? When?"

He looks at his watch. "In about an hour."

"Nate. What are you doing here cutting flowers with me when you need to be getting ready? You're not even dressed."

"I brought my suit with me." He jerks his head toward the bag he carried in with him. "I needed to spend some time with you first. See if this is something I can do."

"What? Prep flowers?" As soon as the words leave my mouth, I realize that's not what he meant at all. I squeeze my eyes shut in embarrassment.

"Yes," he says, completely deadpan. "I needed to see if doing floral arrangements might be my true calling before pursuing a law career."

"Ignore me, that was stupid."

His eyes meet mine. "I don't think I could ever ignore you, Macy. That's part of the problem."

What does that mean?

We stare at each other for a moment before he breaks eye contact and shakes his head. He curses under his breath. "I've got to go."

"Right now?" I'm not so delusional that I thought our friendship would be easy, but we'd been having a pretty decent conversation before I mentioned the interview with my dad. Now he's telling me he has to go?

"I'm sorry." He turns and starts walking toward the door.

I stand there in shock as he gets closer to the exit. He's not bluffing. He's really leaving.

"Wait." I run past him and put myself between him and the front door. "You can't just leave."

"I have to."

"Because of the interview?" I ask, hopeful that I didn't scare him off. "You can get dressed in the back room so you don't have to go wherever you're rushing off to."

"I'm rushing off to tell your dad I'm withdrawing my résumé." He sighs. "I know you want to be friends, and I know that I agreed, but I don't think I can do this."

My stomach drops. "What?"

He turns his face toward the wall so he's not looking at me. A muscle in his jaw ticks. "How can I work at Wagner and Stein? I can't even stand to be in the same room as you."

His words are a hard slap to the face. I've been so focused on how hard it is to be around him because I'm still in love with him, that I didn't stop to think about how he might have been holding a grudge against me. I feel so stupid. I know I have no right to be upset, but I am. He doesn't know the reasons I did what I did, but it was never because I hated him. I don't want him to hate me. And I don't want him to not go to that interview because he can't be around me. I silently beg him to look at me. He doesn't.

"So you're throwing away a potential career because you can't stand to be around me?"

He steps past me to walk toward the door.

I sidestep and put my hands on his chest. I'm so stunned by the hard muscles beneath my palms that I barely register how inappropriate it is to be touching him this way. It's not how you touch someone who can't stand to be in the same room as you.

"Please, just stop and talk to me for a second."

"I thought the distance would help. I thought the time might help. But nothing"—he stops and looks at me, the gold flecks in his eyes are practically glowing—"*nothing* has stopped the ache I feel without you in my life, Macy."

My breath catches.

He puts his hands over mine and pushes them tighter against his chest. "Do you feel that?" His heart pounds beneath his ribs. "I thought I'd come get flowers for Catherine, and I'd realize that we could do the platonic friendship thing. But I can't do it, Macy."

My eyes search his. "What are you saying?"

"I'm saying I still love you, and it's killing me to be in the same room as you and not be able to do anything about it." His gaze goes to my mouth and stays there a moment before he releases my hands and takes a step back. "I've gotta go before I do something stupid."

I lift my chin. "Stupid like what?"

He looks down at my mouth again. "I think you know what."

I'm shocked into silence. This past week, I've thought that Nate wanted closure, I've thought he wanted to be friends, and just now, I thought he hated me. But I was wrong about everything. He still loves me. He still loves me and wants to kiss me. The thought nearly kills me.

He rubs the space between his eyebrows. "That's what I thought. You'll never want me the same way I want you. You'd think I would have figured that out by now." He storms toward the front door once again.

"You think I don't want you?" I call after him, my voice cracking.

He stops. "If you do, you have a funny way of showing it." Then he turns to face me. "Don't forget you're the one that broke up with me, Macy." He takes a step forward. "You're the one who refused to return my calls." Another step. "The one who ignored me when I showed up at your doorstep begging to know what I did wrong."

He's standing just a few feet in front of me.

My heart is pounding. I need to say something before he thinks I'm cold and unaffected by his presence.

"That's because—" I was broken in more ways than one. Because I refused to drag him down with me. Because I wanted him to have a shot at happiness. "I never stopped loving you, Nate."

"Then why are you avoiding me?" he asks, his voice

growing louder. Frustration laces every word. "Why do you find an excuse to run every time I show up?"

"Because I can't stand to be in the same room with you either!" My shout echoes through the studio and we both stare at each other, chests heaving.

I'm not sure who moves first. Maybe we move at the same time. All I know is one minute we're both standing firmly rooted in place, and the next we're moving toward each other at breakneck speed. His hands find my cheeks seconds before his mouth crashes down on mine. He gently cradles my face, but his lips are much more demanding.

They push against my lips, almost punishing, before I open to him and his tongue brushes against mine. A moan escapes the back of his throat when they finally touch, and I'd sigh right alongside him if my lungs would work.

Four years. It's been four long years since I've kissed this man, and the sensation of doing it now is both exciting and comforting. It's like coming home after being away for too long.

His hands slide down the side of my neck, down my arms, and to my backside. Without breaking our kiss, and with little effort, he lifts me into his arms. My legs hook around his waist and he starts carrying me to the floral table. When we get there, he sets me down and continues his exploration of my mouth.

The aroma of roses fills the air—Evie's wedding flowers. I'm sure we're crushing them. I don't care. I'm feeling lightheaded from our kiss. I can't think straight.

His lips leave mine and he kisses a line down my neck. I tilt my head to give him better access. As he gets closer to my shoulder, he pulls the collar of my shirt to the side. His lips barely touch my collarbone before his entire body goes rigid.

I know exactly what made him stop pressing his lips against my skin. If I'd been smart, I would have stopped him before he got that low. I would have dragged his face back up to mine and let him kiss me until my lips were swollen and bruised. I would have let him kiss me and never stop.

Now, I have no choice but to hold my breath and stay still as Nate pulls away from me. He moves the fabric further away from my neck, revealing the space between my collarbone and shoulder.

"What is that?" His eyes narrow.

My voice is a whisper. "You know what it is."

Nate's staring at the small tattoo on my chest, right next to my shoulder. The tattoo no one sees because it's usually covered by clothing.

His fingers brush my skin. "Andromeda."

The constellation he tried desperately to show me. The one I finally found after staring at the sky for hours after leaving his house. I looked at the sky every night I was in New York for that stupid leadership conference. I still look for it every time I'm outside after sunset.

"You got a tattoo of the Andromeda constellation."

I nod.

His nostrils flare before his lips crush mine with a renewed fury. He runs his fingers through my hair and then stops at the back of my head. He pushes his mouth harder against mine. I push back. I can't get close enough. It'll never be close enough.

I lean back, pulling him with me. A thorn pokes my

back through my shirt. I think it's broken the skin, but I don't dare say anything because it will break the spell.

Nate is leaning over me when the bell above my door chimes. He jumps back like he's just touched fire—I feel like I'm on fire—and faces the back of the store. I sit up and brush the leaves and pieces of stems from the clothing. I run my hands over my hair and look at the front door.

A middle-aged man is standing there, his eyes wide. He clears his throat. "I'm sorry. I saw the lights were on and the door was open, so I thought I'd come in and pick up some flowers for my wife on the way home."

My legs feel wobbly when I jump from the table. My face is burning. I cannot believe a customer just walked in on me making out with Nate. I'm twenty-three, not some lovesick teenager kissing in the backroom while the boss is away.

I am the boss.

And I'm in the studio. On full display.

I'm so embarrassed, I can't look the man in the eyes. My heart pounds as my mind struggles to come up with something to say. "Right. Um, if you give me a few minutes, I'd be happy to put something together. On the house."

It's not like I can just send him away after what he walked in on. My hope is that if I give him a free bouquet, he won't leave a terrible review about how unprofessional I am. After all, this is still my business, and I need it to do well.

"Yeah. That would be great." He stands there awkwardly for a moment. "Should I, uh, wait outside?"

Oh, my goodness. This is so humiliating. "No. It'll just

take me about five minutes and then I'll get you outta here as quickly as I can."

His eyes widen.

Oh shoot. I squeeze my eyes tightly, hating how that sounded—like I can't wait for him to leave so I can start making out with Nate again. "I mean, so you can get home to your wife."

I rush to the floral fridge and grab out some of the flowers I prepped this morning. They're for Evie's arrangements. Between these and the flowers Nate and I accidentally crushed, her arrangements will be a little smaller than I originally planned. But Evie gave me full creative control. For all she knows, they'll be exactly how I envisioned them to be.

"Will you grab a vase for me?" I ask Nate, who is still standing off to the side, looking at the wall. When he drags his eyes in my direction, I point to a pretty frosted teal one. It will complement the bright colors of the roses and ranunculus I'm using for the wedding.

He hands it to me before moving to the side of the room. He leans against the far wall and watches me out of the corner of his eye.

I start with a little greenery and start placing flowers in the vase until an asymmetrical bouquet materializes. Despite my hands shaking the entire time, I'm able to put together something beautiful—and in five minutes, as promised.

I lift the vase and carry it to the man, who is still standing fairly close to the front door. I bite the inside of my cheek, unsure if I should say something about what he walked in on, or if I should beg him not to tell anyone what happened.

He grabs the flowers from me. "These are beautiful. Are you sure you don't want me to pay for them?"

I frantically shake my head. "Really, I insist. I'm sorry about—"

He lifts his hand to stop me. "You don't have to say anything." He pauses. "And I don't plan to either."

My shoulders relax and I let out a long sigh. "Thank you."

"No worries but, um, maybe lock your door next time."

"Of course."

My blush returns at full-force as he walks out the front door. I turn the lock as soon as it closes. Once I'm sure it's safe, I spin and push my back against the door, and look across the room at Nate. He's staring at me, but looks completely shaken up.

I can't say I blame him. That was the most absurd thing that has ever happened in my floral shop. "I can't believe that just happened."

He rubs his hand over his mouth. "No kidding."

I press my lips together. "I bet he tells his wife."

"I bet he tells her over dinner with your flowers in the center of the table," he says.

My eyes widen. "Oh no. You're right." I picture what that would look like in my mind. This man and his wife, sitting on opposite sides of the table enjoying their meatloaf and mashed potatoes with my bouquet on display.

Suddenly, it's all too much—the rush of desire for Nate, the adrenaline of getting caught, and the relief of knowing that guy isn't going to report me to the Better Business Bureau for lewd behavior but will probably joke about it with his wife for the next decade.

A giggle threatens to burst from my chest. I cover my mouth in hopes of holding it back, but I can't. I start laughing.

Nate starts laughing with me. "I bet we're a story they tell when their friends come over for game night."

"I bet they never look at flowers the same, and laugh every time they see a bouquet."

"Even at funerals, and everyone thinks they're terribly rude."

"But they're just traumatized by the floral shop downtown."

"And their children will have a personal vendetta against florists for the rest of their lives and make a career in weed killer just because they like to watch plants wither and die."

We're not even making sense anymore, but we're both laughing so hard by the time we're done, we're gasping for air. Tears form in the corners of my eyes and the muscles in my stomach hurt. I wrap my arms around my waist to ease the pain.

When we finally collect ourselves, we're smiling at each other. We just had the hottest kiss I've ever experienced in my life, the most embarrassing moment I can imagine, and we're still able to look at each other with pure joy on our faces. There are no words to describe how good it feels to just be with Nate again.

"I do actually need to go though," he says.

My smile falls.

"If I'm going to make it to the interview, I mean."

Nate's going to the interview?

He grabs the duffle bag from the ground. "Is it still okay for me to use the back room to change?"

"Yeah." I smile. "Of course."

After I show Nate where he can get dressed, I go back to my storefront to give him some privacy—and to clean up. My studio is always messy when I'm working, but this feels particularly disheveled. Probably because I know what was happening just moments ago. My cheeks heat up and press the backs of my hands to my face to try to cool it. I can't believe we just kissed. And then got caught.

I try to focus on sorting through the remaining flowers on the table. Some of them still look good, but most are crushed or limp. I put the salvageable ones in my floral fridge and toss the rest in the garbage. Then, I grab my push broom and start moving the leaves and stems into a pile while I continue to wait for Nate.

I'm just getting the dustpan when he reappears from the back. He's wearing a gray suit that hugs his body, and a navy tie. He looks perfect, except for his hair, which is tousled from earlier.

I press my lips together to stop the smile.

"What?" He looks down at himself. "What's wrong?"

I point to my head. "Your hair."

He runs his hands through it, but it's still sticking up. He raises his brows. "Better?"

It's a little flatter, but still doesn't look great. I shake my head and lift my hands. "May I?"

It feels funny to ask if I can touch his hair when I'm the one who messed it up when we were kissing, but that moment was . . . intense. It doesn't even feel real.

When he nods, I reach out to fix it. Touching him now feels so much more intimate in a strange way. I finger-brush his hair so it looks more polished. When I'm satisfied, I step back to make sure I didn't miss any rebellious strands.

"How do I look?" He holds his hands out at his sides, a nervous smile on his face.

He looks good. Other than his lips being slightly swollen, he looks like the embodiment of a professional lawyer. "Like you're ready for a second interview at Wagner and Stein."

His smile falls. "Is this a terrible idea? Would you prefer I don't go?"

My brows shoot up to my hairline. "In what universe does a recent graduate get an opportunity like this?"

"You're right." He reaches out and grabs my hand. "But we should probably talk about what happened. I don't want to kiss you like that and then disappear. Doesn't feel right."

Of course he's concerned about my feelings, even though he has a potential life-changing interview rapidly approaching. Nate has always been too considerate for his own good. He's a great man, the best, but that was never the problem.

I shake my head. "It's fine."

"Maybe they can reschedule my interview."

"Absolutely not." I pull my hand back. "You have to go."

He watches my face for any hint of hesitation. I hope the smile I give him is enough to convince him to go. I'm not sure if it's a terrible idea for him to go for the second interview. It might be. But it really is an opportunity of a lifetime. Wagner and Stein isn't some puny law firm. They're one of the largest in the city, and this would be an amazing way to launch a career.

His eyes search mine. "Okay. But promise me we'll talk when I'm done."

I look down at the ground.

"Macy. Please look at me."

I lift my head.

"That kiss . . . " He blows out a long breath. "That was amazing. But only if it actually means something. I need to know that you're not going to hide from me again."

A corner of my mouth lifts into a smile. "You know where I work. Where am I going to hide?"

He levels me with a look. "You know what I mean."

I sigh. "Yeah, I know."

His hand reaches out to cup my face. "That kiss meant something to me."

My heart skips a beat. The way he's looking at me right now. It's not the way you look at a friend you accidentally kiss in the heat of the moment. No, Nate is looking at me like a man in love. It's both wonderful and terrifying at the same time to know I'm on the receiving end of those feelings. My eyes sting, and I blink my eyes a few times to keep the tears at bay.

"Please," he says. "Just promise me we'll talk."

"Okay."

"Okay." He leans down and gives me a quick kiss. "I've really gotta go if I'm going to have any shot of making this interview, but this isn't over. I'm not walking away. Do you understand?"

I nod, and he stares at me a moment longer before finally turning to leave. As I watch him walk out the front door of Oops a Daisy, I turn over the words he said. That kiss meant something. This isn't over. Can he really mean that after everything that happened between us? Can there be a second chance?

My fingers press against my lips as I contemplate what just happened. It's a dangerous thing to allow myself to be filled with hope for something I can't have, but I'm left with heaps of it while I stand there thinking about Nate.

What if we really could try again? There was a time when we thought nothing could get in the way of forever. Not time. Not distance. We thought we'd be able to weather any storm and come out on the other side unfazed. That was back when the storms weren't as big as we thought they were. Now, they're much bigger. So much has happened since we told ourselves that we would make it through anything. Is it possible that these last few years were just another obstacle that will feel small when we're on the other side?

I'm not sure. But I hope so.

12

THE PAST

SENIOR YEAR OF HIGH SCHOOL

"What are you up to?" my dad asks as he takes a seat next to me at our dining room table. He sets two mugs of coffee on the table. The smell of coffee is a welcome one.

I've been staring at a screen for hours trying to find the right words to describe why I would be a good candidate for the schools I'm applying to, and I am exhausted. It's shockingly difficult to fit your life into six-hundred words. I sigh and close my laptop. "College stuff."

"How are you feeling?"

"Good."

"Do you feel ready?"

I touch the charm of the necklace I always wear—the one Nate gave me the first time he told me he loved me. It's become a bit of a habit of mine. Whenever I'm feeling overwhelmed, I rub my thumb and forefinger over the cool metal and instantly feel better. "I think so. I have my letter of recommendation and I just finished my essay. Now, all I have to do is actually start applying."

"I'm proud of you for staying on top of it." He leans

back in his chair. "But I was thinking about more than just the application process. I'm wondering if you're ready for all the changes college might bring."

I take a sip of my coffee. My dad's already put caramel creamer in it, and it's perfect. "What do you mean?"

He taps his finger against the wood of the table. "I'm just thinking about what happens when the acceptance letters start coming in."

I laugh. "Assuming I get accepted to the schools I apply for."

"You have great grades and test scores, you've lettered in tennis all through high school, you have hundreds of service hours, and have been involved in multiple leadership programs. You're going to do great."

"Thanks." A trickle of unease moves through me despite the compliment. "So what do you mean when you asked if I was ready?"

He looks down at my laptop before he answers my question with one of his own. "How many schools are you applying to?"

I'm not sure where this is going, but I answer him anyway. "Um, three."

"Only three." It's not exactly a question, but there is a hint of disbelief in his tone.

"Well, they're the only three Nate and I want to go to."

He raises his brows.

"We both made lists of our dream schools separately, and then compared them. These are the only three schools in common." Our individual lists were much longer. We had state schools and private colleges, in-state and out-of-state, but there were only three that we both wanted to go to. It's fine by me, really, because I can't imagine spending the next four years living in separate cities. We've already done that. Our entire relationship has been long-distance. I hate it. I'm ready to be in the same place as Nate. I don't care where it is.

"Have you thought about what might happen if you don't get accepted into the same school?"

"Of course I have." It's why I've been working so hard on my college essay. I need to get three acceptance letters. I need to make sure I'm not the reason we don't end up together.

He sighs. "I think you should apply for all the colleges on your list. Don't worry about application fees or tuition. I have enough money tucked away to send you wherever you want to go. Dream big. You can still apply for the schools you have in common, I won't stop you, and maybe you'll end up at one of those schools next year. But I think you need to make sure you have lots of options."

"There's no point in having all those options if Nate isn't there."

"I think you shouldn't worry about Nate."

I jerk back. "What does that mean?"

"I'm worried about you throwing away your future for a boy."

My chest tightens painfully. I press my palm to it in an attempt to ease the ache, but it doesn't work. "What are you talking about? Nate's not just some boy."

My dad sighs. "I know you think you love him."

I push my chair back and jump to my feet. "I *do* love him."

He rests his elbow on the table and rubs his temples.

"You're seventeen, Mace. You can't know what real love is. Not yet."

It feels like I've been slapped. "You don't think I know what love is?"

He sighs. "I think you know what young love feels like, but you have your whole life ahead of you. I don't want you to end up in some hard situation because you can't see things clearly."

"So what are you saying?" I take a step back.

"I'm saying I think you and Nate should consider taking a break so you don't end up making a decision you'll end up regretting."

A decision I'll regret. Like his relationship with my mom? I know that's what he's implying, but that's not fair. This situation is completely different. "Just because you and Mom didn't stay together, doesn't mean Nate and I are doomed."

"I'm not saying you are." He turns the coffee mug in his hands. "I loved your mother. And in her own way, I know she loved me too. But it was because of our feelings for each other that we thought we'd be fine to push our own plans to the side." He pauses and looks off into the distance wistfully. "Once the reality of our different dreams sunk in, she couldn't handle it. It was too much for her."

He's talking about the fact that my mother never actually wanted to be a mom. I'm not sure what my dad said to her to convince her to marry him and start a family, I only know that motherhood was "stifling her creativity." She couldn't fully immerse herself in her art if she was busy packing lunches, taking me to school and keeping up with pediatrician appointments.

I spent many nights lying in my bed listening to them argue—argue about how she couldn't do this anymore. How she wasn't a good mother and it was better if she wasn't here. I listened to them argue until one day she left, leaving me a painting of a mother and daughter embracing each other.

As if a painting could replace her.

But Nate and I are different. Neither one of us is trying to force the other into a box the other hates. That's why we made separate lists of schools. We're trying to find ways to be together without stifling each other.

"I'm not her," I say, my voice shaking.

"I know you're not."

"And he's not her either."

"I know."

"Then why are you telling me to take a break?"

"It can be a dangerous thing to mold your life around another person at such a young age."

"That's not what's happening."

"Really?" He raises his brows. "How many schools were on your list that you won't apply for because they weren't on Nate's list? How many schools were on Nate's list that he won't apply for?"

"It doesn't matter. The schools on our mutual list both started on our individual lists. They're places we both want to go to already."

"I don't want you to settle."

"I'm not settling." At least I don't think that's what's happening. We're talking in circles at this point, but the more my dad argues, the more I wonder if there's a sliver of truth in his words.

I grab my laptop from the table. "I have to go."

"Where?"

"I've gotta talk to Nate. I . . . " I don't feel like I owe my dad an explanation but I give him one anyway. "I just need to see him. Talk to him about all this."

He waves his hand in front of him. "By all means."

I storm out, not sure if I'm angry with my dad for planting doubt in my mind, or at myself for thinking he might be right. Either way, I need to see Nate. And I need to see him now.

DUST KICKS up behind my wheels as I drive down the long dirt road that leads up to Nate's house. I got here in forty-five minutes instead of my usual hour, and I have no intention of going back home. I've been stewing in my anger toward my dad, and I don't think I'll be able to look at him the same again after what he said to me.

Nate's sitting on the front porch of his house when I get out of my vehicle.

As soon as I see him, the tears I've been holding back start falling down my cheeks. My slow steps become a jog as I move toward him. He stands up to move toward me, too, but barely makes it off the bottom step of the porch when I collide into him. Nate stumbles back before steadying himself and wrapping his arms around me. He pulls me close and I breathe in the familiar scent of earth and pine. I push myself into his chest as hard as I can.

I'm so glad I'm here. I'm so glad to actually touch him. It's been a couple of weeks since I've seen him in person, and I didn't realize how much I needed it.

My quiet crying becomes body-racking sobbing. Nate

makes shushing noises and runs his fingers gently through my hair even as I fight to push myself closer to him. The tears continue to fall in never-ending streams as the weight of everything hits me.

I'm angry that my dad would suggest that Nate and I take a break. I'm sad that my mother abandoned me when I was younger. I'm so in love with Nate that it hurts, and if I'm being honest with myself, I am a little scared about what the future holds. Senior year is going to be stressful enough, but I worry that it's going to be even harder if I break up with my best friend, the only boy I've ever loved.

I stay in his arms until I can't cry anymore. When I finally pull away, his shirt is wet. Not just a couple of wet spots. It looks like someone spilled a drink all over him.

Looking at the darker fabric of his shirt—the place where my face just was—I sniff a couple of times. "I'm sorry."

Nate looks down at his tear-soaked shirt. "I've had worse."

I wipe my eyes with the back of my hands. "Oh yeah?"

"Okay, maybe not." He bites his lip. "But I don't care about the shirt. I care about you. What's going on?"

I didn't tell Nate the reason I was racing over because I wasn't sure I'd be able to come up with the right words to explain what was happening. I just needed to see him in person. So I texted him from my driveway that I was on my way and I hoped he was able to talk.

"I love you," I say.

His smile is hesitant. "Uh, gotta be honest here. The idea of you crying like that and then telling me you love me is a little terrifying. Are you breaking up with me?"

"W-what? No. I don't think so." I don't want to unless this is a situation where I'm holding him back. Then maybe I'll have to do it for him.

He grimaces. "Not super reassuring."

None of this is going how I wanted. I push some stray strands of hair out of my face. "Do you want to marry me?"

Judging by Nate's expression, he's just as shocked as I am that I just asked that. It was on my mind, but I assumed we would ease our way into it. Now that the question lingers between us, I need to know. Am I making a big fuss over nothing? Or does Nate want the same things as I do?

"Um . . . like, right now?" He's shifting on the balls of his feet.

"Not right now." I clear my throat. "I mean, is that something you think you want? With me?" He reaches out to grab my hands, but I step back. I need an answer before I let him touch me. "Do you see a future with me?"

He throws his arms out. "Isn't it obvious?"

It would be easy to assume that means yes, but I need him to spell it out for me. I need to know without a shadow of a doubt that he feels the same way about me that I feel about him. I need to know there is no miscommunication between us. "Tell me."

"Macy. You're it for me. And one day I'm going to marry you if you let me."

Against all logic, the stinging behind my eyes has returned. I didn't think it was possible to cry anymore. But maybe it's because these tears stem from a completely different place. "You promise?"

He takes a few steps toward me. This time, when he

tries to take my hands, I let him. He leads me to the porch and we sit next to each other.

"Wanna tell me what's going on? What's got you doubting things all of a sudden?"

I tell him about what happened with my dad. I tell him about how I'm worried I'm going to turn into my mom. I tell him that I don't want to hold him back from whatever plans he has for life.

He squeezes my hand. "You're not holding me back. If anything, I've had to fight like hell just to make sure I'm worthy of you."

My forehead wrinkles. "That's just as bad."

"No, it's not. I want to make sure I give you the life you deserve, Macy Wagner. You're used to living a life of luxury."

I open my mouth to argue.

"It's okay. I don't think less of you for it. It's just the way things are." He jerks his head toward my SUV. "That's the second vehicle you've owned since I've known you."

Wait. Is he saying I'm spoiled? My first car was a Toyota. Brand new, but nothing special. Nothing like some of the cars my classmates pulled up in after their sixteenth birthdays. My dad only upgraded this one for me as a reward for getting a near perfect score on my ACT. My temper flares before I realize that my dad's doubts are already driving a wedge between us. I take a deep breath.

"What do you mean?" I ask, hoping I'm misunderstanding everything. Afraid I'm not.

"I'm going to have to work hard to be good enough for you, but it's worth it."

I relax. "But I don't want you to have to change for me."

"It's not changing. It's becoming a better version of myself. There's nothing wrong with that, and I'm not going to resent you in twenty years for pushing me to be successful."

"Twenty years?"

"Longer than that. I want to be that old couple whose kids plan a big fiftieth anniversary party because they know how much their parents love each other."

My heart swells with his words. He wants a future with me. He's already planning it in his mind. I bump his shoulder with mine. "And just how many kids are we going to have?"

He smiles wickedly at me. "At least a dozen. Maybe two."

I roll my eyes, but then turn serious. "Really, Nate. How many kids do you want? I'm an only child and you have six brothers and sisters. What if we have different ideas?"

"Macy . . . I don't think we need to figure all this out right now."

Doesn't he understand? It was the kid thing that eventually led to my parents' divorce. I'm still angry at my dad, but I can't deny he's done a great job of raising me. Even so, the fact that my mom wasn't around made for a difficult adolescence. If Nate and I are on different pages when it comes to a family, we can't start planning out our fiftieth wedding anniversary. My eyes plead with him. "How many kids do you want?"

He turns it back around on me. "How many do you want?"

I'm left speechless. I don't know. I don't have a hard number because I've never really thought about it.

He looks at me in question. "Do you want kids?"

I nod. "Yes, I do."

"Great." His face lights up. "We don't need to have six like my parents, but you want more than one, right?"

I nod again.

"Four?"

My eyes widen.

"Three?"

I shrug.

"Two just feels so lonely and I want to be outnumbered."

I giggle at how excited he is. I assumed he wanted a big family, but didn't realize how excited and into it he would be. "Three sounds nice, but I don't know."

"That's fine. We both want kids, but we don't have a set number yet. That's okay. We can figure it out as we go. What's next?"

He makes it sound so easy. "Okay, I want to be a stay-at-home mom. I know that I don't know what that looks like, but I want to try."

"You're going to be a great mom. I want that too."

"But I don't want to homeschool."

I can see the hesitation in his expression. I know he loves being homeschooled and somehow he's turned out pretty normal. He bites his lip. "Are you sure? I feel like you could rock a denim jumper."

I laugh. "Well, obviously."

"And you're smart enough and so fun. You would be great at it."

I don't even know I'll be a great mom, but when he

looks at me like that, it's hard not to get caught up in his enthusiasm. "We can talk about it when the time comes, but I want a get out of jail free card."

"Get out of jail free? Is that what you think homeschooling is? A jail?" His face scrunches up in concentration. "Wait . . . " Nate sticks a finger out for me to wait as he mentally works through whatever is going through his head. "If that's the case, then that means I'm a prisoner, which means I'm a bad boy. Who knew?"

I roll my eyes because he is the furthest thing from a bad boy—and I love that.

He grins at me. "Fine, I'll let you have a get out of jail free card, but can it still be an option?"

"It's an option."

"In that case." He shrugs, like it's no big deal. "What else?"

A rapid-fire question-and-answer session definitely wasn't what I was expecting when I came over, but I like that he's willing to do this with me so I can feel better about where we're heading. I touch my necklace as I think of what else might be important when thinking about a future with someone. "Where do we live? Do we stay in Florida? Do we move across the country?"

He presses his lips together and breathes out his nose. "I'd like to stay close to my family. I love my parents and my siblings. I like the beach and the warm winters. I like the open sky and summer thunderstorms. If it was up to me, we'd stay. But I'd figure it out if you wanted to move."

I breathe a sigh of relief. I want to stay here too. My dad is the only family I know, and I doubt he'd ever want to leave Wagner and Stein. I don't want to leave him.

"Me too. I want to stay in Belview, but I'd consider living in Oak Ridge too."

"I could live in Belview."

"Or Oak Ridge."

He smiles. "I'd be happy in either. What's next?"

"What about college?"

His smile falls. "What about it?"

"What if we don't get into the same school?"

He sighs. "The thought has crossed my mind."

"Really?"

He nods.

"So what do we do?"

"Macy." He turns to face me and takes both of my hands in his. "We've lived an hour away for as long as we've known each other. We can handle long distance a little longer."'

I shake my head. "No, I don't want to do that."

He snorts. "I'm not saying I want to do that. I'm saying I'm willing to do that. I'm not going to stop loving you just because we live far away from each other. I'm not going to break up with you just because we have to wait a few more years."

I lean forward so my forehead is resting against his collarbone. "My dad thinks I should apply to more schools."

He stiffens. "Is that what you want to do?"

"No."

"I wouldn't be upset. Like I said, I want to be near you. I hope we get into the same college. But I'm not going to be upset if there's someplace you want to go that's not on our mutual list." I don't respond right away and he takes my hesitation as a sign of uncertainty. "I can apply to more schools if it'll make you feel better."

I sit up. "Do you *want* to apply to more schools?"

"I only want to apply for other schools because I'm afraid of what happens if I don't get into one of those three. I want to go to school with you, but I think I need a backup too."

I didn't realize he was as afraid of not getting into those three schools as I am. We were so worried about making sure they were the same that we never stopped to talk about how we were feeling about the possibility of getting rejection letters from all three.

I rub my hands down my thighs. "Okay, what about this? What if we apply to our three schools? If we get into them, we go together. But we also apply for a couple of backup schools as a contingency plan."

"I think that might be a really good idea."

"Well, I guess we can thank my dad for that," I say begrudgingly. My conversation with him is the whole reason I came over here in the first place. It's the reason Nate and I were able to talk through some really big things and come up with solutions to potential issues. I was angry when I left, and I'm still hurt that he would suggest that Nate and I take a break, but I guess I should also be thankful that he was the catalyst leading to this conversation.

"Okay. So that was some heavy stuff," Nate says. "Anything else?"

I can hear the hesitation in his tone. He's got to be feeling as exhausted by these topics as I am. But I don't want to brush off his question either. I force myself to think about it because I don't know when we'll talk like this again.

After some consideration, I tell him that I think I'm good.

"You sure?" he asks.

I'm sure there are a lot of things to figure out when building a life together. Things I can't even think about right now, like who sleeps on what side of the bed, and what happens if we both want to watch something different that comes on at the same time. I'm sure the future is filled with discovering all of those things, but they don't feel as big as everything else we discussed.

I let out a huge breath. "Yep."

"Good." He pulls me close to him. "I want you to feel like you can come to me with anything. We'll figure it out. No matter what it is."

I believe him. I believe him with every fiber of my being, and in that moment, I know Nate is my forever.

13

THE PRESENT

FRIDAY

I'M GETTING ready for Evie's bachelorette party when my phone buzzes with a text from an unknown number. My hair is wrapped in a curling iron, and I've been getting so many *we will pay cash for your house now* texts lately, I almost ignore it. But there's something familiar about the string of numbers that light up my screen that gives me pause.

I hastily tug my curling iron out of my hair and drop it on the counter. I hold my breath as I pick up my phone and open the screen.

I think the interview went well.

There's only one person who would be texting about an interview.

It shouldn't surprise me that Nate found a way to text me. I've had the same phone number since I first got my phone in high school. What is surprising is the fact that he still knows it. After we broke up, I deleted his contact from my phone so that I wouldn't be tempted to text or call in a moment of weakness. I forced myself to forget.

My fingers hover over my screen. How does one react when the man she's been in love with for longer than she cares to admit might be getting a job in the city she lives in? And said man literally kissed her right off her feet the day before . . .

I type out a quick, generic response and hit send before I overthink it.

That's awesome. When do you find out?

There's a pause before a text bubble appears.

Soon.

Cool.

Cool? I kick myself for sending such a lame response. Maybe I can send a high-five GIF while I'm at it and establish even more of a bro feel to our text conversation. I'm trying to think about how I can salvage that when my phone starts buzzing—this time with an incoming call from Nate.

I just sit and stare at my screen at first. It's one thing to keep bumping into him around town with all the wedding festivities, and to accidentally kiss him when he visited my shop, but answering now feels like a big step. Do I want to take it? Do I let it go to voicemail? When my phone buzzes for a fourth time, I finally swipe my screen.

"Hello?" I bite my lip.

"I was wondering if you were going to pick up," Nate's voice says from the other end.

I squeeze my eyes shut, thankful he can't see me right now. "Yeah, sorry. I was just getting ready for Evie's bachelorette party."

"Want me to let you go?"

"No," I answer quickly. Too quickly. "But do you care if I put you on speakerphone so I can keep getting ready?"

"Go for it."

I put him on speaker and set the phone on the bathroom counter. "Can you hear me okay? Is the echo too much?"

"I can hear you just fine."

"Awesome." My hands shake as I section out the next piece of hair and wrap it around my curling iron. Even though he can't see me, I'm still incredibly nervous to be talking to him.

"So what time do you leave for the party?" he asks.

We're not going out until later, but I've been filled with so much anxious energy I started getting ready early just so I had something to do. "I actually have a couple of hours until I have to leave."

"It takes you hours to get ready?"

"No, but I didn't have anything else to do, so I thought I might get an early start." I release the fresh curl and section out another piece of hair and wrap it around my iron. "What about you? What are you up to right now?"

"Pretty much the same thing."

"You're curling your hair?"

He laughs. "I mean, I'm just hanging out at my

parents' house, waiting to go out for Matt's bachelor party. I have a little time, so I thought I'd call you."

I smile at my reflection in the mirror. "What are the guys doing tonight?"

"Deep sea fishing trip."

My smile falls. "You're kidding me." I set my curler down and wait for him to respond. The Nate I knew wouldn't step foot on a boat for a million dollars.

Nate releases a long breath. "Yeah. It's a six-hour trip."

"Stop it."

"I wish."

"Do you still get motion sickness?"

"Yep."

"Oh, Nate. I'm so sorry." I rest my hands on the counter and stare at the phone. "Is there a way for you to get out of it?"

His voice is completely flat when he says, "You're asking me if I can get out of my sister's fiancé's bachelor party. That would be bad enough even if I wasn't a groomsman."

"Well, when you say it that way."

His laugh is self-deprecating. "I think I'm going to pop some Dramamine and hope I don't throw up over the side of the boat the entire trip."

"Good luck with that."

"I'll survive."

"I hope so."

"What about you? What horrors await for the bachelorette party?"

"It's not nearly as horrific as yours." I fluff my hair out in the mirror and turn my head back and forth to make sure I'm happy with how it looks. "We're going to St. Pete for dinner and a walk on the beach at sunset."

"Dry land. So jealous."

"But we are wearing sequins." Every. Single. One. Of. Us. "It's going to look like a herd of disco balls roaming the city."

"At least you'll be *Stayin' Alive.*"

I laugh. "Seriously? A Bee Gees joke? I'm embarrassed for you."

"Yeah, well, it's not the most embarrassing thing that's happened to me this week."

My hands, which were reaching for my makeup bag, stop. I look at my reflection with wide eyes. Is he talking about . . . ?

"I can't stop thinking about it." His voice is a deep timbre I feel all the way down to my toes.

The tone of our conversation takes a sharp turn and I take the phone off speaker. I put it to my ear as I walk out of my bathroom and sit on the edge of my bed. My voice is a whisper when I say, "I can't either."

I know I'm breaking all kinds of rules by admitting that to him. It's generally understood that you're supposed to play it cool when dating, but we aren't dating, I don't think? And this isn't just some guy. It's Nate.

He's the only guy I've ever dated. Not because I haven't tried to move on. I've gone out with a couple of guys over the years, but never made it past a first date. I was constantly comparing them to Nate in my mind, and there was always a level of anxiety simmering beneath the surface, like I wasn't sure if I would be able to fully trust them.

It's always been Nate, even when it wasn't.

"Macy."

"Yeah?"

"We need to talk about what happened."

He's right. We really do. Not just about the kiss, but about everything. "I know."

"What time is the party bus picking you up?"

"Six."

"That's two hours. If I leave right now, I can get there by five. That gives us an hour to talk before the party bus picks you up. Can I come over?"

Wait. He wants to come to my house. To talk. Right now?

The last time we tried to talk, we did a lot more than that, and that was at Oops a Daisy. What will happen if he comes to my house? An hour is enough time to let things get out of hand and make some big mistakes. I stand back up and start pacing around my room. I'm holding the phone to my ear but I shake my free hand out in an attempt to get rid of my anxiety.

"I want to see you. I want to see your face, but I don't have to come to your house. We can meet someplace if you want. We can even keep talking on the phone if that makes you more comfortable."

I remind myself that this is Nate. He would never pressure me or hurt me. Even my slight hesitation is enough for him to offer me alternatives. I don't want to talk to him on the phone, and I don't want to go to Spill the Beans or any other place around Belview. We are two adults trying to figure out what's happening. Surely, it's okay for him to come over.

"I want to see you too." I release a shaky breath. "I'll text you my address."

There's a sharp inhale through my speaker.

"So we can talk," I say.

I can almost hear the grin on his face when he says, "Okay."

I spend the next hour finishing getting ready for Evie's bachelorette party—other than putting on my sequin dress—and speed-cleaning my house. It's not terribly messy, but I clean the clutter I have sitting on my coffee table, I put the dishes on my kitchen counter into the dishwasher, and I put all my dirty clothes in the hamper.

I've just finished doing a walk-through to see if there's anything I missed when I hear a knock. Nate is here. At my house.

I look at myself in the mirror one last time before going to the front door. I run my hands over my athletic shorts, and put a smile on my face before opening the door.

As expected, Nate is on the other side.

Not as expected, he's dressed like a middle-aged fisherman. He's got cargo pants, a long-sleeve fishing shirt, and heavy work boots. I raise my brow. "That's an interesting look."

He looks down. "I'm going straight from your house to Matt's."

"So this isn't some fashion statement?"

"No." His eyes trail down my body and back up to my face. "What about you?"

I know he's referring to the fact that my hair and makeup look like I'm ready to walk the stage at a beauty pageant, but I'm wearing a t-shirt and shorts. "Oh, this is definitely how I dress now."

He chuckles. "It's special."

A corner of my mouth lifts into a smile. "Do you want to come in?" I stand to the side.

He walks in. "I'm really glad you agreed to let me come over."

"Me too." I think. My heart is racing. I still can't believe he's here. "I know you don't like coffee, but I have some soda if you want to get a caffeine fix before the bachelor party. It's going to be a late night for both of us."

"That actually sounds good. Thanks."

I tell him to have a seat as I go to the kitchen and grab a couple of Cokes from the fridge. I take that moment to take a couple of deep breaths to calm my stupid heart. I lift my hair and put one of the cold cans to the back of my neck. This is fine. I can do it.

When I go back to the living room, I catch Nate flipping through a wedding magazine I have on my coffee table. There's only one copy on display, but I have a whole stack of them in my closet because there's a small picture on page thirty-nine of me holding an oversized bouquet.

Nate has the magazine opened to the page. "You're in a bridal magazine."

I shrug as I sit down beside him, and set our drinks on the table. "They did a special feature for up-and-coming florists. I sent my portfolio on a whim. I was shocked when they emailed me back."

He shakes his head. "I'm not. You have a gift."

My chest tightens. "Thank you."

Nate gives the picture one last look before shutting

the magazine and setting it back on the table. "Can I tell you a secret?"

I bit my lip. "Okay."

"That's not the first time I've seen that picture." He taps the cover.

My eyes widen. "What?"

"When Evie told me you were doing the flowers for her wedding, I looked up your shop." That's not news, he told me that at his house a couple of days ago. "I thought it was amazing, but I wanted to know more. I looked up Oops a Daisy online and that article popped up in the search results. I was so proud of you." He looks down at his hands. "And I thought you looked more beautiful than I remembered."

I blink at him several times. Looks like we're skipping the small talk and jumping right into the swoony stuff.

"I wasn't sure how I was going to come back to Belview for the wedding and have to see you after all this time. And then I heard back from Wagner and Stein the same week asking if I could come down for an interview . . . " His cheeks puff out before he releases a forceful breath. "I wasn't sure what I was going to do."

"I'm confused. You're the one who applied in the first place."

"I didn't actually think I would hear back from them." He takes a sip of his soda.

"But there must have been part of you that wanted to work there if you applied."

"There is." Nate closes his eyes. His face is pinched like he's in pain. "I wanna tell you something, but I'm not sure if I should. You're going to think I'm crazy."

No crazier than I'm already feeling. My body tenses while I wait for his answer.

"I wanted to be near Evie and the rest of my family."

I relax. "That's not crazy."

He shakes his head. "But I also wanted to be closer to you."

All the air whooshes from my lungs. He applied for a job at Wagner and Stein for the possibility of moving back to Belview. To be closer to me. Even after everything that happened.

He leans forward and rests his forearms on his knees. He doesn't look at me. "I told you it was crazy."

I have the strong urge to thread my hand through the space between his arm and body, and join my hand with his, but I'm frozen in place. I don't know what to think about his confession.

"You're not crazy. I'm just not sure if I understand what you're saying."

"I don't know why you broke up with me, but I've had a long time to think about it. I thought that if I went to the best law school and got a job at the best law firm in Belview, maybe you'd look at me differently. I thought if I did enough, maybe I could make you fall in love with me again."

My heart shatters into a thousand pieces. "You went to NYU because you were still in love with me?"

His head slumps forward. "I'm sorry. I know that sounds insane. But after you broke up with me, I felt so lost. I applied for their law school after I got my bachelor's." He sits up and lifts his drink from the table. He takes another sip, but holds the can in his hands. "You know I'd planned to go to law school anyway, just not so far away. But once I got there, I ended up really liking it. I put myself fully into the program."

"My dad says you were top of your class."

He lifts the tab and folds it back and forth. "I did okay."

"And the interview yesterday went well."

He hesitates for the briefest moment before he nods. "Yeah."

A creeping suspicion takes root in my mind. "You were offered a job at Wagner and Stein, weren't you?"

Another nod.

"Did you accept?"

The tab breaks off in his fingers. He sets it and the can back on my table and turns to face me. "I wanted to talk to you first."

"Why?"

"I wanted to know how you felt after yesterday. I wanted to know if there was a chance of something . . . "

"Wait." My brows lower. "You don't want to take the job unless I date you?"

Horror fills his features. "No, that's not what I'm saying." He runs his hands through his hair, leaving pieces sticking up in every direction. It looks so much like his hair yesterday in Oops a Daisy. "That came out wrong." He sighs. "It just seems like everything is happening really fast. Evie's getting married in two days, I kissed you yesterday, then got a job offer today. That's a lot of good things right on top of each other, and I want to make sure I'm not caught up in some endorphin haze."

I laugh. "An endorphin haze?"

He leans back against the couch cushions and closes his eyes. "I don't know. Everything just feels too good to be true. I wanted to talk to you to see if this was one-sided. If I was losing my mind."

I scoot closer to him. Nate keeps his eyes closed, and I lift my hand so that my fingers hover just above his face. They ache to close the distance and touch him. To feel the light stubble on my fingertips.

Nate reaches up and gently takes my wrist in his hand, he pulls it down so my hand rests against his cheek. He leans his head into me. "Tell me you feel this too."

"I feel it," I say.

His eyes open and he stares into mine. "I'm not asking for a commitment, Macy. I'm not saying I'll only take the job if you agree to date me. I'm just asking for a chance."

I can't speak, so I nod.

His lips curve into a smile before he sits up and kisses me. It's gentle, so different from what happened in my shop. If yesterday's kiss felt like it came from a starved man, this kiss is from someone who's just been given everything. He takes his time as his lips move against mine. His fingers gently trace the lines of my face and down my neck until they land on my tattoo. When he reaches the constellation, he pulls back and looks at it. "I still can't believe you got this."

"It just felt right."

He makes a questioning noise in the back of his throat. "When was it?"

I bite my bottom lip. "Three years ago."

"Three years ago." He pulls back even further to look at my face.

I struggle to keep eye contact with him, and I look down at my hands.

"That was a year after we broke up."

I nod. "Yeah."

"You got a tattoo of Andromeda a year after we broke up." His fingers reach out and trace the stars permanently etched into my skin. "I wish we didn't have to go out tonight. I wish we could stay here instead. We could order takeout and catch up on the last four years. I want to know everything."

"I know." I feel exactly the same. Our friendship was always destined to fail. Seeing each other, spending time together. It's impossible to resist him.

He drops his hand to scoot closer, then lifts it again to cup my cheek. "I don't have to race back after the wedding. I can stay in Belview while I figure things out. Maybe we could spend some time together when everything dies down."

I turn my face so I can kiss his fingertips. Touching him, kissing him. It feels so natural, like my body has memorized what to do and has been waiting for this moment for the last four years.

Nate leans in so his lips are brushing my ear. "Promise me you'll spend some time with me so we can figure things out."

"Okay," I say breathlessly.

He turns my face so our lips are touching and we kiss again. And it's the most glorious thing in the whole world. We kiss for so long, I lose track of time. We kiss for so long, I forget about the bachelorette party until my phone buzzes.

"Oh crap." I pull back from Nate and look down at the screen.

10 minute warning! Par-tay bus is almost there.

I look at Nate with wide eyes. "Evie's almost here. I have to get dressed. She has the whole night planned out and I don't want to be the reason we're late to dinner." I jump off the couch and run to my bedroom to grab the sequin monstrosity off the hanger. There's no time to check my hair and makeup, and I practically rip my cozy clothing off and slide the dress up over my legs. I twist and turn as I struggle to get my hands behind my back to zip it up but can't get it all the way.

Thank goodness Nate's still here. I race back out to the living room. He's still sitting on the couch. He looks up at me with a funny expression on his face. "You really do look like a disco ball."

"Shut up and help me get this thing zipped before your sister shows up at my door." I turn so my back is facing him.

He stands and pulls the zipper all the way up. He even manages to land a kiss on my shoulder before I turn to face him. "What do you want me to do? Do you think I should leave?"

I stop my frantic rushing to get ready. "Uh . . . " I really don't know. It's not that I'm embarrassed to get caught with him at my house, but I want to figure out what's going on before having to explain myself. I need time to process it all, and preferably not under the scrutiny of a bunch of Evie's other friends.

A corner of his mouth lifts. "Don't feel like explaining yourself all night?"

I laugh. "How'd you know?"

"I told my parents I was going apartment hunting because I wasn't ready to have that conversation."

"That makes me feel a lot better." I sigh in relief. "Thanks for understanding."

"Of course." He leans down and kisses me. A quick peck, but his lips hover over mine. "I hope you have fun tonight."

I lean up and kiss him. "I'll be having more fun than you, Skipper."

He stands up and groans. "Don't remind me."

"You'll be fine," I say. "But make sure to put those cargo pants to good use and stuff some saltines in your pockets."

He rolls his eyes.

"Just think, it's only six short hours."

"It's going to feel like an eternity."

"Speaking of eternity, we don't have it. We need to get you out of here. Now."

He moves toward the door, but stops and gives me one more kiss. Then he's running down my driveway, jumping in his car, and peeling out of my driveway. It's not a moment too soon, either. As soon as his car is out of sight, the party bus pulls up.

14

THE PAST

FRESHMAN YEAR OF COLLEGE

I HATE SAYING goodbye to Nate. It rips my heart out every single time.

You'd think I'd be used to the long-distance thing after doing it for the last few years, but the fact that we ended up at different colleges at the last minute really sucks. The strain on our relationship feels harder than ever.

At least we have Saturdays.

Every week, I drive back home to Belview. In the morning, I stop by my house to see my dad and do my laundry while we eat breakfast together. Then, I spend the rest of my day with Nate. Sometimes we go to a movie. Other times, we sit together and talk for hours about our week. Regardless of what we end up doing, saying goodbye keeps getting harder and harder.

Today, we've spent most of our day outside. Nate took me on a picnic, with delicious baked goods from his mom, and we've sat in the shade of a giant oak on the edge of his parents' property ever since. As the sun begins its descent and the sound of cicadas fills the air, I know that we're getting closer to one more goodbye. Dread pools in my stomach and I silently will the sun to stop in the sky for just a little while longer. I think if I could get just one more hour with Nate, I'd be satisfied. Deep down I know that's not true. If I got one more hour, I'd want another and another and another. There will never be enough time with him—at least not with our current situation.

I lean my head against his shoulder and breathe in his scent. I want to bottle it up and take it back to Gainesville with me. "I hate this."

He releases a long sigh. "Me too."

"I wish there was a way to make these days last forever."

"At least we won't have to do the long-distance thing forever. One day we'll be near each other again."

He tells me this every time, and I want to believe him, but it feels impossible right now. There's always something that gets in the way of us being near each other. "You promise?"

He reaches down and laces his fingers with mine. "I promise."

We sit in silence for a few more moments. The last of the light slowly disappears from the sky as we both get lost in our thoughts. My mind focuses on his promise that we won't be doing this forever, but it feels impossible. I so badly want him to be right and try to imagine what things will be like when that time comes. One day, I won't be holding onto minutes of daylight, watching them fall through my fingers like I do now. I hate this so much I can barely stand it.

When it's finally dark, it's my cue to leave. Reluctantly, I stand.

Nate does the same, but when I start to walk back toward his house, he grabs my hand again. "Not yet," he says.

My gaze goes between him and to where my car is parked beside his house. I can barely see it across the distance in the dim lighting. "Please don't make this harder than it already is. I already don't want to leave, but it's a two-hour drive back to campus and I don't want to get in too late."

"I just..." He clears his throat and looks down at his feet. "I just want to talk to you about something."

The hesitation in his voice gives me pause. "What's going on?"

His eyes meet mine, and he stares intently at me for a moment before he takes a step back and releases my hand. He goes down on one knee. I stare at him in utter shock. My heart stops beating and my lungs forget to work. This isn't what I think it is, *is it*?

Nate closes his eyes and takes a deep breath before looking up at me. "Macy. I've been sitting here thinking about how to do this, but I don't know if I'll ever be able to come up with the right words. All I know is I love you. You're the best thing to ever happen to me. I knew it the first time we met." He runs his hands over his jean-covered thighs. "I can't imagine spending my life with anyone else. I know we're only nineteen and people think that's too young, but I don't want to wait until we reach some mythical age." He reaches into the pocket of his jacket and pulls out a small box.

I can't breathe.

Nate opens the box. Inside is a gold ring with a plain band and a small diamond solitaire. "Macy Wagner, will you marry me?"

My eyes burn, and I blink to stop the tears forming in them. "Yes, of course I will marry you."

His smile is wide and brilliant and perfect as he stands back up and pulls me into a hug. He lifts me off my feet. "I love you so much," he says into my neck as he pulls me tight against him.

When Nate finally sets me down, he pulls the ring from the box. My left hand shakes as I stick it out toward him.

"I wish I could give you the whole world, Mace, but I hope this will do." He slides the ring on my finger, and it's a perfect fit.

I don't want the whole world. I just want Nate. This piece of jewelry is the promise of forever with him.

I look down at my hand fighting to see the ring in the dark. It's small and simple, but I know Nate had to have saved for a long time to pay for it. It's the most beautiful ring in the entire universe.

I've wanted to marry Nate for a long time. Now, I get to. We just have to get through the next few years of college since my dad won't let me get married until after I graduate. Then we can get married, we'll officially be Mr. and Mrs. Delaney, and I won't have to say goodbye ever again.

When he takes my face in his hands and kisses me, it feels like anything is possible. That this crazy long-distance college romance is possible. I can't help but squeal as his lips move against mine because I can't believe I'm going to marry Nate.

15

THE PRESENT

FRIDAY

"EVIE'S GETTING MARRIED!" Lillian yells.

The lights inside the bus are dimmed, but there are enough blue and purple LED strips running over the ceiling that I can see the bridesmaid in question dancing with the same enthusiasm she had the first three times she yelled the same exact thing. Her movements send her dark hair flying all over the place.

Meanwhile, I'm just trying to stay upright. The driver is pedal-happy, and I've almost fallen onto one of the couches that line the sides of the bus twice because of his hard and sudden braking.

I'm currently leaning against the wall to steady myself as we head to Evie's bachelorette party, but I can't stop thinking about Nate. My lips feel puffy and I'm afraid they'll be a dead giveaway of what I was doing before the bus showed up. If I don't stop touching them, I know they will be.

Lillian wraps an arm around my shoulders and pulls

me close, shaking me a little. "Come on, we're celebrating."

"I know."

"Really?" She arches a brow. "You don't seem excited."

I step out from under her arms. "I am. I'm just not really a woo-hoo girl," I say, trying to keep my balance.

Her face scrunches up. "A woo-hoo girl?"

"You know." I punch the air and shake my hand like it's holding a pom-pom. "A woo-hoo girl."

She rolls her eyes. "Just because you're allergic to fun doesn't mean you need to bring Evie down with you."

This isn't the first snide comment she's made to me tonight. While Lillian and I have never been great friends, she's not usually this rude to me. She's been acting weird since dinner the other night, and I'm not sure why.

I look past her to where Evie is talking to Joanna. She's not close enough to hear the conversation between me and Lillian—and I'm glad. If Evie could hear us, she'd hurry to my defense. I don't want her to feel like she has to choose between two of her friends during her bachelorette party.

I plaster on a cheesy smile when I look back at Lillian. "You're right." I dare to lift both hands and hope the driver doesn't gun it as I yell, "Woo-hoo!"

Lillian's pained smile reflects how I feel at this exact moment. "Whatever." We move closer to the rest of the bridal party, and spend a few minutes talking before Lillian eventually pulls out a bottle of champagne and plastic flutes. "Let's get this party started!"

Evie grabs her glass as Lillian pops the top off the bottle. The cork lands at my feet. I look at Lillian and she shrugs. I didn't realize it was possible to be so accurate with a cork, but it definitely feels intentional.

When she tries to hand me a glass, I hold up my hand. "No, thank you."

"It's not like we need a designated driver," Lillian says. "You can have a glass of champagne to celebrate your *best friend* getting married. It's almost like you don't care that you're the *maid of honor*."

And there it is. The reason Lillian is acting more over-the-top than usual. It's funny. If anyone was going to be jealous of my title, I was sure it was going to be Joanna. She's Evie's sister, after all, and still has a bit of a vendetta against me for breaking Nate's heart. But as far as I can tell, she's been fine to be a regular bridesmaid.

Lillian jerks the glass in my direction once more, causing a few drops to spill over the rim. I'm thankful they didn't land on my shoes, but I wish she'd stop pushing.

"I'm not the only one not drinking." I point to Joanna. "She's got a bottle of water."

When Joanna looks at me, her face is tired. "That's because I'm pregnant."

Evie smiles in a way that tells me she's known for a while, but the rest of the girls squeal in delight. A chorus of congratulations fills the air. Joanna touches her belly and grins. "It's still really early, thank goodness. No one wants a pregnant bridesmaid."

Evie pushes her sister's shoulder. "Oh, shut up. You could be nine months pregnant, and I'd still want you up there with me on my wedding day."

Joanna laughs. "But I would hate how puffy my face

looked in all your pictures. I'm glad I'll only be ten weeks along when I walk down the aisle."

"So now that we've solved the mystery of why Jo isn't drinking, you can take this." Lillian hands me a champagne flute. "Unless you have some news you want to share?"

I hold the glass away from me. "I'm not pregnant, if that's what you're implying."

When she smirks, I feel like I'm going to lose it.

It's not that I have a moral issue with drinking, or that I'm a recovering alcoholic, I just don't want to do it. I wish there wasn't so much pressure to drink to have a good time. I wish Lillian would let it go.

"To Matt and Evie," she yells. "May they be in love forever!"

Everyone lifts their glasses—Joanna lifts her bottle of water—and cheers. I lift the glass to my mouth, but don't tip the glass enough to actually take a sip. The smell of the alcohol makes my stomach turn. We're already in an enclosed space, so I've had to deal with it on top of the wild driving, but having it this close to my face makes it harder.

I swallow the excess saliva in my mouth, the telltale sign that I'm about to be sick, and hope that Lillian won't monitor the liquid in my glass the entire time to make sure I'm actually drinking.

Evie downs her champagne, walks over to me and discreetly swaps out glasses. She leans in and whispers, "You don't have to pretend. I love you just the way you are."

"I love you too."

"I'm sorry about Lillian. I'm not sure what's going on with her tonight."

I do, but I'm not going to get into it tonight. Maybe never. For better or worse, Lillian is Evie's friend, and I'm sorry that she's letting her personal issues with me get in the way of Evie's night. Regardless, I refuse to add fuel to the fire. I smile at my best friend. "It's okay. Tonight is going to be so fun."

"You're right, and you know why?" she asks with a sly smile.

"Why?"

She steps back and yells, "Because I'm getting married!"

The entire bus erupts into cheers again, and I can't help but laugh. It's a joyful laugh because Evie looks so happy right now. She has every right to be happy. Matt is a great guy and the two of them are perfect for each other. They are going to have the best marriage ever.

I'm happy for her. I really am.

I keep waiting for a pang of regret to hit me, or a wave of sorrow to overcome me because of my past with Nate, but it never comes. Maybe it's because I'm too happy for her to feel any sadness.

Or maybe it's because there might be hope for me and Nate.

Regardless of the reason, my best friend is getting married in two days, and I can't wait.

Forty minutes and several sharp corners later, we're sitting down at a table in the back room of the steakhouse. I'm getting water so I start looking at the food while everyone debates which cocktail sounds the best. This place is famous for its aged steaks, but carbs are calling my name tonight. I find a chicken pasta dish that sounds amazing and set my menu down as the server comes to take our drink order.

As soon as she leaves, everyone else starts talking about the ride over.

"I still can't believe how bad that driver was," Evie says.

"Right?" Lillian sets her menu down. "That was one wild ride."

Joanna laughs. "There were a few times on the ride over I thought I was going to be sick."

"The room is still spinning," I say. "I've never struggled with motion sickness, so this was a first for me."

After the words leave my mouth, my mind goes to Nate and the night ahead of him. I never understood how hard it must be to struggle with something like that. The fact that I'm still feeling bad and the drive was only an hour makes me worry for Nate. When everyone picks up their menus to look for what they want to eat, I pull out my phone and send a quick text to him.

Are you sure you're going to be okay tonight?

His response comes back right away.

Awww. Are you worried about me?

You know I am.

I don't know what to say. This is all so sudden.

I roll my eyes and look up to see if anyone is paying

attention to me. Their attention is still focused on the menus in front of them. I send him another message.

Seriously. I got motion sickness on the drive over. I can't imagine doing that for six hours.

I'll be okay.

You sure?

If I said no, would you come rescue me?

I smile at his response. It's just so *him*. And things feel so normal. It's scary how easily we're slipping back into these roles, and I wonder if it's really possible for us to try again. Every part of me is screaming for me to go for it except for the small voice in the back of my mind telling me it's a bad idea. I ignore it as I type out a response.

You know I can't, but I wish I could.

"Who are you texting?" Evie asks.

Guilt claws at me for not telling her about Nate, and I panic. I quickly turn off my screen like there's something incriminating on it.

Her eyes narrow at me. "What's going on?"

"No one." I clear my throat. "Nothing. Just some flower thing for your wedding." We kissed on her flowers and, if you do a lot of mental gymnastics, that makes what I say almost true. It's not that I want to lie to her, I'm just not ready to have that conversation yet. It's why I kicked Nate out before she could catch us together.

My phone lights up with another text. Thankfully, I

haven't saved Nate into my phone yet, so it's just a string of numbers. Not so thankfully? The words **I miss you** are clearly visible.

I know this because Lillian is so kind to read it out loud and then add, "Why would the flower people tell you that they miss you?"

I pull my phone off the table and shove it into my purse—sorry, Nate, you're on your own now—and ignore the dirty look coming from my best friend. "I don't know. Weird."

I ignore the buzzing that comes from my purse and let out a sigh of relief when the server returns with our drinks. She places everyone's cocktails in front of them and starts taking orders. When she walks away, I turn toward Joanna and ask, "Have you had bad morning sickness this time around?" before anyone can mention my texts again.

With any luck, the table will allow the abrupt subject change and forget about my weird relationship with the "flower supplier."

She looks taken aback by my sudden interest and gives Evie a questioning glance before looking back at me. She shakes her head. "Not really."

I prop my elbow on the table and rest my chin in my hand. "Weren't you really sick with Caroline?"

"Uh, yeah," Joanna says, clearly still confused by my line of questioning. "I puked every day when I was pregnant with her. I didn't think I'd do this again, but here I am."

"I can't wait to have kids, even if that means going through morning sickness," Lillian says. She takes a sip of her drink and turns toward Evie. "What about you?

How long do you think it'll be before you and Matt have kids?"

"I don't know." Evie looks down at her fingers as they trace the stem of her wineglass. "I'd like the cousins to be close in age, and since Joanna is already on baby number two, I guess we'll have to get started pretty soon."

"Considering your family and its propensity to having kids, you'll have a few chances," Lillian says.

Everyone laughs. I even manage to crack a smile.

Lillian looks at me. "What about you, Macy? Do you want kids?"

I shrug. "There was a time I was sure I was going to have them."

"It's totally fine if you don't," Evie says quickly. "Not everyone wants kids."

"People always say that, but I don't think I believe them," Lillian says. "I always wonder if it's an issue of not wanting them or being single."

My toes tap violently beneath the table. I plaster a smile on my face. "I never said I didn't want them, just that there was a time that I thought I wanted them. But yeah, being single is a bit of a roadblock."

"It's only a roadblock if you want it to be," she says and takes another sip of her drink.

What is she suggesting? That I go out and ask some random dude to knock me up? I choose to ignore her and that ridiculous comment.

Thankfully the conversation quickly moves onto something new. Lillian and Rachel start talking about work. Lillian works in real estate and Rachel is a teacher. On the surface, they have nothing in common, until Lillian realizes she's trying to find a house for the family of one of Rachel's students. Then they start off on a long rant about how weird the mom is. Evie and I, of course, have no clue who they're talking about, but by the way the two of them are laughing, it must be really funny. Personally, it makes me feel a little icky teasing someone mercifully behind their back.

I turn to Evie. "Have you heard from Matt yet?"

"Yeah. He even sent me this picture." She taps her phone until an image of Matt and his groomsmen fills the screen. She laughs as she turns it so it's facing me. "Isn't this ridiculous?"

I look at the picture. All the guys are wearing similar outfits as Nate—cargo pants, fishing shirts, hats. They're standing next to the pier with Matt in the center. There's a giant grin on his face. His brother is next to him, and Nate and the other groomsman are on either side. Everyone is smiling, but you can see the pain in Nate's eyes if you are looking for it. I feel so bad for him.

"I thought you'd be laughing your head off," Evie says. "They look like a couple of alpha dads ready for a day on the yacht."

"Yeah, it's pretty bad." I force a smile as I continue to look at the picture. Nate's not looking at his phone, but I can see it in his hand, which hangs limply at his side. I think of the unread text messages on my phone and wonder if he was sending them right before they took this picture. "I just hope Nate took his Dramamine."

"You remember his motion sickness." Evie clicks the side of her phone, making the screen black.

"Yeah, and when he said he was going to be on the boat for six hours, I told him he needed to take some crackers with him too."

She narrows her eyes at me. "When did you tell him that?"

I realize my mistake too late. "Uh . . . "

"What were you looking at?" Lillian asks, her voice carrying loudly in the space.

I turn away from Evie and look at Lillian. "Evie was just showing me a picture of the guys from their bachelor party."

"This, I've got to see," Joanna says, reaching out her hand for Evie's phone. She taps the password—since everyone knows it—and stares at the screen. "I can't believe Matt dragged Nate on a fishing trip."

"Why's that?" Lillian asks as she looks over Joanna's shoulder. "Oh, they look so cute."

I highly doubt any of these guys would like the idea of being called cute by Lillian when they're about to go deep sea fishing.

"Hey, Macy," Lillian says, her eyes still glued to the screen. "Didn't you and Nate used to date?"

I clear my throat. "Uh, yeah."

She looks up. "It was a while ago, though, right?"

I nod. "It's been four years."

"You're not, like, still hung up on him, are you?"

Spots appear in the corner of my vision. I know alcohol has a way of stripping away inhibitions, and normally, I'm content to sit and enjoy the conversation while others drink, but having it directed toward mine and Nate's relationship feels like a line is being crossed. It's none of her business whether or not I still have feelings for Nate. It's not a question I want to answer, but I'm also completely aware of the way Evie and Joanna have gone completely still while they wait for my response.

They might not be the ones asking the rude questions, but they want to know the answer just as much, if not more, as Lillian.

"No, I'm not," I say because I'm not still "hung up" on him. I love him. And he loves me. And after we get through this wedding, we're going to figure out what that looks like. And it's not going to be any of Lillian's business.

"Oh, good. Because I might have a little crush on him." She snatches Evie's phone and looks at the screen like a lovesick teen.

"You have a crush on Nate?" Rachel asks.

"Yeah." Lillian sighs. "He's got a chiseled jawline, muscles for days, and just graduated from law school. Nate is the total package."

He is. But he's mine. A wave of possessiveness moves through me. I'm not jealous, necessarily, I know how Nate feels about me. But I don't like the fact that I can't say anything to anyone. Not yet. Not until Nate and I figure it out.

"We talked a little at dinner the other night," Lillian says. She means the dinner at the Delaneys'. The one where Nate and I talked on his front porch and looked up at the stars together. "I think we really hit it off."

I cross my arms over my chest, and because I can't help myself, I say, "Oh, yeah?"

She nods enthusiastically. "Uh-huh. We like a lot of the same things. Movies, music, food. And the fact that he might be moving back was the icing on the cake. He's new, and nobody knows he's here yet. I get first dibs."

The cleverness in her eyes is surprising. I didn't think she was sober enough to plot out how she was going to swoop in and take Nate before the unsuspecting ladies of Belview even know he's here, but she is. I have to give it to her, she's a mastermind. Even though I know she's already failed, the urge to mark my territory gets stronger, and I want to rip the phone from her hands and tell her he's mine.

"And if things go the way I'm hoping they will, Matt and Evie won't be the only ones getting lucky on Saturday."

"Ew." Joanna covers her ears with her hands. "Please don't talk about my *baby* brother like that ever again."

Rachel laughs, but I am seeing red. I can't sit here anymore and listen to Lillian talk about how she wants to hook up with Nate. Forcing a smile, because this is still Evie's bachelorette party, I excuse myself to the restroom. I grab my purse as I walk away because I need to see my phone. I need to see the texts that Nate sent while I couldn't respond. I need to know that I'm not imagining things.

I make it around the corner of the hall leading to the bathrooms and pull it out. I lean against the wall of the narrow hall so that I'm out of the way. My breaths are coming in shallow pants, and I hold my phone like a lifeline as I look at the messages that fill my screen.

We're about to get on the boat. Quick! Help me think of an excuse to stay on the shore. Do you think they need a lookout?

I'm sorry if I scared you off with my earlier text.

But I don't regret sending it. I've missed you for a long time, Mace.

I take a deep breath and feel my heartbeat begin to slow. This is real. What is happening between me and Nate is real. My fingers tap out a quick response.

I've missed you too.

There she is. NOW THAT I'M ALREADY ON THE BOAT.

Sorry, I was listening to a certain bridesmaid tell me about how she can't wait to get lucky with you.

Is it you? Are you "certain bridesmaid?"

You wish!

Uh . . . obviously.

I bite my bottom lip as a blush starts moving up my neck and to my cheeks. I don't know how to respond to that, so I don't.

Too much?

No.

Good. Because I can't wait to see you.

I can't wait to see you either. But I can't text you anymore tonight. I think Evie might suspect something.

Plus there's that "certain bridesmaid" you need to look out for, that I'm still not convinced isn't you.

I roll my eyes.

I'll see you tomorrow.

Not if I'm claimed by the sea tonight.

I'm trying to think of a way to reply that includes mermaids and them keeping him as his prisoner when Evie appears.

"I was starting to wonder if you fell in," she says flatly.

I shove my phone in my purse. "Yeah. Sorry. I'm coming."

She jerks her head at it. "Flower people again?"

"What?"

She presses her lips together. "That's who was texting you earlier, wasn't it? The flower people?"

I'm saved from answering right away as a guy walks down the hall toward the men's room. Evie and I push ourselves against the wall so he can get by. When he's safely inside the bathroom, and Evie and I are alone again, I still don't know what to say.

"I'm not an idiot, Macy. I know it's not the flower people." She pauses. "Is it Nate?"

My shoulders sag.

"I don't care that it is." She stops and shakes her head. "No, actually I do care if it's him, and we'll talk about that later. But why are you lying to me?"

"I'm not lying. I just don't want to talk about it tonight. This is your bachelorette party and I'm trying to keep it about you, despite the fact that Lillian keeps asking me about babies and Nate and . . . " I throw my hands out.

She grimaces. "I think maybe she's had too much to drink."

"You *think*?"

"Okay, I know she's had too much to drink." She laughs nervously. "I'm really hoping we don't have a puking situation tonight."

"Me too." But mostly because I don't want to end up cleaning it up. Evie is the bride-to-be, so there's no way it's going to be her. Joanna is pregnant, and I wouldn't let her do that either. Rachel isn't drunk, but I don't know how well she'd be able to handle it being impaired, so that leaves me. Having her word-vomit all over me before actually vomiting would almost be poetic, but I'll cross that bridge when we get there. I wrap my arm around Evie's shoulder. "I'm sorry your party is going this way."

She rests her head against me. "No, I'm sorry. I don't know what's gotten into Lillian."

I still think it's the maid of honor thing, but I say, "Maybe she's just excited about the wedding."

"Maybe," she says slowly. "But back to you." She pulls her head off me and steps back so she can look me in the eyes. "You're talking to Nate, aren't you?"

I chew the inside of my cheek. The bathroom hallway wasn't exactly where I planned to have this conversation. "Yeah."

"And what does that mean?"

"I don't know." I grip the strap of my purse with both hands. "We're trying to figure it out."

"Romantically?"

I think about our time at my apartment before the party bus showed up. "I think so."

"Do you think that's a good idea?" Her voice is gentle, and there's no unkindness in it, but it still feels like a punch to the gut because deep down I know it's the furthest thing from a good idea.

"I still love him. He loves me." My voice cracks and we stand there in the hallway while a song about breaking up plays over the speakers.

Evie's face softens. "Love was never the problem."

The words linger in the air and, as much as I don't want to admit it, she's right. It wasn't lack of love from either of us that made me push him away. My eyes sting as I nod. "I know that."

"I hope so, because if you're not careful, I think you two might end up more hurt than before."

Again, she's not wrong—except for the fact that it might already be too late. I squeeze my eyes shut and blurt, "I kissed him. He saw my tattoo."

"Oh, honey."

"I know."

When she pulls me in for a hug, it feels more like a finishing blow.

I'm an idiot for kissing Nate and imagining that we could have a second chance. This is just something else to add to a series of unfortunate events that cannot be undone. A series of events that started our freshman year of college and forever changed our futures. A series of events that made it impossible for me to be the person Nate needed and deserved.

I've spent countless nights thinking of all the things I could have done differently. I have a list of all the things I wish I could take back. But sometimes things happen in life that cannot be fixed no matter how badly you wish they could be.

In the afterglow of kissing Nate, I imagined we would find a solution together. But as I step out of Evie's hug and take in her sad expression, I realize I was wrong. Breaking up with Nate four years ago was the only solution, even though it hurt more than anything I'd ever done. Even though it still hurts.

Lillian comes stumbling around the corner, a drink in her hand. "There you are." Her words are slurred as she waves her free hand at Evie and me. "We were wondering where you went."

I force a smile. "Just some stomach issues, but I'm better now."

"Okay." Lillian looks at my torso and wrinkles her nose. "Well, I just wanted you guys to know that the food came out."

"Thanks," Evie says from beside me. Her voice gives nothing away.

I don't know if it's the way Evie is trying to cover for what we were just talking about or if it's the fact that is Lillian standing there, without a care in the world after I had such a gut-wrenching realization, but something in me snaps.

I'm tired of caring about Nate. I'm tired of hurting over our past. And I'm tired of feeling every damn thing.

I walk past Evie and grab the drink from Lillian's hand. I have no idea what it is, but it's colorful and smells like fruit. I hold my breath as I lift her glass to my lips and chug it as quickly as possible. I down it in three big swallows. The taste of pineapple does nothing to stop the burn as the liquid slides down my throat. Just like the last time I drank, the liquor turns in my stomach. I don't love the way I feel right now, but hopefully the next drink will help. And, yes, there will be another one because I want to stop feeling.

I hand Lillian back her empty glass. “Good. I’m starving.”

I don’t see Evie’s expression. I don’t need to see her to know she’s giving me a disapproving look as I move back toward the dining area of the restaurant.

But Lillian is positively giddy. “Finally, we can get this party started,” she says, as she follows closely behind me.

The party has definitely started, and maybe I’ll forget for one night.

16

THE PAST

FRESHMAN YEAR OF COLLEGE

"Are you being serious right now?" Nate's irritated voice comes through the speaker of my phone. "We're supposed to leave tomorrow morning."

I step out of my dorm room and out into the hallway so I can have a bit of privacy from my roommate. It's not that she's a bad roommate. Lin doesn't stay up too late, keeps her side of our room clean, and has a pretty friendly disposition. We're both focused on doing well in our classes, and it's worked out well so far. But ever since I came back from Belview a few weeks ago with an engagement ring on my finger, she's been telling me I'm too young to be thinking about marriage. I don't want her to overhear me and Nate arguing because I don't want to give her another reason to try to convince us to break up.

I lower my voice. "I know I said I was going to come this year, and I'm sorry, but I have so much work to do. I can't take a week off to go to the Rendezvous."

"But we go every year. You can bring your work with you. There will be plenty of time to do it there."

I think of all the assignments that keep piling up and what it would look like trying to do them from a tent without electricity. I lean against the concrete wall and sigh. "Unfortunately, none of that time includes technology."

"We'll figure it out," Nate says from the other side of the line. "I'll take you to Starbucks for a day. I'll take you to Culver's and feed you and just keep you company while you do your work. Whatever you need. But please, just come. Don't make me go by myself when everyone is expecting to see you. I don't want to go a week without talking to you."

I hold the charm on my necklace and run it back and forth over the chain. It's not like I want to stay here at school and work on my assignments. I don't. I'd much rather be with Nate and his family at the River Rendezvous, but I barely squeaked by last semester. I need to make sure I start this one off right. "I can't."

"You can. You just don't want to." Nate makes an irritated sound on the other end. "Do you know how hard it is not to be able to see you?"

"Of course I do," I say a little too loudly. A girl walking down the hall stops and turns to make sure I'm okay. I give her a reassuring smile and she continues on her way. "Don't forget, I don't get to see you either because *you* chose to go to community college."

"Wow." He laughs bitterly. "You're never going to let that go, are you?"

I thought I had, but I guess I haven't. It's not the fact that he's going to community college, it's the fact that he gave up his spot at UF last minute to take care of his dad after a surprise surgery. And yes, I realize how horrible it is for me to be upset. It's amazing that Nate was willing to put his life on pause to take care of his dad. But I miss him. And I hate that we're doing the long-distance thing for another year when we worked so hard to make sure this exact thing didn't happen.

"Nate . . . "

"Do you think it was an easy decision for me to make? I had to choose between you and my parents. The people I love more than anything else in this world. Do you know how hard it was to choose to stay?"

"But it was still a choice," I whisper-yell into my phone. "And that's what I'm doing. I'm making a difficult choice."

"It's a little different, don't you think?"

"That's not really fair."

"You want to talk about fair? How's this for fair? I never asked you to stay home with me, and I've tried not to make you feel guilty for going to Gainesville because I want you to be happy. I'm not asking for some great sacrifice on your part, Mace. I'm asking for a week. You're motivated. Great. You want good grades? Cool. But you're taking it too far."

"What's that supposed to mean?"

"It means you talk about how horrible it was for your mom to leave you to pursue her art, and it was really shitty for her to do that to you. But maybe you should look in the mirror because that's exactly what you're doing right now. You're choosing your future career over your future family."

I almost drop my phone when he says this. His words hit straight to my core. "You think I'm like my mother?" The woman who abandoned me.

There's a pause before Nate says, "I shouldn't have said that. Of course you're nothing like her."

I shake my head. I'm furious. "There must be some truth to it, if you said that."

"Macy, no." His voice is cracking. "I'm so, so sorry. I'm frustrated, and I miss you, and I said something stupid in anger. You are amazing, and you're going to be a great mom one day."

His voice is so earnest, I know he really believes that, but I can't help the thread of doubt that runs through me. Is there a chance I'm like my mom? Am I wrong for wanting to focus on school instead of spending time with my future family? I don't know. But what I do know is that he hurt my feelings and I don't want him to know just how badly his words wounded me.

"I gotta go," I say with an almost steady voice before I turn my phone off.

My phone immediately buzzes and his face appears on my screen. I ignore it. I can't talk to him right now. I don't know what to say and need some time to think about it all.

I shove the phone in my pocket and walk back inside my dorm. Lin isn't exactly watching me as I walk in, but she's staring at her phone a little too intently. She's sitting a little too still, like she's trying to see my reaction without making it obvious. Maybe she's right. Maybe I'm crazy for getting engaged at such a young age. I sit down on my bed and take my engagement ring off. I turn it in my fingers for several moments before I turn to her. "Do you want to go to a party with me?"

She sets her phone down and looks at me like I'm

crazy. Maybe because we've never done anything together in our time as roommates. "When?"

"Tonight."

"Tonight?" She nods her head once to punctuate the question.

"Yeah." I shrug, like it's no big deal. "I know a guy who's having a party off-campus." The guy in question's name is Jake, and we went to high school together. We aren't exactly friends, but it's nice to have someone familiar now that I'm so far away. I'd originally told him no, but he texted me the address in case I changed my mind.

"You sure your *fiancé* won't care?"

I tuck my ring under my mattress instead of putting it back on my finger. "Right now, I don't care what my fiancé thinks." My phone screen lights up with notifications—all texts from Nate. I scan them. He's sorry he said that. He feels horrible. He wants me to call him back. But I'm still too upset to talk to him.

I put on a dress I bought impulsively when I was shopping for college. It's short, tight, and black—not the type of thing I would normally wear, but it felt right at the time. And it feels right now. This is my life-is-hard-and-I-want-to-feel-better dress.

I'm surprised when Lin puts on an even flashier dress. It's just as short, but it's bright red. It compliments her pale skin and black hair perfectly. When she does her eyes with a perfect cat eye and completes the look with red lips that match her dress, she looks like a completely different person. She's a knockout. In an effort to look as good as she does, I do a smokey eye, complete with fake lashes.

Once Lin and I are satisfied with the way we look, we load up in my car and follow my phone's GPS instructions. The directions lead us to a house that is a couple of miles from the university—right in the middle of the suburbs. There are a lot of cars lined up on the street when we pull up. I park behind another one, careful not to block any driveways, and we get out.

"I love this song," she says as we walk up to the house, toward the sound of loud music. It's still early, but I'm surprised no one has called in a noise complaint yet. The fact that it's so loud we can make out the lyrics before we even get inside makes me wonder what the neighbors must think.

"Should we make a pact that we leave together?" I ask right before we walk inside. It's been years since I've been to a party like this—actually, the last party I went to was the one I threw and got grounded for. I don't really know if this is a real girl code thing or just something they do in movies.

Lin scrunches her face. "Really?"

Okay, so definitely just a movie thing. I give her a sheepish smile. "I just wasn't sure how you felt about it."

"I feel like this is going to be the best night ever!" She lifts her hands above her head and screams before opening the front door and stepping inside.

A few beat-up couches surround an outdated coffee table. The only decor is a few posters of girls in bikinis taped to the walls and a framed picture of *Scarface* in what should be the dining room. Even if I didn't already know this was a student house, it would be completely obvious by the décor alone.

The loud thumping of the bass is deafening as Lin

walks past small groups of people standing in circles with drinks in her hands. She moves through the crowd and leads me straight to the kitchen like she's done this a hundred times. People are huddled around all kinds of bottles—liquor, wine, sodas, and mixers.

Lin grabs two red solo cups and pours something into them. Then she grabs two cut up lime slices off a paper plate and a salt shaker. She sets down her collection of items right down in front of me. "Let's do tequila shots."

I look around the kitchen to see if anyone is looking at us. I lean in and ask, "Do you think it's okay to take these? Maybe I should try to find Jake first?"

She laughs a laugh I've never heard from her before. "Oh, Macy. You're so adorable. It's a house party. Literally, nobody cares."

As I watch her lick the top of her hand and pour salt on it, I realize I *really* don't know this girl standing in front of me. I thought we were the same because our life inside our dorm room has looked so similar since we arrived last August, but we've never talked about what we do when we're not there. I gape at her as she takes my hand and licks the spot right between my thumb and forefinger and pours salt on it too.

"Ready?" She shoves a red solo cup into my hand and smiles.

"Um . . . "

She licks the salt off the back of her hand, tips back the cup, and shoves the lime in her mouth. When she's done, she smiles. I feel like an idiot because I've never done anything like this before, not even the one time I threw a party when my dad was supposed to be out of town, and I'm not sure that I want to. But it looks simple enough and she's watching me expectantly.

Salt, tequila, lime. No big deal.

I lick the salt off the back of my hand, lift my cup to my lips and choke down the tequila, then pop the lime in my mouth, thankful for the relief it gives after the burning of the liquor.

"Woo!" she yells. "Let's do another."

I shake my head. "I think I'm good." It's been so long since I've drank, and I don't know how I'll react to it. Plus, I need to drive us back to school later.

"Suit yourself." She pours tequila into her cup, sprinkles more salt on her hand, and holds the same lime from her first shot between her fingers.

"Macy?" comes a deep voice from behind me, and I turn to see Jake. His blond hair is shaggy and almost hits his eyes. He's wearing a polo shirt and jeans, like most of the guys here, and has a red cup in his hand. His eyes rake over me. "I didn't think you were coming tonight."

"I didn't think so either." I nod and jerk my thumb at Lin who just finished her second shot. "I hope it's okay that I brought my roommate."

His eyes go to Lin and back to me. "The more the merrier. I'm glad you're here." Jake looks down at my empty hands. "Can I get you a drink?"

"I actually just took a shot." I grimace. "I hope that's okay."

"Of course it is." He sweeps his hand over the various bottles. "This is for everyone."

Lin is eating from an open bag of chips on the counter, but overhears this. She smirks as lifts her hand in triumph. "I told you."

I tuck a strand of hair behind my ear. "I guess I just don't do a lot of parties."

Jake smiles at me. "Then I'm honored that you came to mine."

"I'm just glad to know someone here."

Lin seems perfectly content with her snacks while I talk to Jake about our classes and how our first semesters have been going. Jake has been having a hard time with his classes, too, and while I'm not happy to hear anyone is struggling, it's nice to have someone who understands how difficult the transition from high school to college can be. Sometimes it feels like I'm the only one who is fighting to keep their grades up.

After a few minutes of conversation, Jake looks down at the empty cup I've been clutching like an emotional support cup.

"Are you ready for another drink yet?"

"I think I'm good on booze, but maybe something else?" I bite my lip as I wait for his response.

He frowns, but quickly recovers. "Yeah, okay. What do you want?"

"Maybe a soda?"

"Sure, no problem." He looks me up and down before smiling. "I'll be right back."

When he disappears, I turn to Lin. She stopped eating and . . . wait, is she taking another shot? "Whoa," I say, and put my hand lightly on her arm. "Maybe slow down for a minute. We haven't been here that long."

She rolls her eyes at me. "It's fine. Alcohol doesn't really affect me. I have to drink a lot before I feel anything."

"And three shots isn't a lot?"

I've only had the one, and I can already feel more relaxed. Nothing major, the room isn't spinning, but I know enough to know I should stop here.

She laughs and pats my arm. "Don't worry about me. I'll be fine." Then she walks out toward the living room.

I'm left standing by myself in the kitchen wondering what the heck I'm doing here. I was mad at Nate and wanted to do something, but it feels too much like the days when I tried really hard to fit in with all the cool kids at my school and forced myself into a box I didn't fit in.

I continue to stand awkwardly in the kitchen for another minute until Jake returns. He's got another red solo cup in his hand now. When I look down at it nervously, he smiles. "No booze, I promise."

I sigh with relief and take it from him. "Thanks."

"Where did your friend go?"

I point toward the living room.

"Wanna go make sure she's okay?"

I nod eagerly. I might not like the way the night has gone so far, but I can't just leave her alone. "Yes, please."

Jake leads me out to the living room where Lin has already joined one of the small groups we saw when we came in. She's laughing loudly at something and looks like she's having a great time. At least one of us is.

I don't actually like parties. I don't even know that I like the idea of parties. I just wanted to escape for the night. Now that I have, all I want to do is go home. Unfortunately, I'm stuck here, at least for a little while. I can't leave Lin by herself, especially when she's taken back-to-back shots. And it doesn't feel right to make her leave when we've been here less than fifteen minutes.

There are two open spots on one of the couches, and

Jake and I quickly grab them before someone else does. I take a sip of the drink he brought me. I look down at my cup. "You sure there's no alcohol in this?"

He lifts his hand. "I swear. Why?"

"It tastes a little funny. Almost bitter."

"Hmm." He scratches his chin. "It took me a little while to find some soda, and the only thing I found was some off-brand thing."

I take another sip and swish it around my mouth. There's no burn, and it definitely still tastes like a cola of some sort, so that must be it. I lean back and look at the room. Everyone, including Lin, looks so happy. I'm not sure if it's the alcohol lowering their inhibitions, or if they've discovered some secret to life that makes them feel more comfortable in situations like this.

"What are you thinking right now?"

I snort. "That I still don't belong."

"What do you mean?"

I wave my hand at the room. "I wasn't good at this in high school, and I don't feel any better at it now."

"You're kidding, right?"

"I don't know if you remember high school, but I always felt like I was on the outside looking in. I never felt like I was part of the in-crowd."

"You could have been part of the in-crowd." He scoots closer. "You were certainly hot enough to be popular, but you were always hanging out with that weird homeschool kid."

I touch my necklace. "You mean Nate."

"Yeah. Nate." He looks at where my fingers touch the charm. I drop my hand. "Is that from him?"

"Yeah."

"And you guys are still dating?"

I take a sip and nod. "We're doing the long-distance thing this year."

And even though Nate really hurt my feelings, I still love him. And I miss him. I think I'd rather be with him working things out than here feeling like an idiot. If nothing else, I wish I would have kept my engagement ring on. The guilt of leaving it behind gnaws at me.

I look up and find Lin's bright red dress. She and one of the guys from the group have split off from everyone and are standing close to each other and talking. I wonder if she'll end up hooking up with him—if she's the type of person who does that. I still don't know.

"So he's not in Gainesville at all?"

I shake my head. The room spins with the movement. "He stayed in Oak Ridge this year."

"So, it's just you and your roommate?"

"Yeah," I answer slowly. Or maybe it just sounds a little slow because I've got a slight buzz from my shot.

"You okay?" Jake is looking intently at my face.

I put the back of my hand to my forehead. "It's been a long time since I drank, and I think that shot hit me a little harder than I thought."

"That's probably it." Jake stands up. He put his hand out for me to take and lifts me. "Here, come on. I have some water in my room. It'll make you feel better."

I let him hoist me off the couch and I follow him down the hall. Maybe the water will make me feel better. I hope so because I don't feel so good right now. The room spins and I stumble into him when he stops at his door.

He takes my hand and leads me to his bed. "Just stay there. I'll be right back."

It strikes me as funny that he would say that. Where am I going to go when I'm having such a hard time just sitting up straight? I lean back and fall against his pillow. I'm just so tired. I don't know what's going on. How can one shot affect me so much when Lin was doing just fine? I'm not sure. But wondering what's wrong with me is the last thing that goes through my mind before my body goes limp and everything goes black.

17

THE PRESENT

SATURDAY

It's late when I wake up the morning after the bachelorette party. Just like the last time I drank, my head is pounding and my skull feels like it's going to crack open. My throat is so dry I can barely swallow, but the very thought of drinking water makes me want to puke.

Unlike last time, I'm waking in my own bed.

I run a hand over my face and use some of the techniques Dr. Shay taught me to ground myself. It's been a long time since I've felt this helpless—and this sick.

I groan as I turn toward my nightstand. My clock says it's ten o'clock. I can hardly believe I slept so long. Usually, I wake with the sunrise, if not earlier. Today, the sun has gone on without me.

When I look at my phone, it's filled with notification after notification. There are several pictures from Lillian. In them, we look sloppy drunk. Our eyes are glazed over and we're barely looking at the camera. We're making kissing faces, our tongues are sticking out, and we're drinking shots.

Ugh. I don't even want to think about the number of shots we took together. I've never consumed so much alcohol in my life and I don't know my limits. I send up a quick prayer that I didn't end up in the hospital getting my stomach pumped.

There's a text from Evie telling me to call her tomorrow when I wake up—meaning today. I ignore her for now and read the many texts from Nate instead.

> You'll be happy to know I was not claimed by the sea. I'm safely on dry land, and only puked once.

> Does that make me less attractive?

> Because I totally didn't puke. I was manly the whole time.

> I hope your night is going well with the girls.

> I still miss you.

My stomach churns as I read through them all. I miss him too, but that doesn't mean I can be with him. Nothing has changed, and it took another night of drinking and passing out for me to realize that. It's not like part of me didn't realize this was going to end badly, but last night served as a twisted refresher to remind me that I do not get a happily ever after with Nate.

I do not want to have this conversation with him, not after everything that has happened this week. But he deserves to know the truth. The reason I broke up with him the first time, and the reason we can't be together now. I need Nate to know that I love him, but it's not enough. You can love someone and also know that there's no future together. That's what it will always be for me and Nate, no matter how badly I wish it wasn't.

I reread our texts from the last twenty-four hours and look at the picture he sent of him and the rest of the groomsmen. I let myself pretend I can have him—just a little while longer—but I know I need to call things off tonight. This time for good.

I SHOW up to the church for Evie and Matt's wedding rehearsal wearing a nice black dress that I hope makes up for the lack of effort I put into my appearance. A shower washed away the mistakes of the night before, but I didn't have the energy to do much beyond that. My hair has a slight wave from drying naturally, and the only makeup I put on was a single coat of mascara. I didn't even bother using concealer to cover the dark circles under my eyes.

I'm not late, but I still managed to be the last one to arrive. Evie watches me as I walk down the aisle toward the front of the sanctuary, where everyone is congregating. I've ignored her texts and calls all day, which I realize is terrible of me since I'm her maid of honor, but it's been impossible to face her.

I know she's disappointed in me for getting involved with Nate romantically again. I know she's disappointed in me for drinking my weight in liquor last night and having to make sure I got home safe. And I'm sure she's more than just a little disappointed in me for ruining her bachelorette party—and possibly her rehearsal dinner.

I'm a crappy friend, and I'm well aware of that fact.

If I could just disappear, I would. If I could give the

role of maid of honor to Lillian, who looks perfectly put together, I'm sure things would be better for everyone, but the programs for the ceremony have already been printed. I'm locked in, for better or for worse, at this point. The only thing I can do now is try to make sure I do my best to make sure her wedding day is nothing less than perfect.

I try to avoid meeting Nate's eyes, but he makes it impossible when he strides over to me.

"Are you okay?" He cups my cheek. "Evie said you had a lot to drink last night, and then you weren't returning my texts."

I step back. "Yeah. I'm fine. Just not feeling good."

His brows lower. "Are you sure that's it?"

"Yeah," I say, a little too cheerfully, painfully aware that Nate isn't the only one watching me intently. "I'm fine."

"Why does that feel like a lie?"

"I'm fine," I say again, this time more forcefully, and take a step back putting space between us.

He presses his lips together. "Fine." He walks back to where the wedding party is congregating without me, and I have no choice but to follow behind him. As much as I didn't want to make a spectacle of myself during Evie's celebrations, it looks like I did anyway. I feel the weight of his family's stares. I imagine they'd be shooting daggers out of them, if it were possible.

"There she is," Lillian says as we get closer. She pulls me in for a hug. "There's my reluctant woo-hoo girl."

At least she still likes me. I chuckle weakly. "I might have woo-hooed too hard last night."

Her laugh is much more enthusiastic. "No way. That

was awesome. I fully expect you to party with me like that tomorrow at the reception."

My eyes widen as I break our embrace. "I don't plan to ever drink again."

She waves her hand in front of her face. "You're just saying that because you're hungover. Tomorrow will be a different story. You'll see."

I doubt it, but I don't argue the point.

"Now that everyone is here," the wedding planner says loudly, causing everyone to stop their chatter, "it's time to line up in our positions so we can go through the ceremony."

When I stand next to Evie, she raises her brows. "She lives."

"Yeah." I rub the back of my neck. "Thanks for making sure I got home safely last night. I appreciate it."

Her smile is hard. "You have a funny way of showing gratitude. You couldn't text me and let me know you were okay? I was so busy today, and all I wanted to do was drive to your house and check on you. I almost sent Matt."

"I'm sorry." The words feel inadequate, but I don't know what else to say. I don't have an excuse other than not wanting to face today, and wanting to live in a fantasyland where I didn't screw everything up for a little longer.

"You're my best friend, but I'm so angry with you right now," she hisses. "I still can't believe you last night."

Her words feel like a knife to the gut.

"Okay, Evie, now when you and Matt exchange rings, you will hand your bouquet to your maid of honor."

I can't meet her eyes when she pretends to hand me

her flowers. I make the mistake of looking over at the groomsmen. Just like the dinner at the Delaneys', Nate is looking at me. But there's something different about the way he stares at me now. Almost like he knows what's about to happen.

I try to focus on the wedding planner as she walks us through our various places for the ceremony. We run through the entire event three times. Each time, I'm careful to avoid looking at Evie or Nate. I just need to make it through this evening, get Evie's flowers to the church and reception, and get her off to Fiji.

After that, I'll have plenty of time to think about my poor decisions and how I've ruined everything by being impulsive and not thinking through what it would really mean to kiss Nate Delaney again after four years.

When the wedding planner is satisfied that we can make it through the ceremony without getting confused, she releases us for dinner. I've been looking forward to this meal ever since Evie told me that John Boy's BBQ was catering it. They're based out of Tampa and are my very favorite barbecue in the whole world, but the idea of eating still makes my stomach feel uneasy, not to mention the idea of doing it with Evie and Nate.

I grab Evie after she finishes talking to Joanna. I pull her to the side of the church, away from anyone who might be able to hear me. She crosses her arms over her chest. "What?"

I feel terrible for what I've done, and terrible for what I'm about to do. I hope she meant it when she said we'll still be best friends, and I hope she'll forgive me for making such a mess of things.

I take a deep breath and hold it for a few seconds

before releasing it. "I'm sorry. For everything. I shouldn't have had so much to drink last night. I shouldn't have gotten involved with Nate again. I should have texted you back today, and I know I've made a mess of your wedding."

Her face softens.

"I made a lot of mistakes that I can't take back. I'm sorry because I know I messed things up. I'm still messing them up. But I can't go to dinner tonight. Please. I'm asking you not to get mad if I skip the rest of the evening. I need to go home and get myself feeling well for your wedding tomorrow."

She presses her lips together and nods. "Okay."

She's not thrilled, but I'm thankful she's not making this harder than it already is. "And I need you to know that I'm going to tell Nate everything. I'm finally going to explain to him why I broke up with him and why I can't be with him now. I know that puts you in an awkward position, but I hope that coming clean will make it where we can finally move past this."

I tell her this in hopes that she'll know this is not coming from a place of pure selfishness.

She shakes her head. "What happens when he says your reasons aren't good enough?"

There was a time when Evie hoped our breakup was just a break that we'd eventually get over. She thought if Nate and I would just sit down and talk it out, that her brother and her best friend would end up back together. The idea was simple. The reality, not so much. As hard as it was to resist the urge, I pushed through her heartfelt pleas until she eventually stopped suggesting it.

"You know why they are." I bite the inside of my

cheek. "I'm sorry to mar your wedding day with this drama, but I don't know what else to do. I can't ignore this anymore, especially if he ends up moving home. Please don't stay mad at me."

She sighs and pulls me in for a hug. "I'm still angry at you for last night, but not because I'm worried about my wedding day. Matt and I are going to be fine even if everything goes wrong tomorrow. The wedding day is not the important thing. It's the marriage." She squeezes me tighter. "I'm angry because you were reckless and did something you are not proud of."

Tears stream down my cheeks. They're a mixture of sad tears over what's going to happen with Nate and grateful tears for a best friend who has loved me through my hardest moments over and over again. I am so undeserving of Evie, but I hold her close because I refuse to let her go—ever.

"I'll cover for you," she says. "Say there was some kind of flower emergency and that you're sorry you couldn't come to the dinner. But please take care of yourself tonight. I want my best friend by my side tomorrow, do you understand?"

I wipe my nose with the back of my hand. It's not my finest moment, but at least I still have Evie. "Thank you."

"I love you."

"Love you too."

"I'm going to get everyone out the door. Why don't you take a minute to clean yourself up in the bathroom so that you don't have to face them?"

Evie joins the wedding party, and I watch as they move toward the sanctuary doors. I follow behind, and duck into the bathroom for a minute while I wait for them to all shuffle out. When I see my reflection in the mirror, I startle, and not just because of the unflattering fluorescent lighting that highlights every imperfection.

My eyes are puffy, black streaks are running down both of my cheeks, and there's a wet spot toward the top of my dress. No wonder Evie suggested I clean myself up. I splash water on my face and use the paper towels to wipe the mascara off. After a few minutes, the blotchiness has faded, and I don't hear voices in the foyer anymore.

I take a deep breath and step out of the bathroom, only to bump into Nate. My eyes widen.

"Macy."

I glance away and stride past him. I told Evie I would talk to him, but I didn't want to do it until after the wedding. Not if I'm going to keep my promise to Evie to be well for her wedding tomorrow.

"Will you please just wait?"

I stop, but I don't turn around. Instead, I close my eyes as I listen to his footsteps against the tiled floor getting closer.

"You're shutting down again. You promised me we would talk and . . . " He takes a shaky breath. "What have I done that's so terrible?"

I turn to face him. "You haven't done anything."

"Really? Because it feels like I have. One day we're kissing and talking about how we both feel something, and the next you're ghosting me. It feels like four years ago all over again."

All the pain of that time comes rushing back to me. I wrap my arms around my waist. "It's not."

"But you're still planning on breaking things off again, aren't you?"

"I . . . " My shoulders sag and I hang my head. "I'm sorry." I've said those words so many times today, it feels like they're losing their meaning. But I am sorry that things won't work out for us.

"Are you?" he asks. "Because it doesn't seem like you care."

"Do you think this is easy for me?"

"I don't know. Is it?"

"No, it's the worst thing in the world. I hate it more than anything."

"Then why do you keep doing it?" His features are pinched. "Why do you keep making me believe we have a future and then break my heart?"

I rub a hand over my face. "Because we can't be together."

"Of course we can. If I move here, we'll be near each other again. We can figure it out."

"We can't figure it all out."

"What do you mean?" He moves closer to me. "What aren't you telling me?"

I step back. "I can't give you what you deserve. What you want."

"What are you talking about? You're what I want."

I shake my head, the tears falling freely at this point. "No, you don't understand. I can't have kids, Nate. I can't give you the family you've always wanted."

Then, in the church where Evie is getting married tomorrow, I tell him everything.

18

THE PAST

FRESHMAN YEAR OF COLLEGE

I WAKE up groggy to the sound of beeping in the background.

The lights are blindingly bright, and it takes me a few tries for me to open my eyes all the way. As the room comes into focus, the first thing I see is my dad. He's sitting in a chair next to my hospital bed. His hair is disheveled, there are dark circles under his eyes, and his shirt is crumpled. His gaze is vacant as he looks out the window. I've never seen him look this bad—not even when mom left.

It's been weeks since the party, and life has been a never-ending spiral since.

Right now, I'm just trying to remember the events that led to me waking up in this room with an IV stuck in my arm. It's all a blur, and I'm sure my current state isn't helping. I close my eyes as memories come to me in flashes.

I was home with my dad. We were eating dinner.

There was an unbearable pain in my lower abdomen, followed by sudden, heavy bleeding.

My dad sped to the ER.

The doctors said something about an ectopic pregnancy and emergency surgery to save my life.

It all happened so fast, I wasn't able to process everything before I was told to count down from ten.

Now that I'm waking up in my hospital room, I'm hit with the reality of what happened.

I was pregnant.

With Jake's child.

Now I'm not.

A silent sob racks through my body, but the movements are enough to alert my dad that I'm awake. He jumps out of his seat and races over.

"Macy?"

I can't speak.

"What do you need? Are you in pain?"

If he's wondering if the incision hurts, the answer is no. Emotionally, it's a different story. I don't know if I'll ever recover.

I'm sure he knows that because he lifts my hand, kisses the back of it. "I'm so sorry, Macy."

He doesn't say anything else. Neither do I. Tears stream from my eyes as silence stretches on. A nurse comes to check my vitals. Another person brings me a thermos of ice water that I don't touch. My dad steps out in the hall to make a call but returns quickly. It all runs together until the doctor walks in.

She's an older woman with red hair and a kind smile. "Hello, Macy. How are you feeling?"

This time, I know the question is about my physical pain. "I'm okay," I say weakly, even though I'm not.

She looks between me and my dad when she speaks. "I want to let you know that the surgery went well. We were worried you might need a blood transfusion but were able to stop the bleeding quickly enough that you should be fine with some iron supplements and plenty of rest."

"That's great," my dad says.

"It truly is. That's not often the case in situations like this," she says. "But I have some bad news."

My heart sinks. I'm not sure how this could get any worse. I brace myself for what she says next.

"As you know, your fallopian tube burst. It's why we had to perform the emergency surgery. We had to remove the tube."

I can't speak, so I'm thankful when my dad asks, "What does that mean?"

"It means that it will be more difficult to get pregnant in the future." She looks at me. "And if you do, you have a higher risk of having another ectopic pregnancy."

Meaning I'd have to go through this again if I ever got pregnant again?

"I know this news is difficult to hear," she says. "But I need to make sure you're aware of what potential risks there are if you choose to get pregnant in the future."

She continues to talk, but I don't hear the words that she's saying.

All I can think is I didn't *choose* this. None of it. I didn't want to get pregnant at nineteen. But now that I have, I'm learning I might not ever be able to do it again. It's not fair.

One stupid night has changed everything. *Everything.* And there's nothing I can do to change it.

I haven't talked to Nate since our fight. I've been too ashamed to tell him what happened. But now? How do I talk to him when I just found out I may never be able to have kids, and it's all my fault?

Family is the most important thing to Nate. He loves his big family, and I know he wants to have one of his own one day. What happens when I tell him I can't give that to him?

I take a deep breath and try to release it slowly.

I already know what will happen because I know the kind of guy Nate is. Assuming I ever get the courage to tell him what happened, he will tell me it's okay. That he loves me and we don't need to have a family to be happy. But he'd be wrong.

It's not that you need to have a family to be happy, but what you do need is to be on the same page as your spouse. You need to have the same hopes and dreams. I know this because I watched something similar happen to my parents. They were people who loved each other and wanted vastly different things from life. It eventually drove them apart.

If Nate chose to look past this, it wouldn't last. We'd eventually split up. Only it would be harder because we would have had more time together—more time to get closer before the inevitable comes. No, it's better to end things now, when we're already not speaking. Not because I don't love him, but because I love him so much and don't want to bring him down with me. I don't want to doom him to a life of unhappiness.

When the doctor leaves, I turn to my dad and speak

before I lose my nerve. "I need you to promise me you won't tell anyone what happened."

He sits up in his chair. "Of course not. Why would I tell anyone?"

I look him straight in the eyes so he won't miss my understanding. "Not a soul. Not even Nate."

"I wasn't going to." His eyebrows furrow. "But Macy, this isn't your fault. He can't blame you for what happened."

My eyes water and I play with the rough sheet that is pulled up to my shoulders. "I know he won't." I look at him again, even though he's a blur. "Promise me that what happened here, stays here."

He hesitates for a moment before he nods. "I promise."

IT'S another week before I feel strong enough to get out of bed. I've been taking iron supplements and eating foods rich in iron to try to get my energy back, but the process has gone slower than I'd hoped.

It's been hard putting this off after making the decision, and dodging Nate's calls and texts is getting trickier, but it's important to me that I do this in person. I feel guilty for asking Nate to drive an hour to break up with him, but I'm still not confident that I can drive safely.

When he knocks, my stomach drops. I still don't want to do this. My heart literally aches at the idea of living without him, but I know this is the right thing. It will hurt now, but one day he'll meet someone else, fall in love, and have lots of gorgeous babies.

I open the door, and he's there as wonderful as ever. He's wearing a t-shirt and jeans, there are flowers in his hands, and a small, cautious smile on his lips. When he takes in my appearance, a tank and athletic shorts, his smile falters. "Hey."

He waits patiently for me to invite him in, but I step outside instead. I sit down on the wicker couch on our front porch, and Nate sits next to me. He places the bouquet on the glass top of the coffee table and looks at me. His eyes are filled with concern. "Macy, what's going on? Are you okay?"

When his voice cracks, I almost lose my nerve. It's not too late to change my mind. I selfishly remind myself that Nate won't hold any of what happened against me. He'd want to hunt down Jake and kick his ass for what he did. He'd tell me that he would be okay not having kids, even though I know he'd be lying. He would convince me that everything would be okay, even though he'd be wrong.

He doesn't know what it's like to watch a husband and wife suck the life from each other for years before finally separating. He doesn't know, and now, he never will.

I close my eyes. "This isn't working."

"What's not working? The long-distance thing? We only have a couple more months, and then you can come home. Next year, I'll come up to UF with you. I've already been accepted for the fall. We won't have to be apart anymore."

"No." I shake my head. "It's not the long-distance thing, it's us. I've realized that we're not a good fit."

"What are you talking about?"

I look down at my hands, which are clasped in my lap.

"I've changed. I've realized I want different things from life, and you're not part of that."

He jumps up from the patio furniture and paces back and forth. I watch as he opens his mouth like he's going to say something, then clamps it shut. This happens a few times before he stops and faces me. "Is this because I went to community college?"

He's giving me an opening. I could say yes, and be done with it, but I know it's been a sore spot for him. I may be breaking his heart, but I don't want him to feel inadequate in other ways too. "No, I just think we moved too fast too soon."

He kneels in front of me and grabs my hand. "We don't have to get married right away. We can take a break. Whatever you need, Macy. We don't have to break up."

I pull my hand back and turn my face away from him. "We do. I just don't think we're going to work out. Better to end it now before it's too late."

He stands back up and rakes his hand through his hair, holding it back and then releasing it. "It's already too late. It was too late for me when I asked you to marry me. It was too late the first time I told you I loved you. It was too late the first time I talked to you at the River Rendezvous." His arms fall limply at his sides, and he stares at his feet.

My eyes fill with tears. I know exactly what he means. It's been him for as long as I've known him, even before I realized it. I can't imagine ever loving someone else the way I love him. Which is why I have to do this. I have to follow through with my plan for the shot of him having a better future.

I do my best to keep my voice steady as I say, "I'm

sorry. Sometimes things just don't work out. People drift apart."

"This isn't drifting apart. This is about what I said before I left for the Rendezvous. I'm sorry I compared you to your mom. That was wrong."

"This isn't about what you said. I just can't be with you anymore." I stand up and take my ring off. I take his hand and place it in his palm. His fingers curl around it. "I'm sorry."

I look at him one last time before I walk back inside. Once I lock the door behind me, I let the tears start falling. I stay in bed until I can't cry anymore. And then I block his number and delete all the pictures of him on my phone. I throw away every memento in my room that reminds me of him, except for one picture that I tuck away in my closet because I can't bear to get rid of everything.

It's almost like he never existed.

19

THE PRESENT

SUNDAY

I WOKE up with the sunrise this morning. I haven't talked to Nate or Evie or anyone, for that matter, since the rehearsal dinner. It's for the best because there's nothing else to say.

Nate knows everything now. I told him about the party and what Jake did to me. I told him how I was so embarrassed that I wasn't sure how to tell him—but that I did intend to eventually—until I ended up in the hospital. I explained how breaking up with him was the only way I knew how to make sure he didn't end up in a loveless marriage, trapped with a woman who couldn't give him a family.

"I need time to process, Macy," he said, his face impossibly blank. His tone frustratingly even. Then he walked away, leaving me alone in the church foyer.

That was nine hours and twenty-three minutes ago, and still not a peep, not that I'm counting . . .

I spend the morning finishing up Evie's flowers and installing the arrangements at the reception hall with a few of my part-time assistants before meeting Evie at her church. Because she's getting married on a Sunday, I had to wait for the service to finish and the crowds to clear before getting set up. Now that it's officially wedding time, I can bring everything to the church.

The biggest arrangements need to go in the front of the sanctuary, I have a lovely garland for the entranceway, and flowers need to make it to the entire wedding party. I stop by the bride's room first so I can say hi and reassure Evie I'm here and ready for her big day.

When I walk in, a tray of bridal bouquets in my hand, the room is already a flurry of motion. Evie has hired a team of stylists to do our hair and makeup, and all the bridesmaids are in various stages of getting ready for the special day. Evie and Joanna are getting their makeup done. Lillian is fluffing her hair in the mirror, and Rachel sits in a chair while someone curls her hair into loose waves.

"Hello," I say, setting the bouquets on a table filled with various light refreshments. There's a sandwich ring, some fruit, and crackers next to a case of bottled water. "Happy wedding day, Evie."

Her face lights when they take in the bouquets. "Oh my goodness. Macy, those are beautiful."

My cheeks heat at the compliment. I'm happy she loves them, especially with the unexpected drama I've brought to her special day. This was why I wanted to be her florist. "Just wait until you see the rest."

She's practically bouncing in her seat, much to the irritation of the stylist. "Are they set up already? Can I see?"

"Not yet."

“Macy, it’s almost wedding time. And you still need to get ready.”

I look down at my phone. I still have two hours. Installation should take an hour max. Typically, weddings take a lot more time to set up, but Evie wanted to keep the floral design really simple so that the wood and stained glass of the church would shine through. As much as I wanted to go big, I tried to honor her wishes. I just made sure the arrangements were the best they could be within her restraints.

I flash a smile at her. “Let me do a few more things before I make the official transition from florist to maid of honor. I’ll be really quick.”

The stylist sighs. “See to it that you are.”

“Worst-case scenario, I get simple makeup and you throw my hair into a bun.” It’s something I could do in about fifteen minutes, so there’s still plenty of time. I hope.

“Here, I’ll come with you,” Lillian says, turning from her reflection in the mirror. “All I have left is to get dressed. It’ll make it go by faster.”

I nod at her. “That would be great.”

She follows me through the church and out the side to where I parked my work van. Even though I knew the flowers wouldn’t be out there for long, I parked in one of the only shaded spots in the lot.

Lillian follows close behind. “You didn’t come to dinner last night.”

“Yeah. I wasn’t feeling good and told Evie I was going home to sleep off the hangover.” I laugh. “I’m not a good drinker.”

“And you went straight home?”

There's a slight edge to her voice that gives me pause. I thought she wanted to help, but now I'm not so sure that crazy Lillian isn't back. Maybe she never left. I stop at the back of my van and try to choose my words carefully. "Yeah. I left the church, went home, and loaded up on electrolytes before going to bed. It was very exciting." I open the doors and the aroma of roses and ranunculus pours out. I'm thankful for the familiar scents and the small bit of comfort they give me.

"So you weren't with Nate?"

I choke on a cough before spinning around. "What? Why would you think that?"

Lillian shrugs. "Matt's brother said he saw you and Nate talking inside after the rehearsal, and then neither of you showed up to the dinner . . . "

He didn't go to the dinner? I try not to think about what that might mean.

"Well, he definitely wasn't with me." When Lillian raises her brows, I say, "Yes, we were talking after the rehearsal. Just some reminiscing from the past, but I went home, and I have no idea what he did after."

"So you're not getting back together?"

My laugh is high-pitched. "Uh, no. Definitely not."

She releases a long exhale. "I just thought since you two have history and there was all this romantic stuff with the wedding happening, that some old feelings might have resurfaced."

Old feelings resurfaced, all right, but now Nate knows why we can't act on them. She doesn't need to worry about us getting back together. "Nope."

"Oh good. Because he's super cute and I really think I might have a shot with him."

I recall the way she talked about him at the bachelorette party. They liked a lot of the same things. Plus there was the mention of wanting to make babies with him. While the very idea of Nate and Lillian being . . . together . . . makes me want to puke, she would be able to give him what he wants. They might be able to have a future together. “I think you should go for it.”

“Really?”

No. “Yeah, why not?”

“Hearing you say that makes me feel so much better.” Her smile filled with hope. “Maybe getting waxed won’t be a total waste after all.”

I barely repress the shudder that threatens to rake through my body. I make a non-committal noise as I grab one of the arrangements and hand it to her. She takes it with both hands, and I grab another one. I shut the doors to my van with my hip and lead Lillian back inside.

She doesn’t say anything as she follows me, her mind surely filled with images of her and Nate dancing the night away at the wedding reception. It works out well for me because I’m lost in my thoughts as we walk toward the front of the sanctuary. My thoughts also center around the reception, but more along the lines of *how do I avoid talking to Nate?* Or *how will I give a toast to Evie and Matt if I catch Nate and Lillian mid-canoodle?*

I sigh as I set my arrangement on the ground and reach for the one Lillian carries. I move them around until I’m satisfied then go out for more. Lillian helps me carry in the rest of the flowers and even helps me hang the garland. Somehow, she still looks amazing when we’re done, which is shocking and annoying because I’m a sweaty mess.

I thank her and send her back to the bride's room before I go back to the van for the final items—the boutonnieres. I've been avoiding them because bringing them in means having to see the groomsmen.

If I can drop them off quickly enough, maybe I'll be lucky enough not to see Nate in the process and then I can get in the stylist's chair and shift my focus to my maid of honor duties.

I carry the small box of flowers as I walk through the church. The men are congregating in the library, which is on the other side of the building. That way, both bride and groom can get ready on-site without having to worry about bumping into each other before the ceremony.

I take a deep breath as I knock on the door.

"Come in," Matt calls from the other side.

I crack open the door and barely peek my head inside, keeping my eyes on the ground in case anyone is getting dressed. They didn't even ask who it was. "Hey, it's Macy. I have the boutonnieres."

"Oh, good," Matt says, walking over. I look up and I'm happy to see that he, along with everyone else in the room, is fully dressed. "Thanks for bringing these by."

"No problem."

I set the box down on the table in the library. Instead of sandwiches and fruit, the guys have beef jerky and energy drinks. It would be enough to make me laugh if I wasn't so aware of the fact that I'm in the same room as Nate after everything we said last night. He's in a suit while I'm in a t-shirt and shorts. I'm sure there's a Taylor Swift lyric in there if I try hard enough.

I lift one of the boutonnieres. "Does everyone know how to put these on?"

The guys all exchange blank looks. It's obvious not a single one of them does. Usually, I'd be more than happy to put them on the groomsmen, but I know time is starting to get away from me. And that's not even my biggest hesitation. It's the fact that I will need to get close enough to Nate to pin it on him. I will have to touch him. I will have to smell him.

I plaster on a smile. "Don't worry, I've got you."

"Are you sure you have enough time?" Matt asks as he takes in my appearance. "Obviously, I'm no expert, but I kinda assumed the bridesmaids were all getting ready right now."

"They . . . we are. I'm getting my hair and makeup done right after this." I pull out the first boutonniere and beckon Matt to get closer. I thread the pin through the lapel of his jacket until the flowers are attached. When I'm sure I'm happy with how it looks, I call his brother, Joey, over. I attach his boutonniere, then Matt's best friend, and then it's Nate's turn.

He refuses to make eye contact with me as he walks over. His movements are jerky, and I know this is as difficult for him as it is for me. My hands shake as I attempt to pin the boutonniere to his jacket. Thankfully, no one else is paying attention when I drop it, except for Nate, who bends down to get it at the same time as me. His eyes meet mine for the briefest moment, and I can see the pain and regret in them. It would be enough to unnerve me if I wasn't already completely shaken up.

We stand, and I'm about to try again when the door to the library swings open. This time it's the photographer. When she sees me and Nate, she orders me to stop until she can get the angle right. The rest of the groomsmen go back to ignoring us.

"Are you sure you don't want to get me pinning Matt's boutonniere on since he's the groom?" I ask. "We can stage it?"

She waves her hand in front of her. "Nope, I mostly just want to get a detailed shot of your hand and the boutonniere. Besides, I'll have plenty of pictures of the groom, but this might be my only chance to get the florist in one. I usually never see them before the ceremony."

"That's because this one is also the maid of honor," Nate grumbles under his breath.

"What?" The photographer's shriek is enough to bring everyone's attention back to me and Nate. "Why aren't you in hair and makeup? Why are you here doing this instead?"

"Because there's still time before the ceremony."

"Not very much." I swear the photographer might be hyperventilating. "Let's get those flowers on the groomsman, and then get back to the bride's room so you can look decent for the ceremony."

I swallow as I make attempt number two to get the boutonniere on Nate. I try to ignore the clicking of the camera as picture after picture is taken of my hands near his chest. It takes me longer than usual because the photographer keeps telling me to move my hand to the left or to pause. I might be the one hyperventilating now. I can barely breathe this close to Nate. It feels like an hour, when in reality I'm sure it's only been a minute, two tops.

When I'm done, and the photographer is satisfied, I start to walk out of the library, but there's a tug on my hand. It's Nate. I look back at him in question. Did I mess up the boutonniere in my distraction? I look at his chest, but the placement looks fine. It's not crooked, the flower isn't smashed. When I look back at his face, his brows pinch together. He opens his mouth to say something but closes it quickly.

I give him a small, sad smile, and use the photographer's earlier words in an attempt to keep the mood light. "I gotta go, so I can look decent for Evie's big day."

He still doesn't let go. He stares at me. "You always look beautiful."

I close my eyes and whisper, "You can't say things like that to me."

"Why?" He takes a step closer. "Because you don't think we can be together?"

I pull my hand free of his. "You know we can't."

"Macy . . . "

I turn on my heel and walk out before he can finish his sentence. I don't know what conclusions he came to while he was "processing," but whatever he was about to say will only make things worse than they already are. He knows why we can't be together, but it seems like he might still be having a hard time seeing it because feelings have a way of clouding your judgment. What Nate needs is a big push in a new direction to help get the reset he deserves—a push away from me.

By the time I make it back to the bride's room, I think I have it worked out. Nate and Lillian would be perfect together. Lillian already sees it. Now I just need to get Nate on board.

Will it be impossible for me to see? Absolutely.

Do I love the idea? Not exactly.

Do I think it's for the best? Probably.

The next thirty minutes go by in a blur as I think about how I can push them together. My hair is curled, and my makeup done as my thoughts run wild. Things are falling into place, and I've just slipped my dress on, a pale pink number with wide straps that cover my tattoo, when the photographer comes to the bride's room to snap a few pictures. She gives me a look of approval when she sees I'm no longer in my work clothes and has us pose in various ways pretending to get Evie ready for the big day. We adjust her veil and fluff out her train as the shutter clicks over and over. Even Katja shows up before the wedding to make sure Evie doesn't do anything stupid, like wear flats, to ruin her workmanship, and gets in on it.

The ceremony goes by without a hitch. Matt is obviously smitten with his bride when she walks down the aisle toward him. He tries to inconspicuously wipe a tear from his eye. Everyone remembers their spots from the rehearsal from the night before, and nobody messes up by forgetting the rings. Evie even chokes up during the exchanging of vows because she's so taken with emotions for her groom.

It's a really lovely ceremony, and miraculously, I don't think about Nate the entire time. Not until Matt and Evie are pronounced man and wife. The entire church erupts in cheers. I look over just in time to see Joey patting his brother on the back in congratulations. Just beyond him is Nate. He's looking at me and I can almost imagine what it would be like to be up here with him.

I push those thoughts back into the deep recesses of my mind so that I don't let my feelings cloud my judgment. One of us needs to be reasonable, and if I'm lost in the moment, I won't do what's necessary.

As we walk down the aisle for the recessional, I loop my arm in Joey's. I squeeze a little tighter than I normally would because I'm holding on for dear life at this point. I'm hyper aware of the fact that Nate is right behind us, and that Lillian is the one on his arm.

"You okay?" he says through his grin as he continues to walk.

"Totally. Just ready to get out of these shoes."

"Just one of the many reasons I'm thankful to be a guy. Getting dressed was easy. The hardest part was getting these flowers on, and you did all that for us."

"Happy to help," I say, struggling to keep my voice even. Forcing myself not to turn around and see the other happy couple. I don't want to see them together.

"They're beautiful."

"What?"

"The flowers. I know you did them for Matt and Evie as a wedding present. You did a great job."

"Oh." I let out a nervous laugh. "Thanks."

As we walk through the hallway of the church back toward the library, where the bridal party will hide out while the crowds thin a little, Joey turns and looks at me. His brows are lowered. "You sure you're okay? You seem a little tense."

I give him a big smile. "Yep. Never better."

He gives a small shake of his head. "Whatever you say."

When we get to the library, I busy myself with looking at the bouquets to make sure all the flowers still look good for pictures. Lillian is talking to Nate, and I make out snippets of the conversation. Words like "romantic" and "beautiful" come from her, and short monosyllabic responses come from Nate. It's obvious she's doing her best to take advantage of the situation, and I feel bad for her that he's not having any of it.

I brainstorm ways I can push them together at the reception, hating myself more and more with every new idea. It's impossible to look in either of their directions in the library or as we move into the sanctuary to take pictures. I'm working so hard to keep my head from turning in a certain guy's direction that the muscles in my neck are starting to hurt. I remind myself that I just need to make it through the next few hours with a smile on my face—for Evie—and then I can have my mini-breakdown while she's in Fiji with Matt.

With the ceremony behind us, I now just need to get through the reception.

How hard can it be?

20

THE PRESENT

SUNDAY

THE RECEPTION IS in a beautiful historic building downtown that overlooks one of the city's many lakes and is near a botanical garden.

Evie let me go a little more over-the-top for the reception, and because the nearby landscaping is so pretty, my dream was to make the inside of the building look like an extension of that by putting flowers everywhere. There's a giant flower arch when you first walk in, three-foot centerpieces on every table, and a flower chandelier over the dance floor.

Evie never asked to see the final designs and told me to have fun with it, so I know she isn't expecting the inside of the building to look like a secret garden. I'm standing off to the side of the dance floor with the rest of the wedding party as Mr. and Mrs. Matthew Davis are finally announced. The utter joy that follows Evie's shocked expression as she takes it all in gives me a sense of relief I haven't felt in days. I'm so happy she likes it. More than happy. Ecstatic.

She mouths, "This is so amazing," at me as Matt leads her onto the dance floor for their first dance as husband and wife.

"You are," I mouth back, because she is. I'm so thankful to have this woman in my life. And I'm excited for her new adventure.

Matt twirls her in his arms and they start slow dancing to "A Thousand Years." Yes, it's the song from *Twilight.* No, she doesn't care what anyone at the reception thinks. She's come a long way from the girl I first met at the Rendezvous who was embarrassed about enjoying romance. Now, she embraces it, and made sure Matt knew that playing this song was nonnegotiable since *Breaking Dawn* is one of her comfort movies.

To his credit, Matt doesn't seem to be bothered in the least. He stares at her all starry-eyed as they spin around the dance floor while Christina Perri sings about being brave. I'm so happy for Matt and Evie. They are going to be so happy together, I just know it. I wish that those words could be for me and Nate, too, but understand that they can't.

As the song finishes, Evie's parents thank everyone for coming, and Matt and Evie join the wedding party for dinner. We're sitting at a long table that faces the rest of the room, with bridesmaids and groomsmen on opposite sides of the table, which means I won't have to look at Nate for the entire meal. Waiters materialize out of nowhere and start placing salads in front of everyone.

Joey takes this as his cue and stands up from his spot next to his brother. He gives a lovely speech about how Matt was a great big brother growing up. How he always looked out for him and made sure nobody at school picked on him. He talks about the first time Matt brought Evie home and he knew that they were going to get married even then. He wishes them a long and happy future and lifts his glass in cheers.

The room erupts in applause, and I swear I can feel it in my chest. Except, in reality, it's just the violent thumping in my heart knowing I'm supposed to speak next. Public speaking has never been my favorite, so I pull out a small note card to help me get through the next couple of minutes. I grab the microphone and stand up.

"Hi, my name is Macy, and I'm so honored to be the maid of honor for Evie's wedding. I've known Evie for ten years now, and I can say without a doubt she is my best friend. Growing up, I was an only child and didn't have many friends. There were many times I felt alone, and wondered if I would ever feel at home with anyone." My fingers go to my dress, and I tug at the fabric covering my tattoo.

Do not think *about him, Macy. Not right now.*

I clear my throat. "My parents split up when I was young, and my dad never remarried, so a sibling was completely out of the question. Or, at least, I thought it was, until I met Evie." I smile down to where she's sitting. "Even though she grew up in a big family, she found a way to make me feel like I belonged. She made me feel like I was her sister. I can tell her anything and know she won't tell anyone else. I can call her up when I need to cry, though she'll probably show up at my house within a few minutes to give me a hug instead of talking on the phone. I can send her stupid memes and count on her to watch cheesy movies with me. She even was one of my biggest cheerleaders when I started my floral business."

Evie grabs my hand and lowers the mic so she can say, "She did the flowers for this wedding, by the way."

"See? Biggest cheerleader." I pause and smile while the crowd laughs. "Not only that. She's been through some really hard things with me." My eyes briefly flick to Nate. He's staring at me with such intensity, I need a moment to compose myself before continuing. I look down at my notecard to remind myself where I am. "Through it all, she's never made me feel like an inconvenience or a burden because that's who she is. Evie is the most loyal, wonderful, amazing friend a person could have."

The sting of tears burns in the back of my eyes as I think about the way she's loved me through it all. I sniff and blink them away. "So when she started dating Matt, I was nervous. I wondered what it might mean for my best friend to be involved with a guy. Would he be good enough for her? I wasn't sure. But you know what? Matt is amazing. He treats Evie with the love and respect she deserves. He's as loyal and wonderful as she is. And has become a friend to me as well." I smile down at Matt.

"You two deserve to be happy, and I am so thankful you found each other. May your marriage be filled with joy, this day and always." I lift my glass, filled with water, and the rest of the room drinks to Matt and Evie with me.

When I sit down, Evie leans over and hugs me. "Thank you. That was so beautiful. But remember, you deserve happiness too."

"I am happy."

"You know what I mean."

I do, but I don't admit it. It will have to remain unspoken for now.

Indistinctive chatter and light instrumental music fill the space as we finish our meals. The lights start to dim, and the music gets louder. It can only mean one thing: it's time for dancing, and part two of my plan to get Nate and Lillian together.

I ignore the way Nate watches me as I walk around the back of the table and tap Joey on his shoulder.

"Want to dance?" He looks a little confused, so I say, "I want to get out there so other people feel comfortable dancing too. Someone's got to start it, right?"

"Good point." He looks at the rest of the wedding party and nods before he stands. "Let's go."

By asking Joey to dance, I'm hoping others will follow and start dancing. This is the perfect opportunity for Lillian to make her move on Nate. I hope she takes it—for everyone's sake.

"I'm not hitting on you or anything," I say to Joey once we're out of earshot of the rest of the wedding party. "Just so you know."

He laughs. "Don't worry. I know."

I don't see Joey as anything more than a friend. And I don't think he sees me as more than that either, but the laugh seems a little much. I stop in the middle of the dance floor.

"What does that mean?"

"Nothing." He shrugs. "Just that I know you're Nate's girl."

My mouth falls open. "W-why do you say that?"

Joey starts moving back and forth. "Aren't we supposed to be dancing?"

I look around and realize that several people are watching us out here. I start bouncing from foot to foot and move my hands lamely at my sides. I look around before I lean in. "What do you mean I'm Nate's girl?"

"I know you used to date, and the way you two look at each other makes me think there are still feelings." A corner of his mouth lifts into a playful grin and he waggles his brows. "You asked me to dance to make him jealous right?"

My eyes widen. "What? No?"

"Wait? Then why are we dancing?"

"To get this party started."

Joey doesn't need to know the elaborate details of my plan. Mostly because they aren't exactly elaborate, but also, I don't want to feel like I'm more drama than I already am.

He looks over my shoulder. "So you wouldn't be excited about the idea of Nate walking this way right now?"

Before I can stop myself, my head turns to look back toward the bridal table. Sure enough, Nate is walking this way—and he doesn't look happy about it. My head whips back to face Joey. "Oh, crap. That's not what was supposed to happen."

"What do you want me to do?" he asks.

I know Joey's asking because he's worried about Nate, but he doesn't have to be. Nate isn't going to do anything to hurt me because that's not the kind of person he is. But even if he was, there's nothing that can make this hurt anymore. I'm broken when it comes to Nate.

"Nothing," I say, answering Joey's question. "I'm okay."

"You sure?"

Nate appears in my peripheral before I can answer. "Can I talk to you?" he asks, his voice clipped.

I nod at Joey, who walks off the dance floor, then turn toward Nate. "What's up?" I say loud enough for him to hear over the music.

"*What's up*?" Nate looks toward the flower chandelier in disbelief before taking a step toward me and leaning in close. "That's what you're going to say to me after everything?"

"What do you want me to say?"

He rubs his eyelid and lets his fingers drag down his face. Now that we're this close, and I'm actually looking at him, I can see the circles under his eyes. I can see how bloodshot they are as they stare into mine.

"I don't care what you say, I just don't want you to pretend like everything's okay when it's not."

People are congregating on the dance floor now. While they aren't really paying attention to us, I do realize that I'm not moving anymore. Nate and I are standing awkwardly amid others trying to dance to the steady thumping of the music.

"I'm just trying to make it through tonight, okay?"

His eyes narrow. "And dancing with Joey is making it through the night? Are you trying to make me feel terrible as we try to figure this out?"

Everything stops. I was wrong when I thought Nate couldn't hurt me anymore. Hearing that he thinks we're still trying to be together causes my heart to shatter into a thousand pieces. With all his time to *process*, he still doesn't understand. That, or he's refusing to.

My throat tightens. "That's not what's happening, Nate. We can't be together."

A muscle in his jaw flexes, and without another word, he grabs my hand and pulls me through a side door. We leave the noise and the crowds behind as he continues to lead me outside. It's quieter once the doors close behind us, but there are still a few guests congregating out here. Some are smoking. Others are surely looking for a break from the loud music.

I struggle to keep up as Nate continues to drag me behind until we're in the botanical garden. The small gate squeaks as it moves on its hinges, and soon, we're surrounded by trees and shrubs. We're hidden away so that we won't have to worry about being disturbed.

In the quiet of the gardens, our breathing sounds thunderous. We're both worked up, but neither of us says anything. The feelings of the last few days threaten to drag me under, so my voice is filled with irritation when I finally break the silence and ask, "Why did you bring me out here?"

"Because we need to talk."

"There's nothing to talk about."

We did enough of that last night before he walked away so he could process it all. Watching Nate walk away was what I expected. It's what I thought I wanted. In the time since, I realized what I really wanted was for him to pull me close and tell me that everything was going to be okay. And he didn't. I'm angry at him for leaving me alone in the church last night, and I'm angry at myself for still wanting him even as I'm trying to push him away for good. My chest feels heavy from the weight of all these conflicting emotions, and it takes everything in me to keep my lungs breathing in and out.

"Why? Because you said it's over?" Nate shakes his

head. "You keep saying that, but you haven't given me any say in the matter."

"Because I know what you'll say." My voice cracks and I look away.

"What would I say, Macy?" His fingers touch my chin and turn my head so I'm looking at him. "Knowing what I know now, can I tell you what I think about us?"

My breaths come in faster pants. "I wish you wouldn't."

"Why?" His voice is impossibly gentle. His fingers slide up my face so he's cupping my cheek.

I squeeze my eyes shut. "Because I don't think I'm strong enough to stick to my plan if you actually say it."

"So I shouldn't tell you that I love you? That I haven't stopped loving you."

Tears start to slide down my cheeks.

"I shouldn't tell you that I love you even though you pushed me away? Or that I wish you would have let me be there for you during the hardest thing you've ever gone through, and that I hope you'll let me be there for you now?"

"No," I whisper.

"Then I definitely shouldn't tell you that I still have your engagement ring, and that I brought it here with me tonight?"

My eyes fly open, and I step back away from him.

"Don't worry. I'm not asking tonight. I know you're not ready for that." He pats his coat pocket. "But I want you to know I've never gotten rid of it because I still haven't given up hope that I'm going to marry you one day."

"But you can't."

"Why? I love you, and I want to spend forever with

you." His eyes go to where my tattoo is. "I think you want to spend forever with me too."

My hands shake as I tug on the strap of my dress. "I can't have kids. It's the one thing you want."

"Oh, Mace." His face is soft, and he pulls my fingers from the fabric and squeezes it in his. "How can you be so brilliant but not see the truth right in front of you?"

"What truth is that?"

"That you're the one thing I want."

I shake my head. "You say that now, but I know what happens when a couple disagrees about kids. It tears them apart."

"We're not your parents, and we're not disagreeing. We're pivoting. There are other ways to have a family. We can foster, we can adopt, we can be the best aunt and uncle that the Delaney family has ever seen. I don't care what it looks like, as long as you're with me."

My silent tears become full-blown ugly crying. His words are filled with so much honesty, I can't help but trust him. I want to be brave and trust him. I want to trust him to love me and take care of me forever.

"Are you sure?" I manage to get out.

"I've never been more sure of anything in my whole life. Please give us another chance."

This is not the first time Nate has asked me to take a chance on him, but I hope it's the last. I feel like I'm on that cliff again, the one when he first asked me to date him—only now, he's asking for me to let go of my insecurities and trust him to take care of me. If he says he won't leave me because I can't have children, I believe him. If he says he wants to be with me forever, I look forward to growing old with him. "Yeah."

His mouth spreads into a wide grin. "Yeah?"

When I nod, his mouth crashes down on mine. His fingers are in my hair, messing up the curls that the stylist did before the ceremony. I don't care. My own hands hold onto the lapels of his coat for dear life. His kiss is a promise. The taste of forever is on his lips.

Nate loves me. I never stopped loving him either. It's always been Nate. It's always been us. He's my past, my present, and my future. He's my forever.

When we finally break apart, Nate reaches down for my hand. There's no hesitation, like his fingers belong entwined with mine. "Do you think anyone has noticed we're missing?"

I can think of a few. I nod.

"We should get back in there, then."

"Probably."

He kisses me once more before leading me back to the reception hall. Our return trip is much more leisurely than the initial one out to the garden. Our pace is slower, and Nate keeps leaning down to kiss me or pull me close to himself for a hug.

When we finally walk back inside, most people don't notice us. Lillian is all over some random guy I don't recognize, Joanna is chasing Catherine as she runs between tables, and others are chatting in small groups around the room.

Nate leads me into the middle of the room as a slow song starts playing. "Can I have this dance?"

My arms wrap around his waist, with no care for my lack of proper form. I lean my head against his chest and relax to the steady thumping of his heart.

"I love you," I say, though I'm not sure if he can hear me over the sound of the music.

He kisses the top of my head. "I love you too," he says, because he heard me—he always hears me.

We spend the rest of the night celebrating. We celebrate Matt and Evie's new beginning as we celebrate our own. I can't imagine ever being happier than I am at this moment, but the promise of forever with Nate is a great place to start.

EPILOGUE

THREE YEARS LATER

"Are you ready?" Nate asks as we walk up to the courthouse. He's holding my hand as he flashes me his most brilliant smile—the one that only comes out on special occasions. It's my favorite smile in the whole world.

This is the smile he flashed me when he first told me he loved me. The one he gave me when he asked me to marry him and I said yes—both times. The one he gave me when I walked down the aisle to become Mrs. Macy Delaney. And the one I got when we found out we would finally be a family of three.

We've been fostering Luna since she was a toddler, unsure of what her future held. Nate and I have spent many nights crying as we navigated these difficult waters on little Luna's behalf, only to wake in the morning to give her snuggles and kisses and pretend our hearts weren't breaking by the possibility of having to say goodbye one day. I didn't realize how much more my heart could love, and how I would be able to nurture this little girl like she was my own in the midst of so much uncertainty.

My eyes water as I squeeze Nate's hand. "More than ready."

In his free arm, Nate carries Luna, who is now almost four. When he kisses her tummy, she giggles and squirms until the flower crown I made for her almost falls off. He releases my hand so he can adjust it over her dark curls. "What about you, Lu-Lu? You ready to officially be a Delaney?"

She bobs her head up and down wildly. "I'm going to be Luna Delaney and then we get ice cream, right?"

He chuckles. "Yes, we'll go get ice cream after."

We know she doesn't fully understand what's happening today, but she knows enough. Luna knows Mommy and Daddy get to keep her forever, and she doesn't have to worry about changing homes ever again. She knows we love her more than anything and that she doesn't ever have to worry about us ever leaving her. She knows that we are a family, and we work through our struggles together because that's what it means to love someone.

And she knows this because it's something Nate and I live out every day.

Not that it's something I've always understood. It took me longer than it should have to learn that when tough times come, we don't get to decide how the people in our lives respond to it. It wasn't fair for me to push Nate away without talking about what not having biological children would mean for our future. It wasn't fair for me to decide what Nate did and didn't want.

I've had the privilege of nurturing this sweet girl for

the last couple of years, and I love her like she's my own. Soon, she'll really be mine, and I am the lucky one for it.

Nate and I might not have gotten the future we dreamed about when we were teens, but that doesn't mean this life we've built together isn't enough. It's more than enough. It's better than anything I could have imagined. And now we get to share this life with Luna.

"Let's go." Nate adjusts Luna on his hip. "We don't want to be late."

I look at sweet Luna. My heart is so full it feels like it might burst. When you're given a second chance and a sweet gift like this, you don't want to wait a moment longer than you have to. I reach down and grab Nate's free hand. "No, we don't."

ACKNOWLEDGMENTS

This book was a beast to write, and I couldn't have done it without a team of people.

A huge thanks to my family for allowing to me to sit and write as often as I do. The fact that you get excited with me means the world! I love you so much!

Thank you to Daphne James Huff and Kristin Grafton for being the best critique partners a girl could have. Thanks for helping me see scenes in a new light so that I could make them better.

Elle, thank you for editing this book and dealing with my neurotic tendencies. An editor and a therapist in one!

Lorissa, this cover is the most beautiful thing I've ever seen. Thank you for bringing this dream to life!

Shannon, thank you for bringing my characters to life with the audiobook!

To my readers, it's been a long time, but I wouldn't have had the courage to write again if it wasn't for your love and support for previous books. I hope the wait was worth it!

Love you all!

ABOUT KAYLA

Kayla has loved to read as long as she can remember. While she started out reading spooky stories that had her hiding under her covers, she now prefers stories with a bit more kissing.

When she gets a chance to watch TV, she enjoys cheesy sci-fi and superhero shows. Most days, you'll catch her burning dinner in an attempt to cook while reading just one more chapter.

Find me online:
www.tirrellblewrites.com
kayla@tirrellblewrites.com

ALSO BY KAYLA TIRRELL

Varsity Girlfriends:

Courtside Crush

Game Plan

Wedding Games:

The Bridesmaid & The Reality Show

The Bridesmaid & The Ex

The Bridesmaid & Her Surprise Love

Love in the Arena:

Penalty Box

Out of Play

River Valley Lost & Found:

All The Things We Lost

All The Things We Found

All The Things We Were

Disastrous Dates:

Disastrous Dates: A Sweet College Romance

www.ingramcontent.com/pod-product-compliance
Ingram Content Group UK Ltd.
Pitfield, Milton Keynes, MK11 3LW, UK
UKHW042004190726
13854UKWH00005B/2153

9 798869 094315